PLAYED BY THE ROCKSTAR

A Mile High Rocked Novel, Book 1

CHRISTINA HOVLAND

This book is a work of fiction. Names, characters, places, and incidents are the product of the author's imagination or are used fictitiously. Any resemblance to actual events, locales, or persons, living or dead, is coincidental.

For rights information, please contact:
Prospect Agency
551 Valley Road, PMB 377
Upper Montclair, NJ 07043
(718) 788-3217

Holly Ingraham, Development Editor
L.A. Mitchell, Copy Editor & Proofreader
Shasta Schafer, Final Proofreader

First Edition March 2021

For Courtney and Sarah.
The original Tens and the inspiration for so much of this story.

Chapter 1

Becca

Neon beer signs totally signaled a new beginning. Sure, a girl might not think it possible, but Rebecca—Becca—Forrester was out to prove they could. The scent of hops and bourbon paired with the blast of music through the speakers and constant hum of life in the background at Brek's Bar in Denver, Colorado. Outside, the snow had turned to a slushy mess. Inside, the bar warmed her like she'd taken a shot of top-shelf whiskey.

Oh yes, this joint was the perfect place for a fresh start that did not involve anyone else or the baggage they dragged along with them.

"Why do you want to wait tables here?" Brek asked, giving a dose of emphasis on *here*. "I'd have thought you'd prefer some place with tablecloths."

Becca laughed. Brek was as biker as biker got—long hair, leather, and an abundance of tattoos. His wife was…not. She was a financial planner, and Becca's friend.

Becca shook her head. She definitely didn't want to wait

tables anywhere else. "I'm looking for the diviest dive I can find."

The idea to wait tables was a complete one-eighty from her recent past as a certified behavioral counselor, but she wouldn't go back. Not yet. Especially not when she was having a perfectly lovely time at the local go-to spot for great music in Denver, hanging with her friends, and harassing Brek into hiring her as a part-time waitress while she took a life break.

"Diviest dive? Well, I guess this is your place." Brek flashed her a smile.

"Exactly." Becca tucked a lock of her thick, brown hair behind her ear, where it belonged but never stayed. "Until I figure out what comes next for me."

"You can live the dream right here with me." Brek patted the bar top like it was a living, breathing thing. Something he adored.

Sigh. Someday she wanted someone to look at her like Brek looked at his wife and his bar top.

Not now. She was on a break from all of that—the relationships, the responsibility, everything—but, someday, the adoration thing would be fun to have, too.

He'd created the perfect dive bar atmosphere—neon lights on the dark wood over the bar with his name lit up in blue. The wood paneling covering the walls was new enough to make the place look well-kept but beat up enough that it didn't look like he had tried too hard. Aesthetically, nothing matched. Yet everything still worked together. The place was definitely Instagram-worthy.

The darkened room hopped in preparation for the band to take the stage. A vibe she loved pulsed through the air. That feeling right before music blasts and the lights come to life. Yep. This was exactly what she wanted for her present life: loud music and the familiar faces of the bar's regulars, with no further obligation for the mental or physical well-being for those around her.

Also, the best bands played at Brek's Bar. Sometimes, because he had the connections, Brek brought in huge names. Like *huuuge.* Waiting tables here was perfect for a recovering groupie on hiatus from life.

"You can start next weekend?" Brek asked.

"Next weekend would be perfection." Becca glanced at her friends, mingling across the room.

Then *Linx* entered Brek's Bar. Becca choked on nothing but air.

Linx. Walked. Through. The. Door.

Bassist for Dimefront. Hot as all hell. Heartbreak in leather pants when he took the stage.

She, on the other hand, was only hot when she wore a sweater. Definitely not heartbreak in any kind of clothing. Unless... Could a woman be heartbreak in yoga pants? She was sure that wasn't possible. She shook the thought from her head as he moved her direction.

Her mouth didn't just go dry; her entire body froze in time.

Tonight, he'd ditched the leather and wore shredded blue jeans instead. Lanky, with ridiculously long dark hair, stubble that was a half day away from being a full beard, and all the charisma of a man who could get tens of thousands of screaming fans on their feet with one chord on his guitar. He scanned the room like he owned the joint.

Brek may have owned the bar, but Linx owned the room.

"Looks like my current assignment is here," Brek said, offhand with a touch of growl.

"Linx is your assignment?" Okay, she tried to resist sliding her gaze back to Linx, but she failed. Every woman in the house got the Linx grin as he continued his slow saunter through the room.

"I'm his babysitter…" Brek said, glowering in Linx's general direction.

Crumpet crap-ola. Her blood seemed a whole lot thicker and her skin a whole lot thinner when he sauntered toward Brek… and her. The blue neon halo was a nice touch. Well done, universe. Well done, indeed.

She sighed because…. Linx.

All eyes were on him. Every woman in the room got a solid eye canoodle as he strutted right up to where she stood across from Brek. His eye canoodle could likely get a girl pregnant. She sucked in a breath and braced for her turn.

Linx moved less than an arms-length away, and her heart stuttered like he'd asked her to remove her panties. Surely, he wouldn't recognize her. It'd been years since they partied in the same circles.

She held her breath because she couldn't take the risk of his scent. Not because she had any special superpowers that involved scented rock stars—that she was aware of—but she knew he smelled amazing. Rock star heaven and concerts and something musky, like oak trees in the rain.

"Do you want me to wait for the drinks, or do you want to send them over when they're done?" Becca asked Brek, ignoring the fact that Linx was right-freaking-there doing some kind of intense handshake thing with him.

"You should definitely wait," Linx said, blasting her out of her knickers with that smile of his.

Yes, she often thought in British slang that she'd picked up one summer on a European Dimefront tour. She really took to their language choices. Refined, but still rather raunchy.

Like her. Rather, who she wanted to be.

She slid her gaze up the length of Linx—long and lithe. Not beefcake, but definitely built. He had more of a runner's build. Muscle and sinew, but not overdone.

He leaned against the bar top, a look of pure happiness on his face. This wasn't a cat's-got-his-cream smile. This was a cat's-about-to-play-with-his-dinner-before-devouring grin.

"Becca, this is Cedric," Brek said, slinging drinks like a pro.

Cedric?

Right. Sure, yes, she knew that was his given name. Cedric Sebastian, wasn't it? Last name was Lincoln, and all the original members of the band took a nickname that had an x at the end. Together, they made a triple-x, which they found hysterical, as pointed out in multiple Rolling Stone articles.

"Becca," Linx—er, *Cedric*—stretched her name across his tongue and played it like an instrument.

He held his hand out to her. *What to do? What to do?*

She could touch him. She should touch him. He was expecting her to touch him.

Do something already, Becca.

She was overthinking this way too much. So she gave him a solid handshake.

The way he squeezed her palm was nearly erotic. For no good reason, either. It was just a handshake. He didn't make any lewd gestures or anything.

Still, the bar seemed to zip to a pinprick and focus on Linx.

"Becca is a friend of Velma's." Brek tossed Linx a look like her dad used to give her when he thought she was going to use very poor decision-making skills.

Becca extracted her hand from Linx's grasp. She noted how he kept the touch for as long as she'd allow.

"I like Velma." Linx grabbed a pretzel from the bowl on the bar and flipped it into his mouth.

"I do, too." Brek continued working. "That's why I'm making it clear to you that *Becca* is a friend of *Velma's*. Which means stop looking at her like that."

"Like what?" Linx held up his hands.

"Like you want to make her Denver," Brek said with a growl.

What the heck did that mean?

Linx popped another pretzel into his mouth. Somehow, he chewed, smirked, and smoldered, all at the same time.

"She's not Denver. Denver is Denver. Becca is Becca."

Brek crossed his arms. "You and I need to discuss what you're allowed to do and not do while you're visiting."

Linx held his palm to his heart and wobbled dramatically. "I am offended."

For the record, he didn't sound offended.

"It's not visiting if I bought a house. That makes it my home," Linx said to Brek.

He bought a house in Denver? Huh.

Perhaps Becca wasn't the only one in the midst of reconsidering life choices.

"You *bought* a house in Denver?" Brek asked. "I thought it was a vacation rental."

"It was," Linx said with a shrug.

"The landlord was being a total dick about Gibson, so I made him an offer." Linx did the pretzel thing again.

"Who's Gibson?" Becca asked.

Not that she had any real reason to be part of the conversation, but Linx hadn't asked her to leave.

"His cat," Brek said, arms still crossed.

"He's more than a cat." Now Linx crossed his arms. "So what if I bought one little house so he has a place to live?"

Brek shook his head. "Whatever, man. You do you."

"That's my plan." Linx slid his gaze to Becca. "Unless Becca wants to sit here and have a drink with me? Then we can see what happens."

Linx gave her a charisma-soaked smile.

Ah. There it was, her eye canoodle. She felt that stare deep down in her soul.

Yeah. Total player.

A player who went through sex partners like they were potato chips. This was according to his bandmate, Bax, and general female knowledge when meeting a player of his magnitude.

Back when she'd followed Dimefront concerts she'd had her eye on Linx. Something about him was like a magnet, pulling her in his direction. She had wanted him. Full. Stop.

But Linx was bad news for her. He rocked a total love 'em and leave 'em vibe. The kind that made a girl like Becca—someone who tended to see only the good in people and, therefore, fall for the wrong men—step away. He had just the right amount of baggage for her to want to unpack. And he was exactly the type of guy to pick up those suitcases and leave town right after she committed to the unpacking.

So she kept far away from his wandering gaze, preferring to observe him in his natural rock star habitat, and not let her heart, or body, get involved.

Brek handed a bottle of Coors to Linx.

"I've actually…" Becca jerked her head toward her group of friends. "Got to get back."

"That's a drag." Linx shrugged and gave Becca an extra-long, excessively thorough glance.

She shouldn't have done it. But she did. Yes, she totally canoodled him back.

"Becca?" Brek's voice cut through whatever the heck was going on between the two of them.

Brek had, of course, known Becca during her groupie days. Back then, he'd managed Dimefront and she'd been a Ten, the pet name they called their groupies. The Grateful Dead had Deadheads, Justin Bieber had his Beliebers, and Dimefront had their Tens. She'd spent a summer being Queen of the Tens.

This was not something she shared regularly. With anyone. No one else in her real life knew. Not even her best friends. That summer had been her first attempt at a life vacation. And it'd worked. Lucky for her, Brek didn't, and she was quoting here, "Broadcast shit that wasn't his to tell."

She let out a long breath and turned to Brek. He glanced pointedly to the order he'd prepared.

"Thanks." She snatched the remaining drinks and—and this was the hard part—she walked away without looking back at Linx and his neon halo.

Chapter 2

Linx

"You're bored," Brek announced.

Yes, yes, he was. Linx was bored with his life because his bandmates were being tools and not thinking of anything but themselves. Which left him…aimless.

"You wanna hang out with the family and me tomorrow?" Brek asked unnecessarily. They both knew the answer.

Linx nodded. "Sure."

His foot tapped against the lip of the footrest on his barstool to a custom beat the band on stage played. He'd never heard the song before, and he was pretty versed in all the latest rock ballads. His money said it was an original.

A damn good original. These guys could play. He was slightly jealous of their time in the spotlight.

Fine, there was no slightly about it. He was jealous.

Linx wasn't a guy who wanted to remodel a house or adopt pets to fill a void. He was a guy who needed to entertain. It was in his blood—clear back to his great-granddaddy who played the banjo Saturday nights at the community dance hall where he grew up.

"Any progress on finding a hobby?" Brek asked, but he didn't sound hopeful.

Which made sense because he shouldn't have been hopeful about the whole find-Linx-a-hobby thing.

They'd been dancing this dance for a few weeks now, and all it'd gotten Linx was a big fucking hole in the wall of his new house. Turned out, he didn't know shit about remodeling.

Linx shook his head. "That's why I'm here tonight. Got bored hanging with my cat."

Wasn't that just the sad sack of shit making up his present days?

"We'll get you sorted." Brek wiped down the countertop like he really was a barkeep and not one of the most in-demand band managers in the industry.

"Nothing to sort. I'm just killing time until I can make music again."

"Keep tellin' yourself that." Brek clearly didn't buy what Linx was selling. He might not be their manager anymore, but he still stepped in when things went off the rails, like…now.

These days, he took a consultant role for their new management team. Their current band manager, Hans, sent Linx to Denver to hang with Brek while he got Knox and Bax back in the game. Thus, Brek's current consulting gig was being Linx's emotional support bartender.

Settling down and opening a bar instead of traveling the world with the band seemed to suit Brek.

"Maybe I should open a bar," Linx said, offhand. "It worked for you. You're happy. Content. All that bullshit."

"You have any desire to run a bar?" Brek quirked an eyebrow.

"No." Not in the least.

"Maybe think of something else." As part of his current consulting gig, Brek was tasked with driving Linx bananas.

Linx was his "project." This was a form of special torture because Brek was persistent, and he now had standards.

It wasn't like Linx was a blowhard. He just felt that he shouldn't be punished because the other guys in the band were a hot mess.

He wasn't the band member threatening to leave for the bajillionth time because of whatever bug crawled up his ass. No, that would be Knox. But Knox wouldn't leave. He didn't have the balls to do it. He'd just make everyone miserable while he figured that out.

Linx also wasn't the band member asking for an extended sabbatical so he could plan his honeymoon. No, that was Bax. And as soon as the honeymoon was over, Bax would wonder what he needed to do to make some cash. Then he'd realize that meant making a record.

The latest time Knox started bitching about everything, a-fucking-gain, their newest drummer packed up his set and went to play for some no name band. And that drummer had been exceptional. He also wasn't a dick, which meant that he and Linx got along great. Fuckin' Knox.

So yeah, that sucked. Linx hadn't met the new guy the label assigned yet. No use until they were ready to jam again. Besides, he'd probably just ditch them, too, once shit went sour.

All of this combined into one massive shit pile, culminating in Linx's current boredom.

"You know what I'd like to do for a hobby?" Linx asked, staring at the neck of the bottle a beat before glancing to his friend-slash-babysitter.

Brek raised his eyebrows.

On his hobby quest, Linx had adopted a cat, got a motorcycle through a questionable poker game, bought a Porsche, purchased a house, broken it off with Denver (the woman, not the city), and hung out with Brek and his family.

Linx leaned forward, so he held Brek's stare. "I'd like to make some fucking music."

Yeah, right. He couldn't make music because the rest of the band was unavailable.

"There's the stage." Brek did a subtle chin jerk toward the stage where the band of the night jammed to a Dimefront cover in a blatant attempt to woo Linx's attention. "I'm sure those guys would dig having an artist of your magnitude and questionable charm jump in."

That was a negative. "I don't know those guys. Can't make music with a band I don't know."

Brek wasn't the only one who had standards.

"That's bullshit, and you know it," he said.

Linx glanced back to the stage, his lips pressed thin.

Yeah, they were a talented group. With a little push, they could be better than great.

A mix of old and young. The bassist had to be going on seventy, but he was all in with his commitment to rock. The lead looked like he came straight from an office job, but he'd ditched his suit jacket and rolled his sleeves up to his elbows to show off a pretty kick ass array of ink. And the drummer and keyboard guy looked young and cocky, like they had the entire world ahead of them to fuck up.

Ahhh…to be young and naïve.

"Tomorrow?" Linx turned back to Brek and pointedly changed the subject. "I'll bring Gibson to your place?"

Brek's toddler loved Linx's cat. That wasn't a surprise. Gibson was a fluff ball of easy-to-love.

"Works for me." Brek went back to barkeeping, what with his aborted attempt to get Linx on stage failing and all that.

Linx took a swig of his ginger ale. Brek had transferred the fake brew into an actual beer bottle. Linx couldn't go around losing street cred. What sort of image would that make?

He didn't have a problem with it, per se. Didn't have a

problem with other people drinking. He just learned early in his life that he preferred to be sharp. After watching one of their drummers hit rehab for the fourth time, he officially made the call that he was 95 percent dry. He rarely partook in the real deal.

Except champagne.

Damn. He enjoyed an excellent champagne.

That choice didn't really mesh with his rocker vibe, though.

"You should have Velma ask her friend Becca to stop by and meet Gibson." Oh yes, Becca with the brown hair and brown eyes and gorgeous dimple on her right cheek.

"You know you can't go poking your dick anywhere near Velma's friends," Brek said, low.

Linx nodded because, yeah, he knew.

"Can I show her my cat at least?" he asked.

"No."

Okay, fine. Brek was firm on this one. Still, Linx's gaze moseyed right on over the delectable brunette with the gorgeous smile and legs that went on and on for lightyears. There was something about her. Something familiar. Something that tickled the back of his brain.

"You're sure I don't know her?"

And, by know her, he meant had crazy sex with her while he was on tour.

Becca was absolutely Linx's type. All that hair. That body. Those brown eyes. He gnawed at his bottom lip and forced himself to look back at Brek's ugly face.

Brek shook his head because Brek would know. One of the many tasks he'd taken on as the manager of Dimefront—not because the boys asked, but because Brek was good people—was to keep a tally of the hookups that took place. All of them. Which was cumbersome, at times. The guys were careful, mostly. But mostly didn't cut it when a demand for child support came in from someone they'd never met, heard of, or slept with. So Brek had kept that score during the craziest days of their touring.

As they'd aged, they'd matured. Well, Linx had, and he didn't need a manager to keep a little black book for him anymore. He had a system that worked fabulously.

"Well, this is interesting." Brek looked to where Becca and her friends had mingled, and then his gaze traced a path to the stage where the band paused between songs.

Linx looked.

Becca chatted with Mr. Rolled-Up Sleeves. He grinned like he'd won the lottery, nodding along to whatever she said. Then he handed Becca his microphone, and she radiated pure bliss. Becca grabbed the mic and took the guy's hand to get up on stage.

Every part of Linx perked to attention. *What…?*

Back molars gritted, Linx watched as Becca said something to the keyboard kid. Mr. Suit lingered a touch too close for Linx's preference. *Move it along, buddy.*

Content with whatever they'd decided, she turned her attention to the audience. He knew that feeling. Loved that feeling.

The stage was worn from use, but functional. The sound system Brek had installed, however, was brand new and top of the line. Becca held the mic up to her lips and said, "There's been a dare."

Linx choked on his ginger ale.

The women she'd been hanging with went crazed at this statement, whistling and shouting like they were at one of his concerts.

"Unfortunately," Becca continued. "That means you have to suffer along with me."

He couldn't help it—a smile tickled the edges of his lips. Watching this beauty on stage was not a hardship.

The first bars of the Spice Girl's anthem "Wannabe" started, and the bar went crazy. Becca jumped right in with no regard for pitch. What she lacked in ability to carry a tune she made up for with commitment and dance choreography.

The woman's body moved like it was made to conquer that space—and any space she chose. His blood thumped louder in his ears, matching the beat of her song.

He even found the perpetual bounce of his knee turning into a full groove. Best part of the whole thing? He wasn't the least bit bored. The woman couldn't tackle the true metrics of the melody, but somehow, she carried the parts for all five of the Spice Girls.

Her friends lost their minds when her dance moves involved a non-existent pole. They rushed to form a makeshift mosh pit at the front of the stage. Bouncers inched closer to the stage. That's how a rocker knew shit was getting serious and might skip out of hand.

Meanwhile, the band did not mind the fresh change of events. They ate up the attention. Thrived on it.

There it was… His stomach did a pitch and dive, he felt a little lightheaded, and he was ready for the stage.

He ached to be up there with them. Feeling the rush, the ache of entertaining, the pure bliss that Becca elicited from the room.

Becca's enthusiasm? It was infectious. In the best way.

"You want up there." Brek didn't phrase the statement as a question.

Linx nodded.

"Then you should take the next set."

Linx glanced over his shoulder at his former manager, now babysitter.

Brek was right. He should. But he shouldn't wait until the next set.

"Think there's room up there for Becca and me, both?"

Brek grinned a half-smile. "As long as you don't let her use you for a pole, that'd be fine."

And that was all the push that Linx needed. He stepped from the barstool and sauntered into the fray.

He made eye contact with Mr. Suit and pointed to his chest then the stage. The guy had that blank look on his face that fans sometimes got around Linx. Points for suit guy: he managed to shake it off and waved Linx up.

Becca was so involved with crooning to her gal pals that she didn't notice Linx skirting a bouncer to hop up on the stage.

Suit dude grabbed a spare guitar from beside the drummer and handed it over.

While Becca slaughtered the song, not in a good way, Linx waited.

Waited for the right moment to jump in with her.

And when he did?

Magic.

Chapter 3

Becca

Holy. Holy. Holy shit.

Becca was on stage with Linx. She was *singing* with him. Well, sort of. He knew about half of the lyrics. He did, however, hit all the notes with the band while she told him what she wanted. Really, really wanted. Helpful hint? It involved a *zig-a-zig hahhh*.

She'd totally give him her zig-a-zig ha. Uh huh. He could have all of her zig-a-zigs. Any she ever made. Ever. For all eternity.

Her stomach did the clenching thing that she'd become accustomed to that summer when she saw him regularly take command on stage.

Linx brought a bit of gravelly rock and ripped jeans to the girl-band song and it worked. Oh boy, did it work. He and the band rocked the hell out of that pop song. Being on stage with him was a fantasy come to life. Having him sing to her while looking in her eyes? Well, that made her heart pound in a really fabulous way.

He caught her eye as she bounced around the stage. Caught her eye and held it hostage.

Yes, there was a reason she'd put Linx off-limits and this, right here, was exactly that reason. He had jumped up on the stage and wiggled right under her skin.

Her skin flushed and adrenaline spiked. There was no physical contact, but she felt sated, like she'd just had a mind-blowing night with the man.

If she'd had any expectation that she'd be on stage with a rock god, she would've at least worn a skirt and something with a low-cut neckline—not jeggings with a blue turtleneck. She'd definitely need to plan better next time. Although, the pants did make her ass look fantastic.

The song (eventually) ended, and Becca's friends screamed for an encore. An encore she would not be providing. *No, thank you.* She'd accepted the terms of her friend Marlee's dare without fully thinking through the current situation.

Nevertheless, she'd paid up like a good girl who made bad decisions.

"Thank you," she shouted loud enough to be heard by her friends in the front row. She made a set of rock 'n roll devil horns with both hands, tossing them over her head for good measure. Then she held the microphone to her mouth and finished with, "And good night."

Perhaps she should've held out a little longer. As she exited the stage, Linx dove into a Dimefront cover. She wished—really, wished—that she could be on stage with him as he performed.

She wanted him bad; he was that good.

This was just like the old days. She left the stage and became a full Ten again as Linx transformed the small bar into a stadium. Then it was nothing like the old days when Linx pinned her with his stare.

Her scalp prickled. Her skin heated.

And he sang to *her*.

Perhaps, this was actually better than being on the stage with him. Total toss up, really.

God, he could take her behind the bar and do dirty, naughty things to her in the alley all night long when he finished. She wouldn't even care if someone caught them.

Mesmerized, she didn't move. Barely took a breath as he owned the stage, his body making musical promises. Promises to her. Promises she didn't understand. Not at all. Yet, for some reason, she was willing to accept and savor anything he wanted to offer.

Legs braced, mic to his mouth, the sound of the rowdy crowd in the periphery, she stayed fixed in place because this was so, so right.

No smoke machines. No stadium-sized crowds. No mosh pits of other Tens. It may as well just be the two of them in that room.

The spell he cast didn't break until the song ended.

She heaved a huge lungful of air, as he broke the thread between them.

"That was fantastic." Her friend Kellie threw her arms around Becca and squeezed tight while doing a tipsy, moving hug thing that had them both cracking up.

Becca laughed so hard, she snorted. Usually, she would've been embarrassed by that snorting thing. But this was Kellie, and Kellie didn't care.

Blonde hair, blue-eyed Kellie had the bone structure and lithe body of a super model. She had even been approached by scouts once when they'd been together in New York. They were still practically kids at the time. Kellie, however, didn't thrive on that kind of attention, so she became an accountant and hung out in her work cubicle instead of the runways of Milan.

"Are you going to bang Linx?" Kellie asked, her eyes huge, her expression hopeful. "Please tell me you're going to have sex with that man and then give me all the dirty details."

"No." The band took a break as Becca maneuvered Kellie back in the direction of the cocktail table they'd been using, so she could re-hydrate before getting plastered, since she'd be going home alone.

Kellie was lit off her ass, and it took a bit of time to get her weaving and bobbing in the correct direction.

"No to the sex part, or no to telling me about it?" Kellie asked, linking her arm with Becca's. "Because he's totally willing to do the nasty with you. I can tell. I have a radar for these things."

"You have a sex radar?"

Kellie shrugged. "What can I say? It's my gift. That, and my ability to save you money on your taxes in a legal fashion that won't get either of us thrown in jail."

"Hey." Velma nudged Becca with her arm. "That was interesting, huh?"

Becca's cheeks heated. "Interesting. Fun. Crazy. Once-in-a-lifetime. Pick your words."

Velma and Becca had met through friends, but Becca quickly came to adore Velma.

"Linx, huh?" Velma heaved a deep breath.

Becca took a swig of ice water and shook her head. "Not like that. Just a song. Nothing else."

A little line appeared between Velma's brows. "It's never just a song. Not with Linx."

What did that mean? Not that Becca had followed him specifically, but she followed Dimefront. Obviously.

Becca narrowed her eyes a little in Linx's direction. He'd gone back to the bar, engaging in an animated conversation with Brek.

And during her months as a Ten, she learned quickly that Linx didn't do serious. Not according to her observations, and certainly not according to the tabloids. If there was even a whiff of serious going on with a celebrity like Linx, they would tuck a whisper of a story somewhere in their pages.

"How so?" Becca's fingertips fiddled with the thin swaths of leather she'd braided together with glass beads for a bracelet. Tying intricate knots for beaded jewelry helped release the anxious energy she'd bottled up during the last months with her higher-needs patients. The ones who needed extra support, even after office hours. Even when she was living her life outside of work. Dating. Grocery shopping. Spending time on the water.

Some people knitted when they got stressed. Some people drank wine. She tied knots.

"With music, Linx is very much a man who doesn't share his gift with just anyone. But he got right up on that stage with you," Velma said, lips pursed.

"This is true," Linx said from behind them.

His voice was, *oh dear goodness,* right near Becca's earlobe.

Becca nearly jumped out of her skin. She pinched her eyes closed because Linx stood there, every bit of her fantasy. *Oh. Dear. God.* He shifted, so he stood beside her, their arms touching the slightest bit because the crowd smooshed them together.

"Good music is like sex. Good sex," he said because, apparently, that was the truth of the matter. "You've gotta trust your partner for it to be epic."

Was this happening?

"The way we worked up there on the stage? Epic."

She turned to face him. "Good music is like sex?"

That didn't seem right at all. Good music was good music. Good sex was good sex. Bad music was like… Well, the point was easy enough.

Except, being up on stage with him had left her hot and bothered and holding her thighs together a little tighter to make the ache dissolve. So maybe…

"In my experience." Linx rubbed the pad of his thumb along his lower lip. "Yeah."

"Have you considered that you may be having sex with the wrong people?" Becca asked, as though they were in a therapy session and it was her task to help him see reality instead of his self-created illusion.

She realized what she'd said. Her heart paused. *God, no.*

Life vacations did not include questions like that. They were not in session. He was definitely not a patient. And that was a horribly inappropriate comment. Heat spread along her cheekbones.

Linx scrunched his face all up.

Shit. Shit. Shit.

He nodded. "That's probable. The sex with the wrong people thing."

Oh. Okay.

Velma's mouth opened the slightest bit.

"Guess I'll just have to keep looking for the right person." Linx tapped along to the beat of the current song the band played. "Can't fail as long as I'm still trying." He grinned like the rock star he was. "What was it Master Yoda said? 'Do or do not. There is no try.'"

"Did you just quote Star Wars to my friend about your sex life?" Velma asked.

"I did." Linx nodded.

Velma's phone buzzed on the table. She grabbed it. "Crud. Babysitter calls." She tossed an extremely pointed glance at Linx. "Please be careful with her." Phone in hand, she shook her head and scooted between the throng of the crowd in the general direction of her husband.

Becca guessed they were going to discuss their opinions about what had just happened.

"Becca." Linx turned so he was face to face with her. "Tell me about yourself."

"Um..." She slid a sideways glance to her friends. Friends

who were pointedly attempting to appear as though they weren't listening. Becca knew their number, though. They were 100 percent eavesdropping.

"You want to hear about me?" she asked. Repeating his question bought her time, but she didn't know which parts to divulge. There were many facets of a person. Which ones should she share?

"I do." He leaned so close they shared the same breath of air.

He smelled of warm oak and earth. Comfort.

Odd, given who he was and what he stood for: a man who lived the rock star life. That should be exciting, thrilling, taboo. Not…soothing.

But Linx was exceptionally calming. Like a lavender-scented bubble bath with a glass of pinot noir and a bar of high-quality milk chocolate. That Tony's Chocolonely that was her go to when she needed to re-center herself.

Linx wasn't letting her off the hook. He just stood there, patiently waiting for her response. So she told him about herself. The abbreviated version, anyway. He didn't need to know about her lack of luck in love or her inability to cultivate her own long-term relationships because the men she picked all seemed to have excessive baggage and used her more as a counselor than a girlfriend. Nope, she didn't say any of that. Instead, she focused on her job and her family.

"I needed a break from my life. A minute to catch my breath and figure out what I want to be when I grow up. Home seems like a good place to do that. Better than my office in Portland."

"After you get sorted, then you'll go back?"

"Maybe." Becca had submitted her resignation, but the practice encouraged a long, self-care sabbatical instead. When—if—she was ready to return, they assured they'd welcome her with open arms.

They'd even offered a few alternatives to the overwhelming number of in-person sessions on her schedule.

She figured distance would give her time to plan the next steps in her life. Deep down, she didn't want those steps to lead her back to Portland. The idea made her belly ache.

Sure, she cared about her patients and their well-being, but she couldn't turn off caring when the session was done, and her work seemed to follow her everywhere. There was no balance. That's why counseling held about as much appeal as reading the DSM-5 for fun.

Thus, she took the advice she would've given her patients: step away from the problem to create a solution.

"An extended vacation will help." It always did. And maybe after a few more months of holiday, she'd be reinvigorated to get back to her work.

That's why the anonymity of waitressing in a bar held massive appeal. Most of the time, guests didn't even look at the waitress. Not really. They expected nothing other than a smile and quick service. They weren't searching for anyone to help them understand their emotional baggage. They just wanted someone to bring them a beer.

Linx didn't seem convinced of her decision. He dropped his elbows to the table and leveled his eyes at her. "What if the vacation doesn't help?"

She was absolutely not going to consider that. Not a possibility. Nope.

"Then I guess I'm screwed." She tried to toss her hands wide, but ended up nearly whacking someone nearby. She tucked them in front of her instead.

Linx shook his head. "Does your work make you as happy as you were on the stage just now?"

No. Absolutely not. That was a very large negative. Hence the whole selling, leaving, and life-sabbatical thing.

"Can I ask you a question?" she asked.

He nodded. "Sure."

"Anything?" she asked.

"That depends."

So, no. Not anything. Just some things.

"Ask your question, and maybe I'll answer." His proximity had her turned all topsy-turvy.

She tilted her head to the side. "You think I have promise as a musician?"

He choked on his beer but recovered. He dropped his forehead to his hand and smiled. He didn't, however, answer.

"That's a *no*, then." She let out an exaggerated sigh.

"Do you want to be a professional performer?" he asked, like he was suddenly taking her comment seriously.

"God, no," she said, matching the intensity of his tone.

He pinched his lips together and nodded. "That's probably for the best."

She chucked him on his shoulder gently with her fist like she would've done with any of her brothers. He caught her hand and gripped it in response. The maneuver clearly intended to prevent a secondary attack, but instead of doing the brotherly thing and dropping her palm, he held her hand and opened her fist so it splayed against his. The heat between them crackled, the big mitt of his palm against her small hand. This encounter was totally going in her diary. Then he kissed her knuckles and she nearly came on the spot.

Was it possible for a girl to come from just the slightest hand massage and knuckle kiss?

She was certain the answer to that was now yes, yes, it was.

"You know what?" He stared into her eyes like she was the only person in the universe. "I like your plan. I want to help."

"My only rule on this holiday is that everything has to be fun." She extracted her hand from his. Not because she wanted to, but because she couldn't exactly have an orgasm in the middle of the bar. "Which leads to my question… How are you going help me have the time of my life, Mr. Linx?"

"I guess we'll have to wait and see," he said this all mysterious-like. "And call me Cedric."

Cedric. Mysterious and sexy and—

"Dimefront, huh? That's pretty awesome," she said, cutting off her roaming thoughts about his mysterious sexiness.

The expression that crossed his face did not show he thought the Dimefront thing was awesome. Maybe she misread. However, any hint of dissatisfaction was long gone, quickly replaced by the effortless charm of his perma-grin with a dash of smolder.

"I guess I gave myself away up there," he said.

"Were you trying to lie low?"

"I'm always trying to lie low." Up close, he had the slightest of dimples. They weren't the obvious kind, and she'd never noticed them in the Rolling Stone spreads. But here they were, out for her to see. "Unless I'm not," he concluded.

"I don't even know what to say to that." Becca took a sip of liquid courage.

"When I'm not on stage with the band, I'm just me. That's what I mean," Linx continued talking like it was only the two of them in the room.

"Well, heads up. You gave yourself away when you walked in the door."

"Oh, yeah?" The smoldering look he gave her increased his charm factor by a solid 70 percent.

She hadn't even thought that was possible.

How was that possible? Huh.

She nodded. Nodded with a touch too much vigor. *Tone it down…*

"You follow the band?" he asked, like the question was a snake and it might be venomous.

She held her pointer finger and thumb in illustration. "Little bit."

"Who's your favorite member?" Was it her or had his tone cooled?

Uh huh. It had totally cooled.

"I probably have to say you since you're standing here." She futzed with the condensation on her glass.

He leaned closer, in her space but not invasive. "Pretend I'm not."

One small move and she could touch him. And if she touched him, she wasn't sure she'd be able to stop touching him. Unless he asked. But with that heat in his gaze, it was a safe bet that he would not ask her to stop.

"Well, there was the night I spent with Bax in Belgium."

Shut up, Becca. Shut up. Shut up.

Her foray into groupie life involved a boatload of concert tickets, airline tickets, railroad tickets, and an updated passport. Then, ta da, she followed Dimefront around the entire European continent, sightseeing along the way. It was one of the best times of her life, and it ended with her spending an entire night with Bax, their lead singer.

Not like that. They hadn't had sex. They talked. Both of them talked. Communication happened. Like *actual* communication. He'd been struggling. She'd been struggling. They found comfort in each other through conversation, not the slam-bam-thank-you-Becca she'd expected.

"Bax? You're kidding." Linx didn't seem convinced. Which was good because she should've kept her mouth closed. Linx didn't need to know. No one needed to know. It was bad enough Brek knew.

She was 100 percent keeping her mouth closed from here on out.

"Of course, you're kidding. You're way too classy for a guy like Bax." He took a slug from his bottle. "Definitely not."

She sipped at her drink. "Believe what you will."

"Guess I'll have to." Dear goodness, his gaze held her in place.

She needed to get away from him long enough to regain her composure. Not forever. Not all night. Just thirty seconds.

"I need a refill." Becca held up her bottle. "Anyone else?"

A chorus of "No, thank you" and "I'm good" followed her question.

Except for one. "Heck yes."

That would, of course, be Linx.

She shifted on her old platform shoes. They reminded her of a time when she wasn't always so stressed.

He smiled like a loon.

Well, bugger her, because she seemed to have adopted a new puppy. A tall, lanky, semi-bearded, musical savant of a canine.

"What can I get you?" she asked. See? Preparation for her new gig as a waitress was already in play.

He tapped a beat out on the table with the palms of his hands before pushing away. "I'll come with."

Um…that totally negated her attempt at getting a breather.

"Unless you'd rather I sit tight?" he asked, as though reading her thoughts.

"No. Come along. That's perfect," she replied. Which, for posterity, she should point out, was not perfect.

She headed toward the bar. Linx? Oh, man. Linx followed her.

When they arrived at the bar, he stared at his phone. His forehead scrunched.

"Everything okay?" she asked.

He scowled. "No."

Do not ask if you can help. Don't do it. That's not vacation speak. Vacation chat does not include rock star assistance service.

"Hey, I'm sorry. I've got to jet." He thumbed through something on his cell screen, forehead still smooshed in concern, not glancing up.

"Can I help?" she asked because she was Becca and she

couldn't not. She did, however, prevent herself from putting her hand on his arm like her fingers itched to do.

He nodded, the long strands of his overgrown hair brushing the collar of his Metallica tee. "I have to check on something."

"Linx…" This time she actually did put her hand on his arm.

That caught his attention. He tangled her gaze with his and didn't let go.

She felt that look in the center of her chest.

Then he tore through the link, looking again to his phone. "What are the odds you'll give me your number? I can call you after I deal with Gibson?"

"Your cat?" she asked. *Seriously?*

"My cat."

Was he for real? This was a brush off. He was brushing her off for something better but didn't want to relinquish her as a back-up. She got that. That was what guys like Linx did. Guys with all the prospects in the greater Denver area.

It was her turn to scrunch her forehead. "Your cat?"

He glanced back to his phone. "Shit. He's crawling in my wall hole."

"Your wall hole?" Was he actually speaking English? Because this was, quite possibly, the most ridiculous blow off she'd ever heard.

He looked up, eyes wide. "He got in the wall."

No, it wasn't her business, but she still peeked at his phone. On the screen was an image from one of the home-pet-nanny-cam things. If he was making this story up, he was really running with it.

The camera focused on a giant hole in a wall. A black cat with a white nose, and white paws, crawled out of the broken drywall before ducking back into the depths of the wall. The cat wore a leather jacket that made him look less like Muffin-the-neighborhood-tomcat and more badass-rocker-cat.

Linx dressed up his cat. Yeah, he could totally have her number.

Becca opened her mouth to say exactly that, but she was too late. He hurried out of the bar to save his leather-clad cat, leaving his neon halo behind.

Chapter 4

Becca

Week one as a waitress had gone swimmingly. Becca had tucked away a tidy number of tips, kept her stress level low, and got a front row seat to some kick-ass bands. Yeah, she had to keep track of her section during those times, but that wasn't a big deal. She wasn't talking anyone down from any of life's ledges.

Responsibility level, point-five. Stress level, two. Totally within normal vacation limits.

She nibbled at her lipstick, hurrying back to the bar with a fresh slew of orders from her section. She made it a point not to look where Linx sat alone in a booth, listening to the music, and nursing a ginger ale in a beer bottle.

Linx had shaved. She'd dug the scruff last week, but the smooth skin left by a razor worked just as well. It made her itch to touch the smooth planes of his cheeks before the scruff returned.

He, uh…hadn't called her.

He didn't have her number, so that wasn't a total shock. *Brek* had her number though. He could've gotten her information from Brek. Or Linx could've asked *her* again. He visited the bar often, which was pretty ace. He didn't get his flirt on with her again, which was not. Even when she'd checked in with him about his cat. The cat was fine, just a menace to Linx's sanity.

She dropped the orders with Brek, grabbed her tray, squared her shoulders, and marched her sneakered feet to Linx's booth.

She stuffed her notepad into the black waist-apron. Brek didn't have much of a dress code other than a Brek's Bar t-shirt. The apron was optional, and he didn't care if they wore jeans or yoga pants or shorts. She went with yoga pants most nights, since the boss didn't care, and she figured it was more vacation chic than anything else. Since it was winter, shorts were definitely out.

"You know, if you're going to hang out here, you should eventually order something," she said to Linx.

"Fries?" he asked, like it was a question and not an order.

"Do you want fries?" Becca asked, not reaching for the notepad because she was certain he didn't really want fries and was just ordering them so she'd let him stick around.

"No, I don't want fries." Linx shook his head. He'd pulled his hair back into a low man-bun that should've been ridiculous, but somehow managed to be ridiculously *hot*.

"You want to just hang out and listen to the band?" Becca tilted her head toward where the band was setting up.

It was the same band from last weekend when she'd hopped on stage and Linx had joined her.

He leaned forward, elbows on the table, his gaze focused on hers with laser precision.

She squirmed.

A day of clientele barely noticing her made this encounter feel like it was the first time a man had ever given her a once over. She felt his look all the way to the center of her bones, deep down in the marrow.

Which made her want to run.

"How about you let me hang out here without ordering anything tonight, and you stop by every so often to say hello?" he asked once he had her good and melty.

Brek and his abundant muscles moved to stand beside Becca. Hm. This was new. Ever since Becca began working at the bar, Brek rarely left his drink-slinging post. Only a couple of times had he even interacted with patrons at the tables. And now, all of the sudden—

"How about you get your ass up and help me behind the bar?" Brek jerked his thumb toward the bar in question.

"I'm here to entertain Becca." Linx leaned back, sprawling across the booth. "Becca's bored."

This was not true. Even if it were, Linx and his broody musician schtick would not keep her entertained. At all.

"I brought a band in for that." Brek indicated the stage where they set up an amp. "Earn your keep. I'll show you what to do."

Linx rat-a-tat tapped out a beat on the table before nodding, sliding out from the booth, and dropping a hundred-dollar bill to cover his tab. Since he'd only ordered a ginger ale in a Coors bottle, that meant Becca netted a decent amount for her first hour of work. She snagged the bill and headed toward the register.

Unfortunately, this meant that she moved in the same direction as Brek and Linx.

"You and Becca are going to be a team tonight. She'll help you out. She knows her shit." Brek tossed a waist apron and a Brek's Bar tee at Linx. "You'll need this."

"He's my bartender?" Becca asked, because no. No way was Linx her bartender.

"Yup," Brek said, thwarting any idea she had to talk him out of this.

She turned her attention to Linx. He pulled off his current t-shirt, exposing an expanse of cut abdominal muscles that made her really wish they'd connected off stage the other night.

Unfortunately, the view didn't last long because he tugged on the Brek's Bar tee immediately.

"Have you ever tended bar?" she asked.

He futzed with the apron. The guy could play a bazillion instruments, but he was unable to tie it behind his back. "Nope."

Becca saved him by grabbing the strings and tying them. "Aren't you worried he'll screw up orders?"

Brek nodded. "Pretty much. But I need the booth, and this yahoo needs something to do."

Well, it *was* a bar and there *was* a stage and Linx *was* a rocker… perhaps there was a better solution? But before Becca could speak up about that obvious solution, Linx and Brek were already in a huddle about how to pull a beer without getting too much head.

There was the obvious snicker from Linx because he was Linx.

"Okay. This is fine." Becca splayed her hands out in front of her. "We will be fine. I can bartend. Linx will wait tables."

Linx glanced to her. "That's a negative. Tens come in. If I'm recognized, a bouncer will have to follow me around. No one wants that."

"It's true." Brek crossed his muscled arms. "No one wants that."

"You don't think you'll be recognized here?" Becca asked.

Linx pointed to the bouncer. "This is where he stands, anyway."

It took two-point-five seconds for Becca to realize that's why Linx had picked the booth. It was closest to the bouncer. It wasn't a fluke he'd selected that seat.

Of course, it wasn't.

"This is going to be a nightmare." She rubbed at her

temples. Her tight ponytail suddenly tugged her scalp too tight.

Linx draped his arm around her shoulders. Totally natural, like this was what they did. She did her best not to think too hard about the sensations ricocheting throughout her body.

She failed.

Thus, the green flag waved, and they were off. Given that it was Friday night, and given that the band had grown in popularity, and given that word had quickly gotten around that Linx was slinging beer—the bar was packed. The bottoms of Becca's feet burned from the number of times she'd done her rounds of the place.

Brek brought in more security on the fly to handle the number of patrons shoved into the small bar. He placed several security guards near Linx. Brek also had a dodgy smile plastered on his face that had her wondering if he'd planned the whole thing from the beginning. He totally raked in the dough.

Then again, so did she. Her tips were phenomenal.

Even after she gave Linx his cut, she'd walk away that night with plenty of extra.

Perhaps the burn in her arches wasn't *that* bad.

"Becca." Linx caught her attention as she finished the latest round. "Brek says we've gotta take fifteen."

No. It couldn't possibly be time for her break. She pulled out her cell and glanced at the screen. Damn. It was time.

Past time.

She gave a quick nod before giving a briefing to her relief waitress.

Brek kept a break area behind the kitchen. Nothing fancy—just a little room with a chipped wooden table and a small counter big enough to hold a Keurig, microwave, and a dorm-sized fridge. Velma stocked a little basket hung on the wall with snacks, too, so that was nice. Becca mentioned offhand once she liked the salsa flavored Sun Chips, and they'd been included ever since. The best part of the room wasn't the Sun Chips though. The room was removed enough from the front of the house that they could make phone calls or talk with the others who were taking a breather without yelling over the noise of the bar.

Becca dropped to one of the chairs and immediately pulled off her Converse sneakers. She went to rubbing the arches of her feet and stretching her toes simultaneously.

A bottle of water slid across the table and stopped right in front of her. She looked up from her impromptu foot massage. Linx. He took a gulp from his own bottle.

"Thanks." She removed the cap and took a drink. New rule: she had to take more personal moments to rehydrate the next time they had a night like tonight.

"We've had a good night." She nearly finished the liquid in the bottle in just those few moments. "I'll get you your cut when I cash out."

Linx laughed. Full-out laughed. "I'm not working for tips."

She frowned at him. Then she frowned at herself. Linx was likely loaded beyond any comprehension she'd ever have. He wasn't counting tips.

Of course, he wasn't.

"You can donate your portion, if you don't want it," she said. They'd been a team. It didn't feel right for her to keep the tips.

"I'm not the one out there busting my ass." He flipped a chair around and straddled it. "I've got the easy part."

She didn't believe that was true. He worked as fast as she did. "That doesn't mean you shouldn't get your cut."

He locked his gaze on the door leading outside. "I owe Brek more than a night of pouring beer."

"Why?"

Okay, she shouldn't have asked. Not really. It wasn't her

business. But she had *asked.* Might as well see where the unpacking of that question took them. Then she was going to start checking those questions so they didn't raise her responsibility level or her stress level.

"Because he's covered my ass more than a dozen times while we toured." Linx's hands fell to his sides, the water bottle barely hanging on between his forefinger and middle finger.

"Ah." Becca nodded, letting any further questions go. They weren't her business, and this was most definitely not her job.

"Ah, what?" Linx asked, turning the tables right around on her with the questioning.

She shifted in her seat. "Just, ah."

"Seems like you have something else you'd like to say."

"I'm just thinking that you don't owe someone when they do something kind for you. It's not like we're all keeping markers and tallies so we can cash in."

He pinched his forehead tight. "What universe do you live in?"

"A healthy one, I'd like to think." Most of the time.

"Somebody does something for you and you just…take it?" He sounded incredulous at the thought. "With no plans of repayment?"

"No, it's not like that." She shook her head. "I just know that when I pay it forward, it may not be to them. Like Karma."

Ugh. She could totally do a better job of explaining this.

"I guess what I'm saying is that being a good person isn't about keeping tally. It's about being a decent human being." There, that sounded better.

He seemed to chew on that for a moment, staring at the worn wooden table before moving his eyes to meet hers.

*Oh boy, oh boy…*Those brown eyes should come with a warning label.

"Velma says you're a shrink," he said.

Ick. No. She hated that term. She didn't shrink anyone. She built them up. Except, now, for obvious reasons. "I'm trained as a therapist."

That got her a smirk. Full lips accented his grin in a way that did tingly things to her insides. "I'm not one to pry—"

"Says every person right before they pry."

"But what's a beautiful therapist,"—he put extra weight in the last word—"like you doing splitting tips with me in a place like this?"

"I could ask the same thing. What's a hunky rock god doing in a place like this, splitting tips with me?"

"Hunky rock god?" He seemed to savor the words.

First rule of being in the same room as a player: don't compliment them too much. They'll make it a point to raise a girl's stress levels. "Don't let it go to your head."

"I should get that printed on a t-shirt. Or a new tattoo." He was totally letting her little comment go to his head.

"You let it go to your head."

"I asked my question first. You go. Then I'll go."

"Because of your deep adherence to a scorecard?" she asked.

"No," he said, slow. "Because I asked first. Therefore, by the rules of asking first, you have to answer first."

"I am not aware of these rules."

His brows drew together, forming two deep lines. "Your universe is pretty whacked, you know that?"

Yes, she sort of did. Hence, the whole holiday from it.

Now it was her turn to stare at nothing in particular. Nothing being the tattoo ink peeking from under the right sleeve of his shirt.

"I'm here because I tapped out and came home to figure out what I want to do with myself. I already told you this," she said.

He leaned forward, further into her space. "You did, but I think there's more."

"Trust me, there's not." Nothing she was going to go digging through after a long shift, anyway.

"I get it." He cleared his throat. "The figuring things out. You might say that's why I'm here, too. Mine was more of a forced situation, given that my business partners are dumb asses."

He frowned at his water bottle. Deep lines between his eyebrows became more pronounced. There was a lot to unpack there.

"What are *you* figuring out?" she asked, going with the obvious.

"Tonight? How to make a whiskey sour. Tomorrow? How to keep my band from imploding." He ran his palm over his face and shivered.

Dimefront wasn't exactly on her radar, as of late. But they couldn't break up. Not to make his career about her, but it would totally add a dose of stress if her favorite band stopped making music. "Is that a worry?"

"Are you gonna turn around and sell whatever I say to the highest bidder?" The look he gave her was pure intensity with an undertone of fire she'd guess was anger.

"I'd never do that." She used the tone that she used in session to show her patients they were in a safe space to share what they needed to share. "I'm a vault when it comes to secrecy. It's literally been my job."

"I'm not a patient," he said with a hearty dose of grumbling.

"No, but you're a human being, and I have always prided myself on creating space that's safe for anyone who needs it." Even when it raised her responsibility levels, which she'd noted were steadily rising throughout this conversation. She was at a solid three.

"Are you for real?" he asked. Not like he was being a jerk,

but like he wasn't sure if she was a phantom. A fantasy that would disappear in a puff of smoke.

She wasn't, and she wouldn't.

"I think so." She fixed her eyes with his. "That would be an existential question we could dig into, but we've only got a few more minutes before we have to jump back into work."

He paused. She knew this feeling well. The will-he-or-won't-he-trust-me quandry. Every person was different.

Finally, he opened his mouth. Closed it. Then opened it again. "The guys aren't on the same page. Sometimes I think I'm the only one really in this. They show up long enough for a paycheck and everything falls apart. Then they go pout while I sit on my thumbs like a good little bass player until they come back around, ready for another payday."

When she'd talked to Bax years ago, he'd alluded to being jaded with the industry. They never talked about the money. He talked a lot about how he only made music because it was expected. The industry expected it. The fans expected it. He didn't do it because he loved the process.

"You're not in it for the cash?" she asked. "Or the fame?"

He shook his head, the bun at the base of his neck jostled with the movement. "I'm in it for the craft. The art. The music. The rest is extraneous." He raised an eyebrow. "It's nice, mind. But it's not why I play."

She shifted in her seat. He was the real deal. Not that she'd doubted that, but she hadn't really known. "Can't you go solo?"

"I could. I can. Brek thinks that's the way I should take things. Play with Dimefront when it's on, do my thing when it's not."

Brek was very logical in this situation. That would've been her suggestion, too. "You disagree?"

"I don't know." He seemed torn. By what, she couldn't say. To find out, she would have to ask questions. Those questions would add more investment into this conversation. To ask or not to ask. Fudge. She was going to ask.

"Which part don't you know?"

"No one takes me seriously. How am I gonna make it on my own in the industry? I do better when I play team sports." Many people were like that. Being part of a team wasn't exactly a bad thing.

"Why do you figure that is?" she asked because, apparently, the rules she set for herself were now moot. Therapist Becca seeped into her words.

"Because the other guys take my slack when I drop it."

She had a hunch here that he didn't drop a lot of slack.

"They seem to be the ones dropping the slack, not you. From what you said, you're the one holding their slack until they come back around."

He seemed less than convinced. "Maybe."

"Maybe?"

"Maybe." He stood, bounced on his toes, and tossed his bottle into the trash like he played for the NBA. Apparently, they were done.

"We should head on back in before they start their last set." He did another toe bounce.

She finished her water before tossing the bottle in the recycle bin with substantially less style than he had.

"You're easy to talk to, you know that, Becca?" he asked, slinging his arm over her shoulder again.

This caused contact between them. Contact meant heat. Heat turned to intense craving. She wanted to lick him all over like he was covered in lemon pudding.

Mmm. Her favorite. Becca loved lemon pudding.

"Thanks," she said, instead of doing the licking thing.

"You've got some stupid ideas about why people do what they do, and what they want in return." He held up his hands in mock surrender. "But you're still easy to talk to."

She elbowed him gently in the ribs.

He didn't seem to mind. Instead, he skimmed the knuckle of her hand with the tip of his finger. Nothing serious. Nothing that screamed "Hey, take off my pants!" Yet, something about that one brief touch was more intimate than all the others. Her nerves fired and goosebumps erupted all over. The air practically crackled, and he was right there. Touchably there.

"Have you considered teaching?" She heard herself ask, her mind clearly unwilling to acknowledge what was going on with the rest of her body. She cleared her throat. "Music. Teaching music. Since it's your thing."

"Teach who?" He moved his hand away from hers like he worried he'd reach out and trace her knuckles again.

Funny, she was having the same problem. She crossed her arms. "Anyone."

"I'm a performer. Not a teacher." He shook his head.

Even knowing the likely consequence to her bodily systems, and the short circuit her brain might experience, she reached for the biceps of his left arm. "But you could be."

He nodded. "I could be a lot of things. That doesn't mean that's what I want to be."

Wasn't that just the truth?

"Becca?" he asked.

She glanced up to him. "Yeah?"

"Have you considered teaching?" he asked. "When your vacation is over?"

She glanced down to the worn vinyl tile of the break room floor.

"Maybe," she echoed him from earlier.

He held the door open for her. "Maybe?"

She slipped her shoes back on.

"Maybe." She was definitely, absolutely not thinking about that now. Thoughts of future work had no place in her holiday.

Chapter 5

Becca

Becca climbed into her car, locked the door, and waved to the other waitress who had helped close up for the night. The other waitress had seniority, and the key to lock up.

Cold to her core, Becca shook a little in her parka as she turned over the ignition and cringed. She wasn't a mechanic by any stretch. Really, aside from paint color, she didn't know much about cars. But the motor sounded like she'd dropped a fork in the garbage disposal and turned it on. She immediately stopped trying because whatever that was didn't sound healthy.

Blah. Stress levels were definitely rising here.

This was fine. She could 100 percent deal with this situation. One more time. She turned the key and…no. She quickly turned it off again.

Bless Brek for outfitting his parking lot with an abundance of lights and security cameras. Because at the moment, Becca couldn't leave.

Literally. Unless she wanted to hoof it the four miles to her apartment.

The term *apartment* was definitely a loose generalization of the space. It was a makeshift studio that her parents had built above their garage. But it had a separate entrance, an abundance of insulation, and reminded her of simpler times when she didn't have to worry about all of her stuff. Best of all, though, it saved her money.

Unlike her car, which she'd recently bought from what she'd expected was a reputable resale lot. Whatever was wrong would probably cost her a boatload of her weekly tips. She did a quick mental inventory of her bank account. She cringed and immediately stopped doing that.

Okay, solutions. She needed a solution. Unfortunately, internally cussing out *morning* Becca for not charging her phone because *nighttime* Becca could really use a teeny bit of power to call for help, was not helpful. She dug through her purse, hoping morning Becca had remembered to tuck a cell charger there. Morning Becca had not. All nighttime Becca found was her wallet, two old sticks of Doublemint, and several lengths of leather she'd planned to tie into a necklace. She rubbed her hands over her face and slouched further in her seat.

"C'mon," she said to the empty car. She would freeze if the puff of condensation from her breathing were any indication. Yoga pants were officially a bad idea. She needed to stick to jeans or snow pants. Or both.

"Don't do this here. Not now."

Linx's Porsche was across the lot. He'd either caught a ride with someone or, maybe, he was nearby. He'd let her use his cell to help get her home. Though, she'd have to nosh on a little crow because then, according to the rules of Linx, she'd owe him one.

Wasn't this just a pickle?

"Everything is fine." Perhaps if she said that out loud enough times, it would prove true. "Fine. Fine. Fine."

Gloved hands at ten and two, she let out a long breath before turning the key in the ignition one more time. The horrible sound started again.

Gah.

Looked like she was walking.

A light tap hit her passenger window just as she reached for her purse. Her heart beat a staccato tempo. She turned her head to find two of the band members there.

Here's the thing. The parking lot *was* well lit, but her limbic system didn't seem to care at all about that because she screamed like she was in a stupid thriller flick.

Oh. Thank goodness. The logical part of her brain took over, and her heart rate returned to a normal rhythm. They knew Brek. Therefore, they probably weren't murderers.

Keyboard guy gestured for her to roll down her window. Tanner. Yes. His name was Tanner. She rolled down her window.

"Hey." She did her very best to sound upbeat and not like a woman who was dealing with a misbehaving sedan on a freezing Colorado night. Mountain air was great when it wasn't trying to freeze her blood from the outside in.

He said something about her engine, but she only understood about a quarter of the words. Seriously, it was like the guy spoke a foreign language, what with the talk of the crankshaft thingers and cable thingys and blah, blah, blah.

Finally, the other guy must've read the lost look in her expression because he chimed in, "We fix cars. Yours needs fixed."

Oh. Well, this was handy. Maybe she wasn't being screwed by the cosmic universe tonight.

"Well then, yes, my car seems to need your services," she said.

"You know Tanner." Guy number two said. "I'm Mach."

Mach?

"Like breaking the sound barrier," Mach added.

"Is that your actual name?" she asked because Mach was a pretty kick ass name, and it totally fit a rocker. Which probably meant it wasn't his real name.

Mach gestured for her to exit the vehicle. "My dad was really into aviation."

The band clearly wasn't plotting her murder, so Becca opened the door and moved to pop the hood.

"Oh, we can't fix it here. This is going to require the lift at the garage," Tanner said, stopping her before she pushed the hood button thingy.

Seriously? A lift? That sounded… expensive. Weren't all lifts expensive? Eye lifts, breast lifts, car lifts… This was totally going to drain her savings. Drain her savings and lift her anxiety.

She'd meticulously calculated exactly how much money she needed to get through the next six months while only waitressing. She figured that was plenty of time for her to be ready to hop back into life. But if she had to pay for whatever the lift thing was, then she'd be shaving weeks—maybe months—off of her timeline.

Which meant she'd have to sort her shit faster.

Which totally made her blood pressure rise.

This was not a holiday activity. This was a real-life activity.

"Are you okay?" Mach asked, concern clear in his blue eyes.

"You look like people do after we give them an estimate, not before," Tanner added.

Mach had pulled a cell from his pocket—one that apparently had charge—and started dialing. "I'll get Lucky to bring over the tow truck."

"You met Lucky. He sings lead. It's his garage." Tanner stacked a couple of instrument cases beside her tire. He added quickly, "Lucky's not his actual name."

She figured that. But then she figured Mach was a nickname. What did she know?

"Becca?" Linx called, jogging from the sidewalk. "Everything okay?"

"My car won't start." Becca glared at the offending piece of machinery and metal. "These guys make music *and* fix cars, though. There's hope."

Linx pulled a Kit Kat candy bar from the pocket of his leather coat.

"Hungry?" he asked.

Um… She shook her head. Oh, she wanted Linx's candy, but at the moment she was dealing with a malfunctioning automobile.

"Do you always carry candy in your pocket?" she asked, purely for scientific purposes.

Not really, they were for her own purposes but, whatever.

"No." He pulled off his gloves and shoved them in his coat pockets before cracking open the wrapper. He bit off a chunk like a heathen instead of pulling apart the bars first. "I ran over to the gas station to grab some jerky for Gibson. He's pissed at me." Linx held up a Slim Jim in his other hand.

Becca made a mental note that there was a gas station nearby. That gas station probably had an attendant. That attendant likely had access to a working telephone. Therefore, the next time she ran out of batteries in her cell, got locked out of the bar, her car sounded like a meat grinder, and a mega rock star and two auto mechanics didn't show up, she'd know exactly where to go.

"I figured maybe this might help him get over it." The Slim Jim in Linx's hand kind of fell limp to the left. She refocused away from Linx's limp meat back to his face. "Gibson, as in your cat?"

"Uh huh." Linx held the now mangled Kit Kat out to Becca. "I grabbed this for me, but I'm happy to share."

She didn't take it. "If I take your chocolate, will you require reciprocity?"

"No, not this time. Consider it a freebie."

"Why?"

"Why?"

"Yeah, why?"

"Because you look cranky and chocolate always makes me feel less cranky. I don't like being around cranky people, so technically, if you eat it, I'd owe you a favor since it'd be more for me than you." He bit another chunk out of the side.

"That makes no sense at all."

He shrugged. "Let me know if you change your mind." He turned his attention to the other guys. "Where are we at with the vehicle situation?"

"Tow truck's coming," Mach said, picking up one of the equipment cases from where he'd set it on the frozen asphalt. He handed it off to Tanner. "He can drop Becca off on the way to the shop."

Linx gave a little headshake. "Nah. I'll drive Becca home."

"You're trying very hard to get me in your debt," she muttered, low enough for just him.

"I'm trying very hard to make your night not suck." He bit off another heathen bite of chocolate.

"Uh… Mr. Linx?" Tanner asked, shifting from foot to foot.

"Just Linx," Linx corrected. "Or Cedric."

"I just wanted to tell you how much your music has meant to me." Tanner shoved his hands in his coat pockets. "Mach and Lucky and me. We love Dimefront."

"Thanks, man." Linx clapped Tanner on the shoulder. "You guys have a good sound. Not just with the covers, either."

"Lucky writes our songs. He played keyboard tonight. Sang with you last time."

"Yeah, what's up with that?" Linx spread his stance. "Switching the lead."

"We take turns." Mach reached a hand to shake Linx's.

Linx shook it. They did another version of the name thing. Linx, also asking if Mach was his actual name and seeming intrigued that it was.

Becca had started out giving Linx a load of crap about his philosophies, but here he was, shooting the shit with a couple of guys who looked up to him. The yawn she'd been holding back since she left work finally made it to the surface. Knackered didn't even begin to describe her level of fatigue.

Linx narrowed his eyes in her direction, thoughtful, soft. "I should get her home. She's wiped. You guys mind handling the tow?"

They didn't. And even if they did, they probably wouldn't have said anything. He was Linx and they were star struck.

Linx

The last thing Linx expected to find when he got back to his car was Becca. She didn't need his help, but that didn't mean that he didn't dig the fact that she sat next to him.

"What's going on in that head of yours?" Linx asked.

She grunted. "My stress levels are way too high. I'm entering the realm of real-life stress." She grumbled. "I don't like it."

"What can we do to lower your stress?" He used his smooth, hey-it's-all-going-to-be-great voice. The one that worked on his sister Courtney when she was in a tizzy.

The heated seats were doing their job because Becca pulled off her parka and gloves and shoved them in the backseat. "I need to do something crazy."

Well, he could be on board with that. “What do you consider crazy?”

They should set some parameters here because he—

“Have you ever gone sports car skinny dipping?” she asked, turning in her seat to face him as the car moved out of the lot. “I’ve always wanted to.”

“Um…” He slid his gaze to her. “If it involves driving my car into a lake, I’m out.”

See? Parameters.

Turning and leaning her cheek against the headrest, she grinned. “Lakes are frozen. I was thinking more like stripping down to nothing and cruising through town.”

He looked away from the road for a second, squinting at her. Was she for real? That was definitely not what he’d expected to come out of her mouth.

“The windows are tinted, no one will see.” She waggled her eyebrows.

“I don’t want to wind up on TMZ tonight.” He tapped a beat against the steering wheel as he paused at a red light. “I was thinking we stop at Jack in the Box for milkshakes.”

“That’s your idea of crazy?” she asked, clearly appalled. “Will you use your senior citizen discount, too?”

“Ha.” Apparently, Becca wanted to go rock star crazy and snort a line of fire ants or trash a hotel room. But he’d never gotten into drugs and didn’t particularly want to get locked up. Who would take care of Gibson if he didn’t get home?

“It’s gonna snow, so a frozen milkshake is unexpected. Even a little crazy.” He was also going to have to up his rock star game. He *was* acting like a senior citizen. Fine. Okay, they could get naked and go for a drive. They could do that and if the tabloids found out, who fuckin’ cared? He opened his mouth to tell her—

“Cookies and cream.” She settled in her seat and closed her eyes. “We’ll skinny dip another time.”

His dick stirred at the idea of Becca naked. Oh. Well then. Another time, he supposed.

Milkshakes it was.

"You mind if I make an extra stop on the way to your place?" he asked.

"That's fine." She leaned her head against the headrest and closed her eyes. "I'm just going to rest my eyes for a minute."

He bit at the edge of his cheek. Little miss wants-to-do-something-crazy was too sleepy for anything other than milkshakes, anyway.

Maybe he should just drive her home after the Jack in the Box stop. They didn't need an extra pit stop, not really. Although, even if his house wasn't on the way to Becca's, he'd been doing everything he could to make amends with Gibson since he'd taken him to the vet earlier that week. Gibson held a grudge better than Knox.

That was saying something.

Gibson had even chewed through the cord to the pet cam Linx used to keep an eye on him from his phone. Apparently, the feline wanted his privacy to mourn the loss of his nuts.

Also, perhaps, and this was probably more likely—fine, it was the truth—Linx wanted to stretch out his time with Becca because he felt lighter when they were in the same space. The muscles in his shoulders that seemed perpetually tense these days didn't feel as locked up when she was around.

She smelled good, too. Like the chamomile tea his mom was always sending him to help with the persistent neck cramps, mixed with something flowery that made him think of springtime and the cherry blossoms in the suburbs of Nashville where he grew up.

Selfish bastard he was, he would not take her straight home. He merged with traffic, turning the other direction.

"Becca?"

"Hm hmm?"

"I lied to you." He gripped the steering wheel tighter.

She cracked open one eyelid and peeked at him. "About what?"

"Well, I guess it wasn't really a lie since I hadn't said anything. But my house isn't on the way. I want to check on my cat and—" He cleared his throat. "I want to hang out with you."

That got him double peepers opening up and some serious stink eye.

"Are you going to make me talk to you?" she asked.

"No."

"Do I still get my milkshake?"

Of course, she did. He grinned.

"Extra whip?"

"Sure." He grinned. He liked whipped cream, too.

"With a cherry?" she asked, singsong.

"If that's what you want." He pinched his lips together to keep from smiling.

She crossed her arms. "And sprinkles?"

"Would it be a vacation milkshake without them?"

"And you'll let me stay here in this remarkably comfortable, heated seat, drinking my milkshake while you deal with your cat situation?" she asked.

He nodded. "Uh huh."

She shrugged and settled deeper in the seat, even reclining it a touch. "That's fine. This seat is comfier than my futon."

Wait, what?

"You sleep on a futon?" He wasn't super picky about where he slept. Not really. Especially when they were on the road.

At home, though, he was very specific about his mattress—a climate-controlled version that felt like sleeping on a cloud. Somehow, it wrapped around him without even moving.

"Why would you regularly sleep on a futon?" he asked, unable to keep the incredulity from his voice.

"You said I didn't have to talk." She added a touch of grouch to her words for good measure, but she didn't seem too invested in being grumpy.

"Fair enough." He tapped against the steering wheel with his fingertips. "Can I turn on music?"

"Will it be good music?" Her eyes remained closed, even as she spoke.

Would it be good music? He scoffed internally at the suggestion that anything he picked would be terrible. "I'm a professional. Everything I pick will be good."

He even had a hankering to surprise her by turning on a few of the Dimefront demo tracks the label had sent over to him to review.

"Fine." She settled on her side, hands in prayer mode under her cheek, facing his direction.

She settled deep. Didn't hardly move.

When he glanced over, her eyes were closed, forehead relaxed. Her lips parted just a little. That soothing comfort that he'd become accustomed to in her presence took over. This did not suck. No, it settled deep in his stomach in a very, very nice way. Relaxing.

Being with Becca was relaxing.

He let out a long breath and let the rock do its thing through the subwoofers while they hit up the all-night fast food place for ice cream. Becca stirred only long enough to take a long slug of her drink. Then she settled until they hit the winding driveway past the gate to his house.

Not bothering to park in the garage, he pulled right up to the front door, grabbed his Slim Jim, and bounced out the door. Two seconds. He needed two seconds to pacify his feline, and then he'd take Becca home. Hell, he'd even leave the Porsche at her house if she wanted to sleep in it. He could catch a ride home from the app on his phone.

He took the stone staircase up to his front door two steps at a time and let himself inside. Gibson wasn't around.

This was what his life had come to—a beautiful woman who preferred to sleep in his Porsche more than a bed, a cat that hid from him, and a limp Slim Jim in his hand.

Brek was right. He needed a fucking hobby.

"Gibson," he called. "I brought a snack."

The front door opened. He turned to find Becca standing there, eyes wide, taking in the ridiculous marble foyer. White walls, marble every-fucking-where, and gold anywhere that wasn't white. The whole place screamed ostentatious asshole, not rocker-lives-here. He needed to add some black. Some character.

In his one attempt to knock down a wall, he'd run into… er…electrical issues. Those issues meant he had a huge hole in his wall and no idea what came next. It added character alright. Just not the kind he'd hoped for. But he figured life could be a lot worse than marble bullshit and a gigantic wall hole, so he dealt.

"Aw, this sweet guy is Gibson?" Becca leaned down as Gibson walked right up to her.

Traitor.

Slim Jim still in hand, Linx pressed his hands to his hips. "That's Gibson. He's still pissed at me."

"What d'you do?" Becca gave Gibson a solid scratch under his chin that made Linx squirm with jealousy.

He wanted her to touch him like that, too. This was ridiculous. He handed her the meat rope with a jerk of his chin to the cat.

"I took him to get neutered." Linx sighed. "Turns out he didn't want to get neutered."

"Would *you*?" Becca carefully unwrapped the meat, offering a nibble to Gibson.

Neutered? Um…he was a guy who liked his family jewels right where they were, so… "No."

Intuitively, he pressed his legs together. Not that he was checking to ensure the guys remained intact—he knew they were—but relief was his friend since they were still hanging out where they belonged.

"I suppose whacking off his junk would cause a rift." Becca fed Gibson little bits of Slim Jim, breaking off one small piece after another.

"First, there was no whacking." Now, Linx was the grumpy one. "One of the top veterinarians in Denver did the procedure. He'd graduated top of his class from the Colorado State University Veterinary School." He counted off the points on his fingers. "His practice consistently wins awards for patient care, I checked. *And* he listens to Dimefront."

Becca laughed. She spread out on the floor and let Gibson snuggle on her lap. "It doesn't seem like Gibson here is impressed with any of that."

"Yeah, well, my mom always watched *The Price is Right*," Linx mumbled. "It is what it is."

Since she was settling in with his cat, he should probably offer her a warm beverage or something.

"I don't understand what that means. *The Price is Right* thing." Becca's face went blank.

"Bob Barker?" he asked, giving a valid hint.

She shook her head.

" 'Have your pet spayed or neutered? Help control the pet population?' " Linx did his best impression of Bob. It was lacking, but what could he say? It was past two in the morning. He tried.

"Oh." She nodded and positioned Gibson so they were face to face. "Your daddy is a nutter."

"Yeah, well, I'm just doing my part. I bought him a leather jacket and everything to say I'm sorry. He doesn't care." Linx took two cautious steps toward the pair on the ground. When Gibson didn't bolt, Linx sat.

Progress, this was most definitely progress.

"He'll come around." Becca continued scratching behind Gibson's ears. He turned on a full purr motor for her.

Linx scooted closer, now that Gibson was in Becca Heaven.

"Dude doesn't get that I did him a favor." Linx kept his voice bedroom-low so he wouldn't startle the cat. This was the closest he'd been to his favorite buddy ever since the surgery. "Now, he can tomcat around all he wants without responsibility or litters of dependents."

Was he mistaken or did Gibson give him some feline side eye?

"Does he go outside?" Becca asked, still massaging behind Gibson's ears. "Will he have ample opportunity to sow his oats with his newly minted freedom?"

"Unsupervised?" Was she crazy? "No. There are wolves and…stuff…out there."

"Doesn't that make you the worst wing man ever?" The side eye that she gave him eerily resembled Gibson's from a few moments earlier.

Linx rearranged his face in mock horror. "I am not appreciating your judgmental attitude of my feline parenting."

He scooted closer again. This time, his knee kissed Becca's thigh. The air in his lungs seemed thinner. The touch wasn't soothing. This touch felt like the moment before he hit the stage at the Pepsi Center with a full house. She gave a pointed look to his hand at his side and the happily chilling Gibson. Then she reached for his palm, eyes expectant. He held it to her and let the intoxication of her touch fill is bloodstream. She placed his hand on Gib's head. Linx took the hint, petting Gibson and sending up a brief prayer that he wouldn't immediately hiss.

He didn't. His motor just turned up, and he gave a kitty cat smile that was freaking contagious.

"Sorry, man." Linx said, still stroking the fur. "I should've consulted you first."

Becca laughed lightly. Her finger skimmed his as they both went for the same spot above Gibson's ear.

Linx bit at his lower lip and glanced up to her.

Her eyes sparkled in that way they did when she wasn't annoyed or asleep in his Porsche. They glimmered like stars while tendrils of her dark hair escaped from the knot she'd tied at the back of her scalp. She was her own version of a cosmic universe. And his cat had just adopted her.

If she stayed, he'd probably start touching her. Then Brek would get pissed. It would be a whole thing.

"I should get you home." He withdrew his hand and stood.

"You could just let me sleep in your Porsche," she suggested. "I like your Porsche."

He could do much better than heated-leather bucket seats. "Do you want to feel the most comfortable mattress in the world?"

She raised an eyebrow. "Is that your pickup line?"

"Ha. No." He shook his head and offered her a hand to help her up. "If I were using a pickup line, it wouldn't involve mattresses. In that case, we'd definitely go for the Porsche."

"I'm not sleeping in your bed." Gibson still in her arms, she followed him up the staircase where he swung a right at the chandelier.

"This, from the woman who wanted to drive around Denver naked with me?" he asked.

"Those are two entirely different things. Sports car skinny dipping is entirely different than actually sleeping with you."

He opened the door to guest bedroom number one. This was the blue room. If the previous owners had a commitment downstairs to gold and white, in this room they went full-in with their commitment to blue. All the shades of blue.

He hated it.

She followed him into the room. Gibson jumped from her arms and, tail high, did a figure-eight through her calves before he moseyed out of the room. "Seriously, Linx. It's not happening."

He'd need to work on her faith in him.

Yes, there was a time in his life when he was a playboy. But now he had a cat. He couldn't just have random women coming over and meeting Gibson. It'd confuse him.

And Becca wasn't a random woman. She was his friend. She was Brek's friend. She could totally come see Gibson whenever she wanted, and it had nothing to do with the semi he'd been fighting ever since she showed up at his table earlier that night.

"It's not *my* bedroom. This is one of my guest rooms." He pulled back the thick, blue duvet cover. "Hop in."

Her mouth opened and closed. Finally, she said, "I'm not getting in bed with you."

She would be a tough nut to crack.

"For a woman willing to strip with me, you have trust issues, Becca." He cocked his head and waited her out.

She didn't budge. "My mama taught me not to hop into a man's bed just because he asks me to."

What did her mama say about riding nude in a musician's sports car? That's what he wanted to know.

"I told you, it's not my bed." How many times did he have to say it? "I'm getting the feeling that you don't believe me."

"Because I don't believe you."

"I just want to show you the mattress." He made big eyes at her and tilted his head toward the bed.

"You're impossible." She let out a sigh and sat on the edge of the bed.

It did that thing where it molded itself to her body. Her expression went from incredulous to slack to curious.

"What is this witchcraft?" she asked, giving it a little bounce.

"I know, right?" He shoved his hands on his hips. "Lay down. Get the full experience."

She laid down and…oh, yeah…she sighed.

He grinned like a goddamned fool because he'd made her sigh and smile, and it had everything to do with a bed and absolutely nothing to do with sex.

"Linx?" She tossed her forearm over her eyes.

"Becca?" he replied.

"I'm going to take a tiny nap. Will that bother you?"

No, he didn't mind. Not at all.

Chapter 6

Becca

Linx's guest bedroom was bigger than her entire condo had been in Portland. Even with the excessive commitment to the color blue, it totally overshadowed her Denver garage apartment. Nothing here had come from Lowe's or The Home Depot. This was all custom, high end, costs-more-than-her-car décor.

The place was comfortable.

She'd slept better than she had in weeks. The futon was great because she didn't have to make her bed or worry about where she was going to crash. This bed though? Oh yeah. Her body was a relaxed puddle of Becca. She peeled her eyeballs open and glanced around. The remnants of her milkshake were on the nightstand in the plastic cup. Gibson had curled up on the pillow to her right. He wasn't asleep though; he stared at her like he'd been doing just that for quite a while.

"You need to work on your morning-after technique." She reached over and gave him a head rub. "Full eye contact like that is borderline breakup worthy the first night you spend with a girl. That's more in line with third-night behavior."

Gibson did a slow blink but continued staring.

She rolled in his direction, pulling Gibson to her chest to give him a more thorough morning cuddle.

"First night, you rarely want to wake up together," she mused. "Better not to share the whole morning breath thing right out of the gate. You do the deed and you go home."

Gibson purred in response.

"Second night, you could consider staying, but don't do breakfast. You don't want to give the impression that you're clingy."

Gibson stretched and kneaded the pillow with his paws.

"Now the third night…that's when you can finally let a touch of your neurosis hang out. Spend the night, have breakfast. That kind of thing. Wait until the fourth or fifth night if you've got an unexpected kink. That's the time to let it slip. Gently, though. You don't want to scare them all the way off. Because if they're not into it, it just may be too early."

Her gaze snagged on a pile at the foot of the bed.

"Did your Linx leave me clothes?" she asked.

Gibson didn't respond.

But yes…

He. Left. Her. Clothing.

Folded at the bottom of the bedspread, someone—someone who had to be Linx—had left her purse, a phone charger, and a pair of drawstring pants that were probably too big for her, given that they looked to be Linx's, and a Dimefront t-shirt she probably wouldn't return. Ever.

What freaking time was it, anyway?

She released Gibson and looked to the alarm clock. Holy crap, she'd slept all morning.

She bolted straight up, a move that epically ruined the residual *ah*-factor of Linx's most amazing bed. Gibson did not appreciate the abrupt movement, what with the way he leapt right down from the bed and marched his little bum out the cracked door.

Suddenly reluctant to evacuate and leave the comfort of the mattress, she blinked against the slept-in contact lenses not made for that activity. Seriously, she didn't know it was possible to sink into a mattress the way this one fitted around her body. Forget about the best night's sleep in months. Last night may have been the best sleep she'd ever had. Gunky contacts, cat stares, and all.

Getting out of the bed was paramount if she had any hope of moving on with her day. Reluctantly, she nabbed her phone from her purse and put it on to charge, grabbed the change of clothes, and moved to the attached bathroom.

She paused at the doorway.

The room had more marble than downstairs. And that was saying something.

Laid out next to the sink was a brand-new toothbrush, and a brown bamboo basket filled with lotions and shampoos, razors…anything a girl could need. Even, thank goodness, contact lens solution.

If this was Linx's aftercare program, she should just give in, get laid, and sign up now. Because she hadn't even put out, and he was already taking better care of her than 90 percent of her other hookups.

There were makeup remover wipes, too. And not the normal kind from Walgreens, either. These were the kind that you had to go to Sephora to buy. *Sephora!*

He had to have a housekeeper because there was no way a guy like him had ever been to a Sephora. She glanced from the deep claw foot bathtub to the bubble bath peeking from the side of the basket.

No, she couldn't possibly do that. She'd already slept in his bed. She wouldn't open a brand-new jar of bubble bath, too. He'd need that for the aftercare of *his* future hookups.

Women who actually gave him something in return for the use of all of this finery.

The thought of Linx and hookups that weren't her made her stomach turn. Which was unacceptable.

"Bad Becca," she muttered to herself. "No Linx."

Nuh-uh. No Linx for her.

Reason number one? She didn't want to mess things up for Brek. Reason number two—and really, the only one that mattered—she didn't want to mess things up for her.

Didn't want her heart to accidentally get involved because that would equal a whole lot of responsibility.

She took a shower, but she didn't enjoy it. Mostly because she set it to lukewarm, so she didn't get too comfortable. Getting comfortable in Linx's house was one step toward being comfy around the man himself. If she did that, there would definitely be issues. Issues that even his impressive aftercare program wouldn't be able to solve.

Once she finished in the shower, she didn't blow dry her hair. That would imply that she was trying to impress him. She absolutely, most definitely was *not* trying to impress him.

So, yes, on with the wet hair and Dimefront tee. No to any makeup. There had been several samplers included in the basket. Of course, there were.

Gibson met her in the hallway and purred at her feet as soon as she stepped from the room.

"Coffee's in here," Linx hollered from down the stairs.

She followed the kitchen noises, moving around one of the Grecian pillars and down the hallway toward the back of the house. Linx chilled at the eat-in table, feet propped up on a chair, swiping at the screen of his phone.

She gulped.

Oh, hell…He hadn't shaved, so he had an overnight amount of scruff. She liked him bearded, loved his face when he was clean shaven, but the little bit of stubble was officially her favorite. He'd pulled his long hair into another man bun that should not have made her head fuzzy—yet it did. Those were great, but they weren't the best part. The best part was that Linx wore glasses.

Glasses.

Thick, black-rimmed glasses.

Holy. Hell.

"Sleep well?" he asked, glancing from his screen. He asked, but his eyes danced like he already knew the answer.

Because he did bloody well know the answer. He knew the black magic of that bed.

"You know I did." She sauntered toward a stack of pancakes on a white plate near the sink. His kitchen, like the rest of the house, was spacious, ornate, and didn't match him at all. White cabinetry, cream colored stone countertops, and off-white curtains. If there was a shade of white, this kitchen had it going on. It would've been perfect for a magazine spread, but in person it seemed like all personality had been sucked out of the room to make room for a whole lot of expensive nothing.

"Are these for anyone?" she asked.

"For you." He glanced up from his phone. "If you'd like them. They're the protein kind—beware. They're healthy."

"Do they taste good?" she asked, nudging one with her fingertip. It bounced back from the pressure like a normal-enough pancake.

"I like 'em." He lifted a black mug to his lips. "There's coffee, too."

She plated a couple, adding a little of the raspberry sauce in the bowl beside the plate.

"How long have you been up?" she asked.

He kicked back, just…watching her in his kitchen. She wished that felt creepy, but it didn't. It felt…kinda nice. Like he was truly interested in what she would do and how.

"Not long." He went back to sipping from his mug.

"Maybe an hour? I usually stay up late and sleep all morning, anyway. Morning is not my favorite time."

"Why?"

"Mornings are for hangovers. Best to just sleep through them."

She'd believe that if he'd had anything to drink the night before. She knew all he had was ginger ale with a beer facade.

"You wear glasses," she said, instead of quizzing him about non-existent hangovers. Her abrupt change of subject sounded like an accusation, which wasn't her intention. Not when he'd given her the best sleep of her life, pancakes, coffee, and a toothbrush.

He shifted in his seat. "I do."

She said nothing because she liked to think she'd followed Dimefront enough to know if one of them had vision issues. Surely, at some point, one of the paparazzi would've caught a picture of him in glasses. She flitted through her memory banks. Nope, she'd seen no photos of him with anything other than the occasional sunglasses.

They stared at each other for a long beat.

Then he smiled. "I wear contacts most of the time."

"You buy makeup remover at Sephora and mattresses that cost nine thousand dollars." There it was again, that stupid accusation in her tone. She knew better than this. Understood how to monitor her tone. What was wrong with her? Something about Linx was seriously wrecking her ability to self-monitor.

Also, yes, she'd totally looked up the mattress to see about getting one for herself. The cost, however, put a damper on the prospect of buying one.

He smiled wider, teeth and everything. Like he was totally digging this conversation. "Where are you going with this?"

"Why don't you have surgery? That way you never have to deal with glasses and contacts." That's what she'd do if she had as much money as Linx. His eyes continued to dance, but he frowned just a touch.

"They cut your eyeball with a laser." He curled his top lip. Shivered. "That's not happening to me."

"I'd get it done. I hate my contacts." She eyed the coffee.

"Help yourself." He rose and grabbed a ceramic mug from the cupboard, handing it over to her. "Cream and sugar?"

"Both." She nibbled at her bottom lip while he pulled out half-and-half and a little crock of sugar with a dainty spoon.

"If you want laser eye surgery, they're your eyes. Your life. You wanna let somebody slice open your cornea with a laser, more power to you."

She scoffed. "That's not what they do."

"Close enough."

What had her holiday become now that she was barefoot in Linx's soulless kitchen, preparing to eat protein pancakes he'd made for her?

"It's just basic refractive surgery done with a minimally invasive laser to reshape the cornea. It's not *that* big of a deal." It wasn't, she'd investigated.

"You've done your research on this." He looked at her again like she was the most interesting person on the planet.

"I've thought about it."

"Why don't you do it if you want to?" He set his mug aside and focused his full, undivided attention on her.

"Because the surgery costs nearly as much as your mattress." She dropped to the chair across from him. "Which costs more than my car."

"Because my mattresses are awesome."

"And now I have to buy one." She tossed her hands to the side. Either that, or she'd have to convince Linx to let her come sleep in his guest bedroom every once in awhile.

"You elected to sleep on it."

"You knew once I laid down I wouldn't be able to leave."

"That's my evil genius plot." A barely there, lopsided smile accompanied his dry words. "Perhaps, though, I had a suspicion. What with you sleeping on a freaking futon for who knows how long."

Too long. One night on his mattress and she'd officially been sleeping on a freaking futon for too long. His phone buzzed, drawing his attention from her.

"Thanks to your exceptional gift of sleep, the scales between us are now unbalanced," she said.

"They became unbalanced when I bought you a milk-shake with sprinkles." There was a subtle smolder in his tone. A smolder that had heat pooling at her core, and her skin tingling all over. "I guess I'll have to decide how I want to cash out."

"What are you thinking?" She didn't mean for the last word to have a tinge of a squeak to it. Yet, there it was, all squeaky.

"I'm sure we'll figure something out." He winked. He smoldered. And there was a definite eye canoodle.

Oh, she just bet they would figure something out. Except, no. Nope, she couldn't sleep with a guy just because he had excellent mattresses and his aftercare was on pointe.

This time, *his* phone rang. He frowned, clicked the side button to silence it, then tossed it on the table.

"We should probably be clear that I can't have sex with you because you let me sleep here." She forked a bite of pancake and lifted it right to the edge of her lips. "It's against my ethical code."

Or would be, if she really had one.

They'd have to have sex for other reasons.

"You'll have sex with me because you want to. The rest has nothing to do with that." That damn smolder nearly made her climb on the table and let him do whatever he wanted to her.

Her lips parted. And not because of the food. "You're totally cracked, you know that?"

Then again, she was, too.

"I've been told." He kicked his feet off of the chair where they rested and stood. "Oh, and Becca?"

He moved behind her, toward the coffeemaker. She turned to watch him as he poured himself another mug.

"Hmm?" she replied, not using full words with vowels and consonants because her throat was suddenly dry.

"The mattress in the guest room is the second tier of that brand. I happen to have the top of the line model in my bedroom." She could only describe his smile as wicked. A devil's heat that made her entire body crave his touch. "*If* you ever feel the desire to try it out."

Yup, her mouth was dry, her throat was thick, and she was sure she'd blinked more in that ten seconds than she had all morning.

Crap.

She wanted to try out his mattress, but for the life of her she couldn't tell if it was because of the mattress or the man who slept on it.

A sinking suspicion in her gut told her it *wasn't* the mattress, and that was unacceptable.

Chapter 7

Linx

Becca wasn't moving. Like at all. Her mouth gently opened and closed like she was a guppy, clearly rethinking everything she considered saying.

She was adorable. Adorable in a way that made him want to wrap her in his arms and breathe in her scent.

He liked her. *Really* liked her.

He couldn't seem to recall the last time he felt this way toward another human being. How would his mother say it? Right. He was *sweet* on Becca.

The ridiculous old-fashioned saying was *à propos*, given that he wanted nothing more than to taste her. He just bet she tasted like lemon drop candy.

He gulped. These were the feelings, the questions, that made a guy end up buying flowers and shit. Brek had told him about these feelings when he fell in love with Velma. Linx had never really understood before. Now he did.

Becca still hadn't responded to his ridiculous attempt at pickup humor. He gulped again. *Don't fuck this up, man.*

She nodded nearly imperceptibly and took a small bite of

pancake with the precision of a woman about to eat with the Queen of England. In taking what seemed like an extreme amount of time to chew, she finally set her knife and fork beside her plate. Throughout this entire production, she didn't glance up. Didn't give him a hint of what was going on in her noggin.

Which meant. Shit a brick. He went too far.

But with the way she wasn't responding, his own breakfast landed like a brick in his gut.

"Let's talk in hypothetical," Becca said, finally. She adjusted the angle of her fork beside her plate.

Well, hypothetical was better than nothing, so, "Okay."

"If I tried out your personal mattress, would I keep my clothing on while I do it?" She dabbed at the edges of her lips with a paper napkin. Unfortunately, this drew his attention to her lips. He momentarily forgot exactly what they were discussing.

She cleared her throat.

Huh? Oh. Yeah. Bedroom and clothes optional and all that.

"You can do what you want to do." He moved his gaze up from her lips to her eyes. "But I promise you that when you are in my bedroom, you won't want to keep your clothing on."

She quirked an adorable eyebrow. "Maybe I will."

"Then I suppose we'll just work around the clothing." He went back to sipping his coffee. "If you're set on keeping it."

He really hoped when they got to that point, she wouldn't wear clothes. Clothing could ruin his plans. Plans that included tasting, adoring, and giving an abundance of attention to all her body.

He immediately regretted his decision to wear sweatpants. No way was he going to stand in front of her without embarrassing himself.

"I think you're flirting with me," she said as an announcement, which was a touch ridiculous, what with the way he was getting his flirt on.

"Then you'd be right." He shifted to relieve a bit of the pressure in his crotch that started when he thought about her naked skin in his bed.

Sonofabitch. There he was, doing it again.

She scrunched her forehead. "Why?"

He tried to get some blood flow back in his brain to figure out what they were talking about now. "Why what?"

"Why are you flirting with me?" she asked.

Um. Was this a trap? It sort of felt like a trap.

"Because you're a beautiful woman who makes me feel nice." Nice and normal and… he smiled a lot when she was in the room.

"Nice?"

"Yeah, nice."

"Define nice." She crossed her arms over the Dimefront tee he'd left for her as though "nice" was not a descriptor she appreciated.

He made a mental note to ask his sister about that later. He rarely asked her about women because there wasn't much he didn't know. Cocky, sure. But also, true.

In this case, he couldn't quite figure out why nice was a bad thing. He scratched at his ear and filed away the question.

"I like life when you're around," he said. They didn't need to make a thing about it. Usually, when he was on a forced hiatus from the band, he was as grumpy as Gibson coming home from the veterinarian. Whenever Becca was in the same space, he didn't feel…pissed off. Most of the time he straight-up forgot to be pissy. Instead, he bought past-midnight milkshakes and talked about driving his sports car in his birthday suit.

"You're a good guy, Linx." She wrapped both hands around her mug as though she were warming them there.

His own hands itched to reach for hers. Hold them in his

palms. Hand holding hadn't been something he was interested in since he was in the seventh grade.

His phone rang, breaking the moment.

He glanced to the screen. His sister.

"I need to grab this." He pointed to the phone.

Becca nodded while nibbling at her lip, which made him seriously reconsider answering.

Except, sometimes Courtney needed a bailout from whatever predicament she'd tucked herself in, so he made it a point to be available for her. Also, she was a helluva lot of fun.

"Hey," he said into the phone.

"Hey," she said. "You will not believe where I am."

"Yeah, where?" He grinned. She could be at the Piggly Wiggly in Arkansas or the Louvre. "Tell me you're not in Los Angeles."

Because Bax was in LA with his wedding plans, and Courtney and Bax created a chemical concoction similar to mixing bleach and ammonia. Things exploded in a bad way when they were in the same city.

"No," she practically sang to him. "I'm not."

"Don't sing, baby sister. We all like our ear drums unruptured." He couldn't help it. Yes, he razzed her. It was their thing. She was a brat. But she was his brat, and they were two peas in a pod.

He considered himself a non-traditional older brother who, instead of encouraging her to make good choices, supported her bad choices. It'd always been this way. She did the same for him.

It'd worked out for him when he had all the girly shit he kept on hand for her so she didn't have to pack it when she came to visit.

"It's my sister," he whispered to Becca. "It'll just be a second." Most likely.

"Who are you talking to?" Courtney asked.

He ignored her question. "What's up, sis?"

"Seriously," Courtney said, the background of her call slightly muffled. "Who is that? Is that a woman?"

"Yes, it's a woman." He looked to the woman in question. She blinked several times in quick succession. "Her name is Becca."

"Do you want to call me later?" Courtney asked. She sounded excited. Then again, his hookups never spent the full night. And Courtney knew him well enough to know that he likely hadn't been up that long.

"That'd be great. Unless you need me now?"

"Oh, no. Not at all." Courtney sang her words again to mess with him. "Just checking in."

"I'll call you soon."

"No rush. See you soon." She disconnected the call before he could even say goodbye.

See you soon? Shit. Courtney was coming to town. And when Courtney came to visit, so did his parents.

Which meant, if history was any indication, he had about two days to get the guest rooms made up.

"Sorry about that." He set his phone on the counter just as Becca's phone chirped.

They were both very popular at the moment.

She glanced to her screen. "It's my car."

She swiped her thumb across the screen, eyes tracking back and forth over the message. As she continued to read, the lines in her forehead got more prominent. Deeper. Concerned.

This made his stomach dip.

Becca seemed to give things her full focus—something he appreciated. Something he didn't realize most people neglected to do. Something that made his insides go weird.

"Damn." She frowned.

"What's up?" he asked, hoping that it wasn't too bad. The woman slept regularly on a futon. She deserved a bit of a break. A touch of comfort. More than a night in his guest room.

She sighed and dropped the phone to the table. "They had to order a part from Colorado Springs. It's going to be a day to get it here and another day to install."

"That doesn't sound too bad." Two days wasn't two weeks.

She rubbed at her forehead. "I guess not. It's not the worst thing. Just annoying. Expensive. Frustrating. Not a vacation-approved item."

He craved standing, moving to her, and giving her a shoulder massage to ease the tension. He didn't do this because it wasn't his right to do. Yet. He'd have to settle for what he could offer without scaring her off.

"You want to borrow one of my cars? I've got a few in the garage that aren't getting any use."

"You barely know me." She tilted her head to the side. "Why would you trust me with a car?"

"I know you well enough." And he wanted to know her better.

"Thanks. But no." She went back to eating, half-hearted this time. "I'll figure something out."

"You're down again. We need to do something crazy."

"It's too early for milkshakes."

It was never too early for cookies and cream.

He leaned forward, across the table, giving in to the urge to touch her. Cautious, giving her opportunity to withdraw, he linked their hands together. "How about I just drive you everywhere in my Porsche."

She didn't move her hand away. "Like you've got nothing better to do than be my chauffeur."

He feigned being deep in thought. "Nope."

Perhaps this could be the hobby Brek wanted him to find—chauffeur for a woman he was sweet on.

He could think of worse things—like making another hole

in his drywall in an attempt at remodeling. Between Becca and Gibson and bar tending sometimes for Brek, he'd have stuff to do. Not making music, which blew, but at least he'd be busy.

The kitchen door leading to the back of the house opened. Brek stood in the doorway. He glanced between Linx and Becca. "You're going to give me an ulcer, Cedric."

Brek being ticked off that Linx spent time with Becca outside of bar hours was a given. Linx decided he didn't care. He'd already tried to leave her alone at Brek's request. He'd spent an entire week leaving her alone. It didn't work.

He raised his cup toward Becca. "You'll see that I've got company. Perhaps your lecture could wait until we're done with breakfast?"

"Hey, Brek." Becca waved between bites of pancakes.

"Tell me this isn't happening." Brek shoved his hands on his waist and shook his head. He didn't mean it though, Linx was certain. If he knew the kinds of feelings Linx was having, he'd come around.

"Don't worry, nothing happened."

That was Becca, talking with her mouth full. They were past the Queen of England portion of their breakfast together, apparently.

"But have you tried his mattress? It's amazing," she continued.

"Guest room." Linx slid his gaze to Brek. "She slept in the guest room. Alone."

Becca shook her head. "Not true." She held up a one-second finger. "Gibson slept on the pillow."

Linx gave her a look that he hoped broadcast that he needed her to give-him-a-little-here. Help a guy out. All that. "Yes, she slept with my cat."

"Seriously, though, have you tried his mattress?" Becca asked, deadpan serious. Let's just say, he wouldn't want to go against her in any kind of debate.

If he hadn't recognized earlier that he really liked this girl, her insistence on touting the benefits of his bed warmed his heart.

"I have not." Brek strode into the kitchen, helping himself to a cup of coffee. "I also have no plans to."

"You should reconsider. I'll ask Velma." Becca's smile was full cheerleader. "She'll love Linx's bed."

"My wife is not getting anywhere near Linx's bed." He gave Becca a solid once over, pausing at the Dimefront shirt. Finally, he grunted and drank his coffee.

"Did you hear anything from Bax?" Linx tried for neutral, but the hope in his voice was apparent. He really wished he had a newspaper. Something he could stare at besides the wood grain on the table or his phone. He wouldn't stare at the screen on his phone because that was plain rude. His mother taught him better than that. But a newspaper? A newspaper would've been excellent. He made a mental note to subscribe that afternoon.

"Or Knox?" he asked. "Or Hans?"

Linx had been working on egging Bax and Knox into a jam session via Brek and their new band manager, Hans. He figured they needed to feel the magic that he'd felt on the stage at Brek's. Not making music wore him down.

He loved making music. Loved the stage. Hell, he loved his guitar about the same as he loved his cat.

"They haven't gotten back to me." Brek crossed his arms. "I'll keep trying."

Linx had tried, too. Hans, their full-time manager, had tried.

Knox and Bax weren't responding.

"Becca, do you ever have to rely on others for things?" Linx asked.

"All the time," she said. "I mean, that's part of life."

"What do you do when they let you down?" he asked,

"It depends." She glanced at Brek and back to Linx. "Sometimes you have to move forward without them."

Brek sighed. "She's got a point."

That thought made Linx's stomach hurt. He didn't want to be a team of one. There wasn't much about Dimefront that didn't make his gut turn to acid-spiked stakes these days.

"If it were me, and your life were mine, I'd likely quit, move to Denver, and take up waitressing." Becca smiled over the rim of her mug. "I guess that's what I did, so I can speak from extreme experience."

Brek leaned forward, forearms on the table. "You've got to make decisions that work for you, Cedric. If you want to make music, do it."

"Sometimes changing habits is the best way to work through an unhealthy relationship pattern," Becca said, quoting herself from countless counseling sessions. She finished her plate and took it to the sink.

"Yeah, what she said," Brek nodded to her. "Maybe you should keep her around."

Linx glanced to Becca, who had stalled while rinsing off her plate. She recovered quickly, shutting off the water.

"Fine." Linx wasn't sure exactly how this would work, but he would make his own music. Screw the guys who weren't around. "Tanner and Mach seemed like good people. I'll see if they want to do a jam session."

"Seriously?" Brek asked, apparently unable to believe Linx was really going to do it.

"I bet they'd totally love that." Becca eyes were all soft, like this was exactly what she wanted him to do. "They're good guys."

Like a moth to her fucking flame, he stood and moved next to her by the sink.

Brek seemed to pause, his mind clearly musing over something. Finally, he nodded. "The only thing I'm gonna ask is that you not fuck those boys around. They've been through hell. They don't deserve more."

"What kind of hell?" Becca asked.

"That's for them to say." Brek stood. "If they want to."

Ah, yes, Brek and his unwillingness to spill the tea. His locked lips tended to tick Linx off, unless it was a Linx secret he held. Then it was fine.

Brek handed his cup to Linx's offered hand. "I'll give Hans a heads up about your plan. And I'll keep working on Bax and Knox."

"Don't hold your breath." Linx set the mug in the sink.

"Since you've got company, we can talk later." Brek gave a two-finger wave and walked out the door.

"It's okay if you don't have time to drive me around. Making music is more important." Becca said, her voice careful.

He just bet that was her *in session* tone. He wished it grated on his nerves, but alas, it had the calming effect he was certain she aimed to achieve.

Clearly, she was well-practiced.

"No." He turned off the water to the sink and faced her. "I offered because I want to."

There wasn't but a breath of space between them. His body was totally wired by her proximity. This was the same feeling as getting ready to go on stage—the excitement, the adrenaline, the willingness to give a bit of yourself to the world. In this case, his world was Becca.

That made him gulp, breathe in her scent. This morning, she was lemons, vanilla, and pancakes.

"Okay." She nibbled at her lower lip. "I'll think about your offer. I like your Porsche."

He traced his thumb along the bottom edge of her mouth. "I do, too."

Her eyes drifted to stare at his lips in what felt like an invitation. The subtle breath she released as her chest rose and fell faster was further confirmation. Oh, yes, she was inviting him in. The taste of her lips was a hairsbreadth away from his. The flavor of…hope.

"Tell me you didn't spend the night with Bax," he said. He didn't want to play second on this one. He wanted to be a first-round draft pick.

"I can't say that." Becca shook her head. She held his eyes with hers. "But it's not like that. It *wasn't* like that."

His gut clenched. He wanted this with her, so why was he finding it hard to breathe suddenly? What was with the intense desire to rewind time to thirty minutes ago when things were a helluva lot simpler? He liked simple. Simple was easy. But he wanted this. Complicated could be great, too. The past didn't have to matter.

So he kissed her.

She let out a sigh just before his mouth met hers, like she'd been waiting for this very thing her entire life. His own breath vacated his body with the thrill of emotion as their mouths touched.

He could've drowned in her kiss, and he wouldn't have minded it at all. Still, he recovered fast, his chest heaving as her tongue darted against his lips. His stomach fucking fluttered. Rock stars didn't flutter during a kiss. But it felt good. Nice. Amazing. He parted his lips to explore further. His hands roamed along her back to her waist, lower to her ass.

She had a fantastic backside.

And hell, this woman knew how to kiss.

Every inch of his skin tingled in the best way possible. She mewed softly against his mouth. He craved more of her, more than this kiss.

She made the sound again. This time he grunted in reply. Like he was a caveman or some shit.

What kind of chemistry lesson were they having in his kitchen?

The noises they were both making made him want to take

her upstairs and really show her all corners of his mattress. Naked. For hours.

That thought brought the present into quick focus.

This was Becca. He liked her. He didn't want to be the alternate choice because she wanted someone else. He needed to figure out where he was with that. He didn't want to fuck up a shot with her by fucking her when she wanted to be with someone else.

He pulled away. Reluctant as all hell, but he pulled away.

Because he needed to think with his brain—the one in his skull, not the one in his pants.

"Want to help me with something?" he asked, his voice huskier than usual thanks to the remaining hope of a game of horizontal Twister his body held onto, even though his brain said he needed to figure shit out first.

She nodded, and said a breathy, "Yeah."

He felt lighter. Good. This was good. It wasn't sex good, but it'd be fun. He'd promised Gibson he could get out of the house for a while, and he had every intention of following through on that promise.

Instead of pressing another kiss to Becca's lips, he snagged the front pack cat carrier he'd purchased online and shrugged it on. He'd chosen the black version with white accents, since it matched Gibson. Normally, he wasn't into the whole matchy-matchy thing, but in this case, it worked.

"Gibson hates getting loaded. You mind helping out with that?" He nodded toward the glowering feline as he continued adjusting straps.

Gibson had his frowny face on, but he'd turn that around once they bundled up and got outside. His cranky cat put on a good front, but once they got moving, he purred like he still had his testicles.

"You're taking me for a walk with your cat?" Becca asked, her pretty face totally neutral. She was not grabbing Gibs.

"Uh huh." He unzipped the pocket to make room for the cat.

"Last night, when I said we should do something nuts, you bought milkshakes." She waved her hand, gesturing to the front he now wore.

"I did." He nodded because…well… he had.

"But this is totally normal?" She still motioned to the front pack like it wasn't normal.

Um. It was normal. They wouldn't sell them online if it wasn't. "Yes."

"Next time I want to do something crazy, I'm going to ask you to do something ordinary. Because I think you've got your wires crossed." Finally, she lifted Gibs and helped settle him in the pack.

"That's probable." He made kissy faces at his cat. "He doesn't like loading up, but he loves it when we roll."

Becca shook her head, closed her eyes, and chuckled. "Okay, then."

Then they rolled.

Chapter 8

Becca

"I thought you were off men?" Becca's friend, Kellie, brought her a cup of peppermint tea.

Becca's last boyfriend had left her for someone easier to talk to.

Seriously, that's what he said. To his *licensed therapist,* now ex-girlfriend.

That he'd left wasn't entirely unexpected. That he'd said that tidbit as a parting shot? Well, that sucked donkey balls.

She'd decided immediately to go on a diet from men. Then she'd decided to go on a diet from life.

"Officially, yes. But..." Becca curled up on her futon in the Dimefront tee Linx had loaned her, and her comfiest Lululemon yoga pants, with a blanket tucked around her. Since she hadn't blow dried her hair that morning at his place, she tied it into a messy bun at the crown of her head.

"This should be good." Kellie settled in her spot on the carpet since Becca was short on furniture.

She loved her little nook above the garage. What it lacked in amenities—all amenities, really—it made up for in soul.

Bright colors where nothing matched and a warmth that seeped in the atmosphere, even when no one was around. She loved the place. At least, she loved it until she slept on a mattress that made her reconsider how awesome it was to not have any responsibility if it came with that kind of sleep. And Linx.

If responsibility came with that mattress, it would be totally fine if her stress levels tipped to a five.

If responsibility came with Linx? She shook her head. Yeah. She wasn't thinking about that. What she would think about however—

"I'm going to have sex." She'd decided this around the time Linx's mouth met hers in his kitchen. "With Linx," she clarified.

After all, she may have been an award-winning counselor, but he was an award-winning player. She meant that in all ways. Not just women. He played all the instruments—keyboard, drums, guitar, probably even a ukulele, if rumors were true.

"Is the sex thing because you like his mattress?" Sadie asked. "Or because you helped him walk his cat?"

Neither. "It's because I'm on holiday, and an illicit affair is exactly what I need. No promises for the future. Absolutely no emotional growth. Milkshakes, cat walks, and just...fun." Also, hopefully, lots of orgasms. She didn't need to share that part with her friends. It was implied.

"Does he know this?" Their friend, Marlee, asked as she dished up some kind of homemade cherry danish her chef husband had made. She had to use paper plates. Becca hadn't bought real plates, since she never ate there anyway.

Becca shrugged. "Not yet. I'm trying to figure out the best way to approach this thing."

Marlee scrunched up her face. "Did he even use his tongue? Maybe you need to be clearer about what you want?"

"There was tongue." Oh boy, was there.

"What happened next?" Marlee asked, handing out plates.

"Nothing. I was into it. He seemed into it. I figured we'd move to the heavy groping stage, but he pulled away." That's why Becca had called an emergency group meeting of her best girlfriends. "He probably stopped because he wanted to talk about his childhood."

Linx acted like he wanted to take things further with her. And then, when she'd finally made herself available to him… nothing. He'd loaded her up in his Porsche and dropped her at home. Told her to text when she was ready for a ride. And he did not mean the kind of ride she'd been ready for that morning.

Nonetheless, the ride thing led to where she did, in fact, have Linx's cell number tucked safely in her phone. She got the vibe that he wanted her to call and talk.

She didn't want to call and talk. She wanted to call, meet up, and do *other* things.

"'Kay." Kellie sat tall. "Here's what we're going to do."

Becca widened her eyes and waited.

"You work tonight, right?" Kellie asked, splaying her hands along the edge of the futon.

Becca nodded.

"Then call Linx, ask him for a ride." Kellie grinned like she'd just solved the Riemann Hypothesis million-dollar math problem.

Marlee paused mid-danish-to-mouth. "*That's* your solution?"

"Simple. To the point." Kellie wandered to the card table-as-dining-room-table to snatch another pastry.

"Then you pounce on him." Sadie patted Becca's calf. "When you get out of the car, pretend to trip a little, when he helps, do the lip lock thing. This time, make sure you're clear with your body language that you want more."

"I'm not doing that." Becca sighed and scrubbed her

palms over her cheekbones. "One of the regulars tried to pick me up the other night. Maybe I should let him."

He wasn't Linx, but he'd make a decent life-holiday fling.

"No." Marlee shook her head. "He may as well be a co-worker. And we all know that we don't take coworkers home with us."

"Linx and I kind of worked together last night," Becca pointed out, even though it went against what she really wanted.

Marlee shook her head again. "Yeah, but he's not really your co-worker. He was just helping Brek. Different paradigm. Doesn't count."

"But the guy who comes in pretty frequently does?" Becca asked.

Marlee logic didn't make a whit of sense.

"See, she understands." Marlee did a shoulder shrug dance that she probably should've patented when they were teenagers because it was totally Marlee.

"I wish you all could experience the joy of his guest bedroom." Becca fell back on her sorely lacking futon. "Seriously, the bed. The basket. The shower with six nozzles. The man's aftercare program is on point."

"Makes you wonder what stops he'd have pulled out if you had invited him into bed with you." Marlee giggled at her own funny. "What if I da—"

"No." Becca tried to skewer her with a glare. She was certain it was a failure, given that she didn't skewer people often. Usually, she listened with an empathetic ear and an open smile. She'd have to practice skewering to refine. "Do not dare me on this. I need to let it happen naturally." Well… "Mostly naturally."

"Becca?" her mom called from the bottom of the steps leading to the loft apartment.

The one thing this meeting of the minds did not need was her mother.

"I'm here. My friends are over." Becca called back. Otherwise, her mother would continue right on in and make herself comfortable with Becca's girlfriends. And didn't that just sound like she was fifteen again and covered her bedroom mirror in Lisa Frank stickers?

Her mom had always been great about giving Becca and her friends their space. This hadn't always panned out for her. But they'd only wound up in front of a judge the one time, and it was totally unfair. Thankfully, Marlee's parents had deep pockets that paid for attorneys to illustrate the depth of unfair. All the girls got off with warnings and a promise they would wear their shirts the whole time they were at professional hockey games. No exceptions.

The clomp of feet on stairs did not indicate that her mom went the other direction.

The door opened and her mother appeared. "Hey, honey."

Becca smiled. Her mom was so her mom. Super soft spoken—nearly to a fault—but she had opinions, and she had her ways of ensuring that everyone in her vicinity knew precisely what those opinions were. She was also the queen of swinging others to see her point of view.

Also, her mother came off as a bit of a curmudgeon. It was all a show, from the cardigan twinsets to the super comfy orthotic shoes, because Becca had seen the pictures from her younger days. Perhaps she was more comfortable in these outfits, but she had a history. Becca had seen the receipts of that history. She was sure *she* was a receipt of that history.

"Mom." Becca used her super calm voice. The one her mother had taught her.

"Don't you use that tone with me." Mom bustled into the room. "We need to discuss your choice not to text me when you decided not to come home last night."

"I was working. My phone was dead. I slept at a friend's

house." Also, she was a grown-ass adult with multiple degrees and the ability to make her own decisions.

"Which friend?" Mom asked, glancing between the girlfriends all gathered around. "One of these ladies or… someone—" She coughed like she was clearing her throat. "—else?"

Becca should've known her mom wouldn't fall for sleeping at a friend's place.

"I'm a grownup." And sometimes, apparently, her mother needed the reminder.

"Oh, I know." Her mother gave a sly, knowing smile. "I know you've had the sex, too."

Marlee choked on her pastry. Kellie pounded on her back.

"I mean, I hope you've had the sex," Mom continued. "Sex is nice when you do it right." Mom paused, deep in her own thoughts. Which was good because Becca wasn't sure what the hell to say. Neither did her friends, apparently, what with the way they weren't saying anything.

"You know, you don't even have to have a partner if you don't want one." Mom started talking with her hands—which, given the topic, was unfortunate. "Belinda bought me one of these bedroom doohickeys with two ends. I haven't had anything like that since I was in my twenties. I swear to God, I don't even need your father anymore."

Becca blinked. Hard.

Belinda was the preacher's wife at the church Becca had attended growing up. She held lady's luncheons and Grief Share meetings. She also wore orthotics, just like Becca's mom.

"I want to hear more about this doohickey," Sadie—traitor that she was—said. "I like doohickeys."

Great, there was no way Mom would leave now.

"You have Roman," Marlee pointed out. "Why do you need a doohickey?"

"Oh, girl," Kellie said. "Does Eli not use doohickeys with you?"

Marlee shook her head. "We have a baby. There's no time to get out doohickeys when we're having *the sex*. Our window is limited. We've learned to compensate by—"

"Could we all just stop talking about this?" Becca raised her voice. She didn't have outbursts often, so it got everyone's attention. "I don't want to hear any more about doohickeys or the sex."

"She's drying up." Mom sounded ridiculously disappointed. She pulled up a chair, even though everyone else stood or sat on the floor. Except Becca, who took no comfort at all on her futon.

"I'll ask Belinda to get you one the next time she orders," Mom continued. "She buys in bulk because she gets a quantity discount. The ladies' auxiliary just loves her for it."

Becca's heart seemed to stop pumping blood, and the muscles in her face seemed to stop responding to neural stimulation.

"We meet at the church every other Tuesday," Mom kept on talking like she hadn't blown a fuse in Becca's brain. "They asked if you'd come talk to them about your work."

"I'm on vacation." Becca had told her mother this same thing multiple times. "I'm not working or talking about work while I'm on vacation."

"Then talk about that communication stuff you're always telling me about."

"Mom," Becca said, dryly. "I'll think about it."

Because, actually, maybe it would be fun to talk about the various ways human beings communicate with each other. Verbal, non-verbal, body language. Uh huh, that could be fun.

"Now, baby girl, give me the deets about this man who is not meeting your needs." Mom smacked her knees.

"The deets?" Becca asked in confirmation. Had her mother just used slang from ten years ago?

"Details," Mom explained.

"We should get you a slang manual, Bec," Sadie suggested, a tad too serious. "Maybe we could provide that when Belinda delivers your doohickey?"

"I know what deets means." Becca just wasn't used to her mother using it in her everyday speech patterns. "Why are you using slang like that from an alternative generation?"

"Because I'm with it." Mom sat, settling in way too comfortably. "Now what happened? Will you see him again or was it one of those one up things?"

Sadie seemed to choke on cherry danish.

Mom frowned. "If he didn't meet your needs, I hope you didn't give him a blow job. A man should earn that. Ask your father."

Oh, dear God, she was not asking her father about any of this.

Becca's mother was perfectly comfortable discussing intimacy with her kids, much to their forever dismay. This was likely why her brothers moved out of state at the first opportunity.

"I had lots of one-night stands in my day." Mom glanced from friend to friend. "I believe it's important to get around before a girl decides where she wants to land. How else will you know what you want?"

Becca pressed her fingertips to her temples. "Oh, my God."

"I bet that's what he said last night." Mom nudged Marlee again. "Rebecca, darling, your problem is that you've always been a giver. You need to spend some time being a taker."

Marlee was totally into this exchange, given the crazy smile on her lips. "That's what we were just saying."

"Mom. Stop. I fell asleep in his guest room, and it wasn't

a big deal." And it wouldn't be a big deal because Becca would invest in all the doohickeys, and she wouldn't be getting them from the ladies' auxiliary.

"Not a big deal?" Mom asked. "Then why do you look like you did that time your dad accidentally hit a raccoon with his car?"

Fine, it felt like a bit of a big deal. Okay, maybe it was even an enormous deal. She needed some time with her most trusted friends to dissect that.

"We're trying to help Becca figure out the next steps in her catch-a-man, get-laid plan," Marlee said, directing all of her attention to Becca's mother. "We've all decided this guy is *the one*."

"It's true," Kellie added. Which was ridiculous because they hadn't commiserated on their feelings about Linx.

"I do not need help with my fling plans." Becca crossed her arms and stared at the ceiling.

"I think we established earlier that you do." Sadie rubbed Becca's ankle.

"What's the plan?" Mom asked. If Becca wasn't mistaken —and Becca wasn't mistaken—her mom was about to dig right on in and help Becca catch a Linx.

"To call him and ask him to drive her to work tonight, since he offered," Kellie said. Because, well, that was all the plan they'd come up with so far.

"Why aren't you driving yourself?" Mom asked, her eyebrows falling together.

Becca sighed. Better to just get it all out there before her mom started talking about multi-pronged doohickeys again. "My car died. It's being reincarnated in the shop."

Mom pursed her lips. Perhaps there were some things that didn't change. Her mother's distaste for Becca's choice in vehicles shouldn't have been comforting. And yet…it was.

"You know you should've avoided that brand." Her

mother turned on the stern. "We are a Chevy family." She glanced to Sadie. "Just ask her father."

"I like my car," Becca said, coming to the defense of the car even though it had, technically, stranded her ass. She'd loved it until last night. Somewhere around the second grinding noise, she'd slipped from heavy love to like. Unless there were more issues she hadn't heard about, she didn't plan on selling it soon.

Mom thought on that for a moment before saying, "Yes, but dear, sometimes the things we like aren't what's best for us."

Maybe her mother should become the therapist in the family. With a little tweaking, she'd be excellent.

"Now you sound like me." Becca draped her forearm over her eyes. "I don't like it."

"Perhaps it's you who sounds like me," Mom suggested with a touch of an eyebrow waggle.

Becca didn't like that, either.

"Oh, crud." Mom stood and brushed nothing from her pressed slacks. "I totally forgot why I came up. Your dad is having friends over for poker tonight. Try not to make too much noise. It distracts them if they can't focus on the cards."

Huh? "Since when does Dad play poker?" Becca asked.

"Probably around the time the ladies' auxiliary started handing out double-ended doohickeys," Marlee said around a mouthful of cherry filling.

"Poker. Be quiet. Noted." Becca didn't move her arms from covering her eyes.

"We'll keep it down now, too." Sadie was the brown-nosing friend. "Unless you'd prefer we make noise?"

Mom waved off the suggestion.

"Randy is heading out for chips and beer. You can make all the ruckus you want." The shuffling sounds Becca hoped were her mother leaving paused for a moment. "Let me know if you girls need more snacks."

"We're good, Mom." Becca should start an apartment search.

"This is so much more fun than when you were a kiddo," Mom said on a laugh. She continued to giggle the entire way down the staircase. Loud. With absolutely no care to the fact that Becca and her friends could freaking hear her.

"Randy," Mom called as she got further away. "Becca met a man. You should ask him over for poker with your friends."

And I should definitely check out the housing classifieds.

If Becca had a few nights of extra good tippers, she could move into a place with a touch more privacy.

She peeled her eyes open.

Her best friends all stared at her like she was a ticking time bomb and they were going to help her shove all the pieces of herself back together.

"Does anyone else really wonder what this doohickey is?" Kellie asked. "I feel like I need to know. For science."

"No." Becca gave a not-so-subtle head shake. "You're not allowed."

The ache in her heart while she lived away from her family hadn't ever quite gone away, even when she came back this time to stay for a while. She was still the same Becca, but the rest of the family had gone down a different path. They'd changed. Dad played poker and had buddies. Mom's ladies' auxiliary had gone off the rails. Her brothers moved away. They'd all changed.

Yet, she hadn't.

Her mind immediately took her to Linx's house. The place held an abundance of privacy. Privacy and no parents and a mattress to die for. Bah. No. She would not fixate on Linx, his privacy, or his mattress. At least, she would try her best not to.

She'd deal with the futon and invest in a *Privacy, Please* sign.

Or something.

Chapter 9

Linx

Snow fell as Linx pulled into the spot outside of Brother's Automotive and Tire Center near Broomfield. The gray, cinder-block building was well-kept with new paint and shiny windows. The sign had a small crack along the edge but was otherwise in good shape. The buildings surrounding it weren't as lucky. Several were vacant, and the few that held industrial businesses looked like they could definitely do with an overhaul and a solid coat of primer, at the very least.

Linx climbed out of his car. He could've called, but he preferred in-person conversational transactions—even when he planned to give loads of shit away. Shit being his time. But seeing as he wasn't heading to the recording studio soon, his schedule was wide open.

A bell on the glass door chimed when he pushed it open. The place smelled like the semi-sweet scent of new tires. Thick glass windows separated the front of the shop from the back and muffled most garage sounds, though Black Sabbath through the speakers was clear enough for him to identify.

He grinned all the way through his body. If that song was

any sign of what these boys had for taste in music, they'd get along just fine.

The lead singer with the tats—John—helped a lady at the counter. She held his entire attention.

Which made sense because she was pretty. Not Becca pretty, and she didn't make Linx want to rearrange his life and introduce her to his cat, but she definitely had the look of a woman who knew how to get what she wanted.

He could appreciate that in a fellow human being.

Carpe the fuck out of the diem.

"Be right with you," John said, without looking up from her invoice.

"No rush." Linx grabbed a seat in the waiting area and tapped out the rhythm to one of the new songs he'd been percolating.

The beat of his new song almost matched up entirely with Black Sabbath. That was handy.

John looked up. Then he did a double-take before his eyes got comically wide.

Linx gave his best shit-eating smile and a two-finger wave.

"Go back to whatever you all are doing." Linx also waved to the lady checking him out. Given that the only woman his brain was interested in was Becca, he gave her a smile, but nothing else. "I'm in no hurry."

The shop door opened, and the blare of heavy metal followed the motion. Mach strode through wearing blue coveralls with his name stitched on the pocket. A pair of safety glasses held his shaggy hair out of his face. He grabbed a clipboard, looked up, and did the same double-take as John when he caught Linx chilling in their waiting area.

Linx gave another two-finger wave. "Mach. Good to see you."

"Uh." Mach slid his gaze to John and then to the woman. He was a man who sized up the room before committing. Linx gave him extra credit for being thorough.

"Are you being helped?" Mach asked, now that his assessment was complete.

"Nope." Linx stood, giving his limbs a little shake with the motion.

"Car trouble?" Mach asked, glancing out the front bank of windows to Linx's brand new sports car.

Hell no, Portia—he'd finally decided on a name for her—was perfection in metal form.

Linx shook his head. "That's not why I'm here. Have a second? Private?"

"Sure." Mach tilted his head toward the open door of an office. "Do you… um… want something to drink? Eat? We have coffee and there's a snack machine in the break room. They stocked it yesterday, so it's still got Doritos."

"Nope." Linx strode into the office, taking the chair Mach offered. "I came to talk to you—" He pointed at Mach. "—and the band." He rapped out a rhythm on the desk in time with the last of his words.

Mach didn't sit at the desk. He sat on the edge of the desk. Crossed, then uncrossed his arms. He did the same with his legs.

Linx waited until he settled.

"The other guys are all busy in the shop." Mach glanced through the panes of glass that exposed the expanse of the garage. Looked like they had five or six lifts. It was a decent-sized operation. "Monday's are always the craziest. We've got an entire weekend of problems to triage."

That sucked. Linx hoped they'd beg off early to come play music with him at Brek's. Still, he understood. Suckage factor was still the same, though. He stood. "I can come bac—"

"But I've got a few minutes—was just about to take my break. Talk away," Mach settled in again on the side of the desk.

Linx felt like he was seven again, hoping the neighbor kids

could come play in his first stab at a garage band. Back then, they had trashed instruments. That didn't stop them from trying. They'd played on orange buckets from The Home Depot, an old piano he'd pulled off the sidewalk, ready to get hauled to the dump, and his very first cheap ass guitar his grandma bought him for Christmas.

"Brek says you guys want to go next level." Linx leaned forward, arms slung over his knees.

Mach nodded. "Tanner and I do."

Just the two of them? Linx's brows raised right along with his surprise.

"John runs the shop." Mach hooked a thumb toward where John was still helping the lady at the counter. Helping had definitely encroached on pickup territory, by the looks of it.

"He's not interested in record deals. And Larry only hangs out with us because we force him to." Mach smiled in a way that suggested it wasn't too hard to get Larry to play along. "Since he retired, he's been hoping we can find someone to take his spot."

"Gotcha." Linx pressed his forefingers together and pushed them against his lips. "You and Tanner, though? You want to do the whole rock 'n roll-for-real thing?"

"Who doesn't?" Mach grinned wider. "Well, except John and Larry." He added a half-hearted shrug for good measure.

"Well, then you boys are in luck because I'm your fairy fucking-godmother." Linx nodded once in firm agreement with his own statement.

Mach let out a small breath of air. "What?"

"I want to help you," Linx confirmed what he thought had been perfectly obvious before.

Mach didn't seem to buy it. For the first time since they'd entered the room, he frowned. "Why?"

Why? Uh. Because?

"I need something to do," Linx said. That sounded good

enough. "Brek suggested I use my—how did he say it?—'Talents and considerable charm' to help you guys nab the attention of a label. Figure I'll call my agent once you're ready and have him give you guys a listen. We can go from there. See where the road takes us."

"Yeah. Uh..." Mach rubbed at the bridge of his nose. "I don't..."

"You don't want to learn from the best?" Linx asked. He kept his tone light, but what the fuck was wrong with learning from him?

"It's not that." Mach crossed his arms. This time, he kept them crossed. "We want to learn from the best. Tanner and I, though... we don't do the charity thing. We're not interested in a fairy godmother."

"Gotcha." Linx nodded. The logic was sound. "Well, I'm the best. That part's settled. What do you say I do this for you, then you can do something for me?"

"What does a guy with everything need?" Mach asked. He was serious.

Well, hmm...Linx needed a lot of things. At the moment he couldn't remember what they were, but he'd come up with something.

"A marker." He decided. "For future use."

Mach seemed to mull that over. Then he nodded, slow. "If Tanner's in. I'm in."

Linx rubbed his hands together. "Then let's get Tanner in on this, yeah?"

Mach's perma-grin was back and affixed to his face. "Absolutely."

He held his hand out to Linx.

Linx shook the hell out of it.

Linx

The day called for an impromptu jam session at Brek's while the afternoon regulars and their waitress—Becca—watched. Oh, hell yes, this was living.

Rock 'n roll and Becca in the same room made for a very, very happy Linx.

Even with the garage slammed with work, John encouraged Tanner and Mach to take the afternoon off. They balked. Linx backed John, mostly because he didn't want to lose out on an afternoon of making music.

Since John was the boss, they didn't have much choice. He all but kicked them out the door to go make be-au-ti-ful notes with the maestro.

A maestro who ran his fingers over the strings of his favorite guitar, letting the combination of chords seep into his soul. He opened his eyes for a split second and caught Becca's stare. She glanced away, but the flash of her white teeth and half-chuckle didn't escape his notice.

He hadn't felt this feeling consistently in years. The way he felt like smiling all the time. The way gravity felt lighter.

Happy. This was happy.

Happy was pretty fucking nice.

"Right, follow the melody. Let it lead you." Linx closed his eyes while Mach played the song they'd been working on—the one Linx messed around with earlier that day before he went to the garage. Mach was a master with the keyboard, but he could also rock the hell out of a guitar.

Linx thrived on collaboration when he drafted songs. Mach did not disappoint. They worked and reworked the chords until they were perfection on sheet music.

A touch younger than Mach, Tanner was a drummer, through and through. The love for the beat was it for him. As long as someone tossed him some harmony and a melody that needed a solid rhythm, he couldn't give a shit about the rest of it.

That dedication to his particular craft would serve him well in the industry.

Linx figured as long as these two stayed on the straight path and didn't dip their toes into nose candy and Molly, they'd be stars in the rock sky of their own right.

At the moment, these two were a touch green in the rock world, but their passion and talent were obvious in their ability to adapt to anything Linx tossed their way. Brek had been right. With a little guidance and a few connections, they'd be as big as Dimefront. Maybe even bigger if they kept their shit together and didn't go on hiatus every time someone fucking sneezed.

Becca paused at the foot of the stage, unloading another round of ginger ale served in a glass beer bottle for all three of them.

He was about to initiate them into his club and show off his dirty little secret. Hell, it was only ginger ale, but it was better than all the alternatives the industry came up with.

He caught Becca's stare and held it as he sang the song he'd been writing for her about brown eyes and thunder, rain clouds and sun. She didn't know it was for her—he hadn't mentioned it. They hadn't had a second alone since she'd come on for her shift.

He hoped she got it, though. Given the way her chest heaved as he continued to sing the song through toward completion, he thought it was pretty clear.

Mach and Tanner apparently got the message not to push pause this time because they didn't stop to rework a couple of problem bars. Their focus was on the music and on Linx. And since the music was about Becca, his focus was on her.

He didn't close his eyes until the last guitar riff. That's when he poured himself into the music as though he were playing a stadium of thirty thousand instead of a barroom filled with half a dozen.

When he opened his eyes, Becca hadn't moved. It didn't seem like she breathed much, either.

He mouthed, "For you."

Her lips parted, and she swallowed visibly. Unfortunately, the gleam in her eyes seemed more on the terrified side than the thrilled. He'd have to figure that one out. He'd never written for a chick before. This was all unfamiliar territory. Fucking it up was not an option.

"Third chorus is jacked," Mach said, pulling Linx from his Becca haze. "We need to rework that hold."

Mach wasn't wrong.

Linx handed him a bottle. Mach took a swig. He stilled. Then he spit the ginger ale back into the bottle. "What the hell am I drinking?"

Linx handed another bottle to Tanner. Tanner stared at the bottle in his hand and sniffed. "That's not beer."

"No, it is not." Linx grabbed his own bottle and took a long slug. "This is how you stay sober and keep a decent level of rock star respect."

"Can't I just drink beer?" Mach asked. He eyed the bottle like it was ale made from snake oil, not ginger.

"You could." Linx took another drink, making a show of smacking his lips and saying ahhh. "But this keeps you sharp when you're on stage."

Tanner took a little sip. "Can I have beer after?"

Linx nodded. "Yep."

He searched the bar for Becca and caught her looking his way. He smiled. She smiled. There was a whole lot of smiling.

Then Becca stripped her gaze and got back to work. So did he, and it felt amazing.

Chapter 10

Becca

Becca dropped baskets filled with fried pickles and potato skins in the center of Linx's table. Well, the band's table. Linx, Mach, and Tanner were talking music in the far corner booth.

"Your car will be ready tomorrow." Tanner was a touch sheepish for a guy with a decent stage presence. Like he wasn't sure of himself. On stage, he was all confidence and drumsticks. But whenever Becca approached the table, he seemed to stumble over his words and his cheeks blushed red.

He had the sweet, cute, undercover charmer thing going on. Someday, that combination would prove the fatal one-two punch for a woman to fall ass-over-beer bottle for him.

Meanwhile, her body seemed to have a magnetic pull to Linx. Apparently, she liked cocky, charming men who bought their cats leather jackets, didn't do more than kiss her when given the opportunity, and had excessively lavish taste in bedroom furniture.

"Tomorrow will be great," she said. "Then I won't have to call for a ride on the app."

She did her best to make Tanner comfortable, but he just seemed to blush harder whenever she gave him any attention. She diverted her attention to Mach while she refilled his water glass.

"You don't have to do that now," Linx said, low and dark. Rumbly and gravel. "You shouldn't be using an app when you have me."

She cleared her throat. "I don't want to bother anyone."

"I'm not anyone," he said. And wasn't he just the Grumbly Gus tonight? Probably because neither of them had gotten their cookies that morning. Which was totally bologna because he was the one who hadn't taken things further.

"You ever consider that it's more of a bother wondering how you're getting around?" Linx asked, the words soft as a caress.

Given that they weren't more than friends with the very minimal benefit of that morning's lip lock, he shouldn't have been wondering about her transportation.

Becca opened her mouth to say something snarky about his lack of follow-through—his eyes, her lips—but pressed her tongue hard against her pallet. Wasn't she always cautioning her patients to self-check intent?

"Dude." Tanner shook his head. "Don't make her feel bad."

"Listen to the drummer." Becca winked at Tanner.

Unfortunately, that made Tanner's entire face turn the same shade of red as the Coors Light sign.

"Did I make you feel bad?" Linx asked, again with the caressey-caress words.

Becca squinted her eyes and squared her shoulders. "Maybe."

"It's a yes or no question," Linx said.

Dear goodness, if he sounded like this while they were standing in the middle of the bar and used a tone that made all the hairs on her arms tingle, what would it be like if she did finally get to jump on his mattress with him?

"Yes." She absently fiddled with the edge of her notepad before realizing what she was doing and dropping her hands to her sides. "I didn't want to bug you. Perhaps it's you who should thank me for not wasting your time."

Linx pinned her with nothing but his brown, oh-so-very-brown eyes. "I apologize for making you feel bad."

Huh. Well, "Thank you."

"That's it." Mach smacked the table. "I need Linx lessons."

Becca moved her gaze to Mach, ticking her ear a little to the side.

"Count me in, too," Tanner said, expressly not looking at Becca as he spoke.

Mach gave him a brotherly chuck to the arm. "Tanner needs a helluva a lot more lessons than me."

"Hey." Tanner chucked him right back.

"Someday, he'll learn to speak to a woman without his entire face looking like a raspberry."

"I don't look like a raspberry."

"Boys." Linx spread his arms wide on his side of the booth. "There are plenty of lessons for everyone."

"Isn't that just what the world needs," Becca said under her breath.

Mach leaned forward and mock whispered, "If you can get Tanner to talk to a woman and remain his normal shade of pale, then I'll owe you two markers."

"Consider it done." Linx reached across the table and shook each of their hands, one at a time. Then he held his hand to Becca to shake.

She looked at it. Looked up at him.

"I'm not in on this deal." She did however shake his hand so she didn't leave him hanging.

He turned her palm over in his hand and pressed his lips

to the top of her knuckles. The kiss seeped through her body like warm chocolate sauce, flowing over at all of her pulse points.

She drew in a breath.

"Are you two taking notes yet?" Linx asked, giving her hand a little squeeze before letting it go.

Then it was her hand, just sort of dangling there in the space between them. She wasn't moving. Her parasympathetic nervous system shut down, it seemed, because she wasn't even drawing breaths.

"I'll try next." Mach held his hand for Becca's.

Linx swatted his hand away. "Find your own Becca. This one is mine."

"Hey, the only person I belong to is me." Becca shoved her hands on the ties of the apron at her waist.

Linx straight up smirked. "I can respect that."

"Does that mean I have a shot with you?" Tanner asked, the red now a muted pink.

"No," Becca said in tandem with Linx. She grabbed her pen and paper from her apron, needing to scooch along to the next booth for orders. She pointed the end of her pen straight at Mach. "And don't you ask, either."

Mach raised his hands in surrender. "Wouldn't dream of it."

Oh, well. Okay, then.

"Brek asked me to find out if you're playing another set," Becca said, nodding to the next table in recognition when the guy raised his empty whiskey tumbler.

"Sure," Tanner said, his confidence fully restored with the conversation topic shifted back to the stage. Not even a tinge of pink.

"I'm in." Mach gave a pointed glance at Linx.

"What the hell." Linx raised his arms wide again. "Tell Brek he's covering our tab."

Becca smiled. "Will do."

"And, Becca?" Linx asked.

"Yes?"

"Mind if I drive you home tonight?" he asked.

Oh, now he was all charm and requesting permission.

"I'd be grateful if you would." Becca gave him her I'm-a-waitress-and-I-live-on-tips-so-I-have-to-be-perky smile.

"I'll stick around, then."

She rolled her bottom lip under her teeth. Cedric Lincoln was going to stick around and wait to drive her home.

"It won't be late. I'm not closing tonight," she said, as she started toward the next table. "Brek usually doesn't make us close two nights in a row."

"Even better," Linx said.

"Oh God," she said as she turned fully around.

Her girlfriends were asking Becca's other assigned back booth to switch with one closer to the front. Cash seemed to exchange hands. But that wasn't the part that made her heart beat like it was going to come straight through the wall of her chest.

No. That wasn't it. Not even close.

Becca waited for her heart to seize as she watched them climb into the booth, all giggles and excited whispers.

They brought her mother.

"I'D LIKE to know your exact stance on the policy of waitresses drinking on the job." Becca paced between the gas range and the refrigerator in the small commercial kitchen behind the bar where Brek worked with Marlee's husband, Eli. Eli was a chef and sometimes stopped by to help Brek try out new recipes. His creativity was what made Eats Grill one of Denver's best.

"I like my liquor license, so I'd say I'm a hard ass about that one," he said.

"Damn."

"What's going on, Becca?" Eli asked. He was a mountain of a man who always seemed as grumpy as Gibson. Deep down, he was a sweetheart who adored his wife and son.

"Your wife." She tossed her arms to the side. "And my friends."

"Marlee's here?" Eli asked, craning his neck to see out the little window above the door.

"She is." Becca went back to pacing. "And she brought the rest of our friends. And. My. Mother. My mom, Eli. She brought my mom."

"What's wrong with your mom?" Brek asked, covering some kind of bread in a cheese sauce that looked and smelled delicious. "If she's a looney tune, you have to convince her to go. Babushka and her crew already took the front row tables." He squinted and dropped his shoulders. "I don't have the capacity to deal with two locos in one night."

"Mom's not like that. She'll just drive *me* nuts."

"Oh, well, then she can stay." Brek went back to work.

Ugh.

Babushka was Sadie and Heather's Russian grandmother-in-law. She was a battle-axe with a love of matchmaking grandkids and manipulating everyone into doing what she wanted. Actually, she was a lot like Becca's mom in that regard. Maybe that ability came with age?

The last time she and the ladies from her retirement home came for drinks, she kept trying to shove dollar bills in the waistbands of the band members.

Though with Linx onstage, actually…maybe this might be fun.

Becca put on her best confident saunter and walked straight into the neon-lit lion's den. The band was already taking the stage. It didn't take long before Linx started the set with a Dimefront cover. Though it wasn't really a cover if he was singing it, since he was in the original band—was it?

The old ladies hooted and hollered from the front row. They waved dollar bills and tossed them at the stage. For what it was worth, Linx rolled with this development. He even caught one bill in his teeth. An eruption of raucous hoots and several more bills flew in his direction.

A few even threw quarters and dimes. Linx had to duck so they didn't take out an eye or something.

The bouncers did their best to confiscate the change, but it was a losing battle. In all the concerts Becca had seen him play, no one in the audience had ever tossed dollar bills or coins at the band members. Nor had they screamed for him to take off his pants already.

Also, those old ladies could whistle louder than the amps. It was impressive on a large scale.

A tap on her shoulder had Becca glancing behind.

"Which one is the gentleman you're fond of?" Mom asked, linking her arm with Becca's.

Becca was in her standard Brek's Bar tee and jeans, ponytail high on her head. Mom, however, had foregone her standard twinsets for a cute little black sheath dress. She had not swapped out the orthotic shoes, however.

"I'm not fond of him." No, Becca just wanted to shag him.

"The drummer?" Mom asked. "He's adorable."

Gah. No. Not Tanner. Tanner was way too clean cut for Becca's tastes. He was adorable—don't get her wrong—but definitely not her type.

"The one singing at the front," she said.

Mom seemed surprised at that. "He's got long hair."

Becca bit the inside of her lip and said, "He does."

Linx's hair was not tied back, he wore his on-stage leather pants, and he had the two-day stubble that Becca adored. Deep sigh. He was rocker perfection.

"With hair that dark, I bet he's got lots of chest hair, too. Did you ask if he manscapes?"

Come again? "If he *what*?"

Yes, she did know what manscape meant. She just didn't understand why her mother insisted on using words like that.

Becca did, however, know that Linx wasn't a manscaper. The first night he bartended, she'd seen his chest. He also didn't have a ton of chest hair. He had the perfect amount of chest hair.

"You know," Mom said. "Does he take care of it—" She made a circle with her hand in her chest area. "—with scissors and a razor so you've got a little traction but not so much that you'll get rug burn. I tried to get your father to try hot wax, but he refused." Mom frowned. "Which is a disappointment because Belinda says that it would make things much smoother when we get out the Crisco."

"Mom." Becca closed her eyes. She counted to ten then opened them again. "Please don't talk about you and Dad, hot wax, and Crisco."

"I didn't say what we do with it," Mom said in a huff.

"Have you considered that maybe you spend too much time with Belinda?" Becca asked.

Mom nodded. "Your dad said the same thing after the whole Pop Rocks fiasco."

Don't ask. Don't ask. Don't ask. "Pop Rocks?" *Crap.*

"You put them in your mouth before you…you know." Mom cleared her throat and made her eyes get wide. "It's supposed to give a little pop, but I didn't have enough saliva so they didn't dissolve right. It was like sand in my mouth." Mom shivered. "Followed by an explosion when they all popped at the same time. Don't ask your father about that time."

Frankly, Becca had no intention of that.

"He was not impressed," Mom said.

"Okay, well, I gotta work." Becca started toward the bar to get the next orders.

Unfortunately, her mother followed.

"Don't worry, that only happened once. He really thought the yogurt was fun when we tried that."

"Mom." Becca stopped and turned on her heel, so they were face to face. "Please don't tell me any more of what Dad does and doesn't like in the bedroom."

"Oh, it wasn't in the bedroom. We did the yogurt one on the patio."

"Moooom."

"I thought it might spice it up a little if there was a chance of getting caught."

Don't ask. Don't ask. "Did it?"

"Well, Karen and Bob—they're the neighbors to the south of us—got a variance for a full six-foot cedar fence. We didn't even have to pay for any of it. Your father was so happy about that. He said we could do the yogurt thing whenever I want."

"What's the yogurt thing?" Kellie approached from behind Becca's mom, sipping from the red straw in her Crown and Coke.

"Mom will tell you all about it." Becca tried to turn back toward the bar, silently wishing there was a Crown and Coke with enough Crown to wipe her memory of that entire conversation.

It didn't work. Mom grabbed her arm.

"Have you all done the whole pet name thing yet?" Mom asked. "Because I have thoughts on it."

Becca shook her head. "No, because we are grown-ups, and we don't have pet names for each other."

Also, pet names were for relationships, not indulgent affairs of the kind she wanted to partake in with Linx.

"Even grown-ups need pet names for each other. It's half the fun of being in the relationship," Kellie said, waggling her brows.

Becca hit her with some side eye. "We're not in a relationship."

And they wouldn't be. Relationships raise stress levels and responsibility levels.

"Seriously. I've got to get back to work." Becca jerked her thumb toward where Brek had her next set of beverages ready for delivery.

This time, thankfully, they let her escape.

With her tray reloaded, Linx and Tanner and Mach picked that moment to go into a rock-inspired rendition of "Sweet Caroline," with exceptional use of the drums that had the front row elderly getting a little rowdy.

Becca had to do a duck and twirl maneuver with her full tray so it didn't get knocked to the ground by a stray swing of a cane.

Linx nailed a *bom-bom-bom,* and they all went bananas. More bananas.

Someone was totally going to break a hip if this kept up.

Linx was invested in the song. Which was funny because he didn't seem like a Neil Diamond kind of guy. But what did she really know about him, anyway? Nothing about his yogurt and Crisco preferences, that was for certain.

Hell, he might be a Pop Rocks guy for all she knew.

Actually, deep down, she sorta hoped he was. She'd even make sure she had plenty of saliva to ensure—

"Out of the way, hon," one of the older women said when Becca paused to watch Linx sing about hands touching hands.

Yeah, he was eating up the enthusiasm from the retirement home crew. Broad smile, swirling hips, dollar bills hanging from his belt.

Becca shook her head and scooted along to finish distributing the latest round of drinks. She turned back to the stage in time to see Mach complete an edge-of-the-stage, on-the-knees rock move to the last *bom-bom-bom* with his guitar held high. Thanks to the guitar move, the ladies could reach *his* waistband with dollar bills.

He absolutely didn't appear to mind.

"We've got a problem," Brek said from behind her.

She glanced over her shoulder to him.

"I called in a few extra bouncers." He kept his focus on the front row as he spoke. "This group has a history of not taking no for an answer. If things get dicey, you'll want to head over behind the bar. Last time one lady tried to pepper spray one of my guys when he wouldn't let her get on the stage."

Holy crap. "Was he okay?"

"He was fine. The bottle only looked like pepper spray. It was breath spray, and he felt like an idiot afterward. Who knows if it'll be breath spray next time? We had to close early to get a handle on things." Brek's jaw ticked as something of a gray-haired mosh pit formed at the base of the stage—tables and chairs pushed aside for the walkers and canes. "That's not happening again."

One couple tried to dirty dance, but their walkers got in the way.

Four bouncers Becca hadn't seen before positioned themselves close to the stage, forming a wall of bulging men. They were all muscle and sinew, and now several had dollar bills poking from *their* belts.

"Babushka," Brek tapped the shoulder of a woman in a lime green jumpsuit. He said something too low for Becca to hear.

Babushka responded to whatever he said by tucking a dollar behind his ear.

He gave a head nod in the general direction of the biggest bouncers. The man was built like a mountain.

That's when things got a little wonky. Becca took Brek's advice and headed behind the bar while the bouncers moved the wall slowly toward the exit, gently pressuring the group in the direction of the parking lot.

"Becca," a voice called. A voice that sounded like her mother.

Becca searched the crowd for her.

Crap. Somehow, Mom got caught up with the mosh pit and was part of the herd being carefully prodded out the door.

Becca started toward them to rescue her mother.

Shoulders hunched, jaw still ticking, Brek soldiered to his post behind the bar. "You'll want to stick around back here. Let the bouncers do their job."

"My mom's in the crowd." Becca tried to find her again, but she'd lost her in a wave of eighty-year-olds.

Brek closed his eyes and took a huge breath. "Which one's your ma?"

"Brown hair, orange sweater. Not elderly." Becca pointed to the general direction of her mom but couldn't see her. "What's going to happen to them?"

"I have taxis out there waiting to take them home." Brek smiled a smug grin. "Then they're somebody else's problem."

Well, if they were just going to be taking her mom home, it wasn't like it was *that* big of a deal. And, technically—if she wanted to get technical about it—her friends had brought Mom with them. Becca was at work. Therefore, by the laws of technicalities, this was their problem to solve.

"Taxi home?" she confirmed.

Brek nodded.

"That's not bad. Let's go with that." Then there would be no more Crisco conversations. "Also, thank you."

Brek's smug grin turned sly. He gave a slight head shake before moving on to fill orders that had backed up during the past five minutes for disorderly conduct by the Grandmothers Gone Wild.

With "Sweet Caroline" over, Linx and the band had moved onto one of the newer Dimefront songs.

Becca helped Brek fill orders. “Do you do that for everyone you kick out? The taxi thing?”

“Only when they’re led by my best buddy’s babushka. He’d never forgive me if I called the cops on her.” He dumped the contents of a Coors into the sink, rinsed the bottle, and refilled it with ginger ale. “Mostly because then he’d have to go down and bail her ass out of jail. That would mess up his night. Thus…taxi.”

Brek added a couple of bottles of water to the mix.

“Ready for me to hand this off to the band?” Becca asked, already loading the tray.

Brek grunted in affirmative.

“Rebecca,” an all too familiar voice called.

Becca frowned and turned toward the voice. Looked like her mom hadn’t gotten in that taxi after all.

Oh. Well, fantastic. More Crisco conversations.

Yay.

Chapter 11

Becca

Linx held the car door open for Becca like they were in a Cinderella movie. If Cinderella was a waitress and Prince Charming was a rock star.

As Linx ran around to the driver's side, she mentally did an inventory of her tips. They didn't suck, which she mostly attributed to Linx and the way he charmed the pants off everyone when he was on stage. His repeated requests that everyone tip their waitresses well couldn't be ignored. Judging by the bulge of cash in her wallet, his request worked.

He slid into the driver's seat and started the ignition.

As he pulled out of the lot, he said, "I had a great talk with your mom tonight."

Becca groaned. Why couldn't her mother have gotten into the waiting taxi Brek made available? She hadn't even stuck around that long after she came back inside. Just long enough to talk to Linx, apparently.

"I don't want to know what she said." Becca rested her forehead against the passenger door glass. The cold surface offered a reprieve from thoughts of parental embarrassment.

"She said that she likes Dimefront." He kept his eyes on the road, but the brief twitch at the edge of his lips showed that this was not the end of the tea her mom had spilled.

Becca pinched her lips together. "There's no way that's *all* she said."

"You're right." He kept his hands at ten and two on the steering wheel, but the lip twitch turned to a full smirk.

Don't ask. You don't want to know.

"What else did she say?" Oh well, better to get it all out in the open so there wasn't a can of surprise Crisco in her future.

Linx paused, but not like he was thinking. He paused like he was drawing out Becca's misery because he could. The moment should've raised her stress levels. Since it was Linx, the drama made her smile.

She pulled out her ponytail and ran her fingers through her hair. "Spill it, Cedric."

A dimple popped on his right cheek, and his lips twitched again.

He seemed to like that she'd called him by his given name. "She mentioned that you spent a summer in Europe, the same time we did our Penny Pincher tour."

Shut the Porsche door. Her mom couldn't know about that.

Becca had told everyone that her summer European tour was for continuing education—a program on the need for meditation and relaxation in high-stress environments.

The premise of the trip was not entirely untrue. She was stress-riddled because she had spent her days helping others process their intense emotions and avoiding her own. The trip took place after her third year as a counselor and directly following a not-very-nice break-up with her latest boyfriend.

"How did Mom know…?" Ack. It didn't matter. Her mom had ways of knowing all the things. Becca would do better not to ask that question.

"You found out I was a Ten." It wasn't a question. She had stated fact.

He nodded. "Which means you have to follow the Dime-front groupie code."

There was absolutely no such thing as a Ten code. If there was, she would have heard about it long before now.

"What exactly does that involve?" she asked. "Let me guess. First rule is you don't talk about groupie code?"

"No." He turned onto I-70, toward her apartment. "First rule is that a Ten always identifies herself. That way, it does not surprise unsuspecting bass players. We don't like surprises, unless it involves a thousand dollars of free tacos."

She scoffed but settled in for the conversational ride. "Is that a euphemism?"

"No, for real. I've never met anyone in the business who doesn't love a good taco credit." He lifted his hands from the steering wheel in mock shock.

"I can't tell if you're being serious." Oh, she could tell he wasn't. But this was fun.

"I'm always serious." He used a tone that she called total rubbish on.

"Well, you'll be happy to know that I retired my Ten status years ago. Thus, I have nothing to confess." She held up her rock 'n roll devil horns like the groupie badge of honor they were.

He paused. The Adams apple in his throat worked against the stubble. "That thing about Bax? Was that true?"

The words were light coming from his tongue, but she had enough experience to tell the answer mattered to him.

"Yes." She nodded. But also, no, because, "We didn't fool around. We just talked."

The expression on Linx's face broadcasted his distrust of that assertion. "Bax doesn't talk."

"He talked to me." He had. Bax was a good guy with a double helping of confusion. They'd talked it all through.

Linx didn't look like he believed her.

"What? I'm easy to talk to," she said because it was true.

They sat in silence for half a minute, Linx staring at the road as he drove. His eyes glazed over. He was a million miles away. Probably somewhere in Europe, trying to remember the Penny tour.

"Okay," he said, eventually.

"Okay?"

"Yeah, okay." He nodded, as though this made perfect sense.

"You believe me?"

His throat worked again. "I trust you. So, yeah, I believe you." He thought for a long moment before saying, "It's none of my business."

Good. They agreed. Digging deep into the past brought on a whole slew of emotions. Given that emotional distance was key to her holiday fling with Linx, they needed to leave it be.

Too bad the distance mantra sat uncomfortably sideways in her belly.

"I guess it's a good thing we'll both let the past go because I'd really prefer we not go through a full sexual history," he said. "That would take way too much time."

It wouldn't take that much time… not for her, anyway. Sure, she knew he had a history but—

"How much time are we talking?" she asked, nudging him with her elbow. "Like an hour or all night?"

He twisted in his seat, clearly uncomfortable.

"I'm sort of wishing right now that you *had* slept with Bax, if it meant I didn't have to have this conversation." He turned onto a street that was not in the right direction to her place. "Mind if we take a quick pit stop?"

The night was still early, might as well see where things went. "Home to check in on Gibson?"

"No, he's back to ignoring me." He pulled up to a stoplight. The car slid to a halt on the slush. "We got invited to a party."

She didn't recall any invitations being sent her way. "We?"

"Well, *me*." He tapped out a rhythm that sounded a lot like "Sweet Caroline" against the steering wheel. "You're my plus one."

Excitement bubbled in her chest. The parties a rocker like Linx got invited to would be a former groupie's dream. Movie stars, musicians, celebrities of all kinds—she totally owed Brek a thank you for having her work the early shift.

"Where's this party?" And did she have time to change her clothes first? Skinny jeans, a Brek's Bar t-shirt, a parka, and sneakers were not the rock-star-plus-one attire she would ever pick for a Linx-invitation party.

"Um…" He wouldn't meet her gaze.

They were headed toward Cherry Creek, just past downtown, where all the ritzy hotels stood. Ritzy hotels meant penthouses. Penthouses meant…who had she heard was in town recently? She sorted through the vague handle she had on the pulse of Denver's social life. She should text her friend, Marlee. Marlee knew all that went down with the upper crust of Denver.

"Linx," she said, unable to hold the giddiness from her words. "I'm dying over here."

He wriggled in his seat again. "Don't judge, okay?"

"I wouldn't dream of it." That was a fib. She was totally going to judge him. And hopefully that judgement would be amazing because while she adored Dimefront, and they were her "it" band, she also totally had a thing for Blue Night.

"You know the ladies from earlier at the bar?" Linx asked.

Becca didn't think any of those ladies had a connection to Blue Night. "The grandmothers?" she asked.

"Yeah." He nodded, tossing a hopeful grin at her.

"Yeah," she parroted his response. Her stomach sank.

He lifted his hand from the steering wheel for a high five. "They invited the band over."

A high five which she left hanging. Her jaw dropped open and stuck to the floor mats. Was he seriously considering going to hang out with a group of eighty-year-old women instead of spending time showing her his mattress? Or hanging with Gibson? Or introducing her to other celebrities?

"Unless you have a better idea?" He gave himself a high five with his other hand, apparently unable to let his palm hang out in space un-hit before pulling it back. "They said they're making cake and cookies. I like cake. I like cookies. Especially when they're made by people who know how to do it."

Hold the phone. "To be clear." Becca squinted in his direction as she replayed the events of the evening. "I just got off work early. You insisted on driving me home."

"Yes." He bobbed his head along as she spoke.

"But you're not driving me home." She began talking with her hands, a habit when she attempted to make a point. "You're taking me—" She pointed to her chest. "—to a cake party at a retirement home?"

"Yes." He nodded.

This was definitely not celebrities and champagne. Then again, she wasn't exactly dressed for celebrities and champagne. She was dressed to serve up drinks at a bar and have cake with the elderly.

"Will there be chocolate cake?" she asked. If there wasn't chocolate cake, it was probably not worth going. If there was no chocolate cake, there was *definitely* no purpose in attending.

"I'm assuming."

That was not a satisfying affirmative. Certain things required a full affirmative answer—chocolate cake being one of them.

"If there isn't chocolate cake, will you take me to get it later?" she asked.

He immediately nodded. "Yes."

Well, okay, then. "Fine. Let's go to your party."

Linx reached to squeeze her hand. He didn't pull his hand away once the squeeze had reached completion. Instead, he turned her palm face up and linked her fingers with his on the console between them. Her entire arm sizzled at the simplicity of the touch, even though it was nothing but platonic.

Without her permission, her heart rate increased, and her hypothalamus released a slew of hormones that made her wish he'd touch her in other places, too. Intimate places.

Holding hands was nice, but it wasn't running her tongue along the ridges of his pectoral muscles, down toward his belly button, and along the line of hair she expected she'd find there, down to his—

He skimmed his thumb over the fleshy spot between her forefinger and her thumb. This was not platonic.

Not the sort of touch a girl would have with a man who was only her friend.

Also, not a touch she expected from a guy she only intended to shag a few times.

This felt very relationship-y. She pulled her hand away. Hard no on that.

"You okay?" he asked.

"Of course." She smiled and hoped like hell it was convincing. "I'm just thinking about chocolate cake."

Chocolate lava cake and his pectorals...

Chapter 12

Linx

"I brought you a present," Becca said, as they wandered through the lobby of the retirement home, following homemade signs to the multi-purpose room. The mauve Berber carpet muffled their footsteps.

"Oh, yeah?" he asked.

A present and cake? Wasn't tonight just his night?

She rifled through her handbag and pulled out a can of ginger ale. "You'll probably wreck your street cred if you drink this in public, but I like to be prepared."

"You brought me ginger ale?" He stopped to examine the beverage. The gift wasn't anything much, but it felt like a whole lot more than nothing.

She moved until her chest brushed his, just the slightest touch.

"I was hoping you'd have agreed to come inside when we got to my place for a drink before you went home."

Well, hello then. That would have been very nice.

He parted his lips, but it seemed to happen without his

consent or recognition. "You bought me a drink so we could hang out?"

"Among other things." She ran her tongue along the seam of her lips in a way that stirred his body's carnal response like they were backstage in his dressing room after a concert. Or when he was in the zone on stage. Like everything was right in his personal bubble.

The rush, the high of the show, produced an energy that needed release. He'd found…ways.

That idea, with Becca, made his entire body float.

They wandered through the dim hallways until they came to the rec room, following the signs that promised cake.

They had decorated the room with pastel blue and pink streamers like gender reveal parties his cousins were always having every time they got knocked up.

The scent was a mixture of the starch his mom used to use on his shirt collars—it itched—and the cedar chest his grandparents had in their summer home near Lake Michigan. It kept out the moths.

All of that was fine. Next to the door sat a long table filled with the cake they had promised. Another for punch. Along the edge of the room were various tables with arts and craft stations. A guy about his age demonstrated how to arrange flowers, a group of old women knitted, and some white-haired guys tied what looked to be fishing lures. There was also a younger woman instructing partygoers how to decorate cookies.

Wait, were those cookies shaped like penises?

Upon closer inspection, yes, yes, they were.

"Hey, Heather," Becca nodded to the woman giving a tip on how to pipe veins.

That was weird. Not the craziest thing he'd ever seen. But definitely odd.

"You know her?" he whispered.

Becca nodded. "That's Heather."

"I feel like there's a story here." He studied her piping technique, impressed with the realistic nature of her work.

Becca gripped his arm. "That's a story for another time."

One would think that penis-shaped cookies would be the oddest thing about the event.

However.

Usher's song *Climax* played softly in the background and, off to one side, an elderly woman gave instructions to a few others on how to perform a lap dance. He wasn't making this up, though he wished he was.

A bald gentleman in plaid lounge pants had a smile wider than the Mile High City, while the Playboy bunnies, circa 1958, practiced their moves.

He used the term *moves* loosely. They were more like small jerky movements and an occasional attempt at a twerk.

Everything turned sideways, including his stomach.

What the fuck?

Becca turned to him, eyebrows raised high on her forehead.

None of those people eating cake and participating in arts and crafts seemed to care that there were dick cookies or a lap dance lesson happening in the room.

"I just wanted cake," he said, unable to remove his eyes from the scene. "They said there would be cake."

Bright spot of the situation: the trainees were all fully clothed. Thank fuck.

Becca squeezed his hand. "Maybe we should..." She tilted her head to the door they entered. "Hit up a bakery instead."

Then she squinted at something to their left. Her expression turned quizzical.

"Tanner?" Becca asked.

Linx glanced in the direction she stared.

Yup. There stood Tanner, having an energetic talk with a group of elderly women. He seemed to be totally at ease in their company. Raising his red Solo cup to his lips, he nodded along with the senior hanging on his right arm.

Huh. Interesting. Not that Tanner's presence was a surprise, but his fraternization with women wasn't expected. From what Linx had seen, all women seemed to elicit the same reaction from Tanner—red cheeks, inability to speak a coherent sentence. All that.

Not this group.

At Becca's call, Tanner glanced up from the group of women. His face immediately turned pink. He tried to cover it, that much was clear, but would have to get a handle on that if this was his standard reaction around beautiful women. He waved to her, but even his wave was awkward. As though he stopped halfway through to consider whether he should do that or something else.

"What do you call it when you make someone do something to make it not bad for them anymore? Isn't that part of therapy?" Linx asked. He swore he'd seen something like that on a television show. Maybe it was a movie?

Becca looked at him like she didn't understand what he was talking about.

"When someone is afraid of spiders, you make them sit in a room with a bunch of spiders? Isn't that a thing?" He was certain that was a thing. It had to be a thing.

She scrunched up her nose, adorably. "Desensitization?"

"Yeah, that." That sounded right. "Does it work?" He swung their hands between them.

Becca lifted her shoulder and tilted her ears from shoulder to shoulder. "Sometimes. Depends on the case. What are you thinking?"

He jerked his chin toward the drummer. "Tanner needs beautiful women inundating his space. That way he'll get used to it."

Becca seemed to choke on nothing. "You want to put Tanner through immersion therapy with women?"

Linx nodded. Exactly.

Becca shook her head. "No. Whatever is making him nervous with women needs to be handled with a light touch. By a professional."

"I'm a professional."

She scrunched up her nose again. This time she added a cute frown to it. "You're a musician."

"I'm a *professional* musician."

Becca's lips quirked up. "That doesn't count."

"Says who?" He slung his arm around her shoulder.

"Says the one of us with a master's degree in psychology and a license to practice."

Details, shmetails. Tanner just needed a dash of Linx and a lot of experience. They'd call it a scientific experiment to snap him out of this thing.

"He got an invite, too?" Becca asked.

Linx should've grabbed Becca's hand and headed straight for the exit. But the call of cake proved stronger than his urge to flee. "They invited the whole band. Mach's probably coming later."

They'd all received invitations scribbled on their dollar bills in hot pink Sharpie.

Linx wasn't certain, but he was sure that writing on money like that was illegal, and *technically* considered defacing government property. Not that he was a rat or anything. He just figured it was better to know the little things that would keep a guy out of the slammer. No reason to deal with the feds over an inclination to use dollar bills as a notepad. That was his philosophy.

"Hey." Tanner emerged from his elderly groupies. "Do you two want something to drink?"

Linx lifted his fist for a bump. "Yeah—"

"My guest." The elderly woman who'd had the most dollar bills, a lime green get up, and a hefty Russian accent scrambled toward them.

She didn't really seem like the scrambling kind. That didn't stop her. She seemed fragile, but the teeny tiny speck of intuition he'd inherited from his emotionally supportive mother told him that this woman's spine was pure steel.

Or maybe titanium.

Something strong that didn't break.

"Drinks. For my guests." She held up her hand, snapping her fingers at someone behind him. He wasn't sure who, and he didn't look because the lady's presence demanded his full attention.

"I am glad you have come to my party," the woman continued. "I am Babushka. Brek is a good friend."

"Hey, Babushka." Becca gripped Linx's arm, moving closer as though he were a shield. "We've met."

Babushka gave her a once-over that seemed like a full MRI. "Yes, you are friends with my soon-to-be granddaughter, yes?"

"That's right," Becca said.

Her presence so close to him, the scent of her vanilla shampoo, made him wish he'd taken her some place more private. They could have cake anywhere, really.

Not the apartment where she lived over her parents' garage. That involved way too many opportunities for parental interference. Maybe he should call his agent and have a jet sent out to Denver. He could fly her some place when she had a day off. Someplace private. Someplace where they could hold hands and talk.

"Now, you will stay for lap dances." Babushka clapped her hands like she was a majorette in the Fourth of July parade.

Linx chuckled. Lap dances and cake. She was a riot.

"That's funny," he said because it was. "I'm here for cake."

Becca gripped his arm harder. "I've heard the Babushka stories. I think she's serious."

No, she wasn't serious. Although, there was the lesson going on in the center of the—

Shit. That lesson was over.

"What stories?" He kept his words even. Level. Not relaying the fear bubbling in his gut.

Because… uh… if this wasn't a joke, then lap dances at a retirement home party didn't seem like such a good idea. He was certain the Life Alert policies wouldn't cover that activity. Not that he'd ever looked into it. But he didn't want to be the reason for anyone to fall and break something.

"Maybe we should go," he whispered to Becca.

They should definitely get out of there. He had a personal rule ever since other people got interested in what he did with his spare time. That rule was, when somebody talks about stripping or lap dances, he left.

Unless he was alone with them, and he wanted a striptease or a lap dance. Then it was fine.

But not in a public area. No champagne rooms. When a woman started grinding on you for money, odds were not in your favor that some entertainment website wouldn't get ahold of the footage.

Yeah, there were too many unknowns as soon as anyone mentioned a lap dance. Especially when a guy only showed up for cake. The potential for spiraling here became a genuine concern.

"I kinda want to stay," Becca whispered. "I've always wanted to know how to give a proper lap dance."

He had no time to think about that statement because two Solo cups were thrust into their hands. Reluctantly, he took the beverage. The contents smelled like a little fruit punch with lotsa vodka.

He eyed the ginger ale can Becca had stuffed back in her purse.

"What's floating on top?" Becca sniffed the liquid and tilted the cup, examining it closer.

He gripped his own cup tighter and examined the contents. Becca wasn't wrong. A thin sheen of oil seemed to separate into the top of the cocktail.

He used that word, cocktail, lightly. This seemed like something he'd create on accident with fruit scented shower gel and rubbing alcohol.

"What is that?" he echoed Becca's question.

"C.B.D. oil." Babushka over enunciated each letter. "For the joints."

"How much did you put in here?" Becca sniffed her cup and immediately moved her nose away from the opening, coughing.

"Keeps the internal processes in working condition." Babushka patted her stomach. "One moment, I vill return shortly."

He gave Becca his best, hey-help-a-guy-out look.

She smirked and said nothing.

"This is the last time I bring you here," he whispered.

"Because it's the last time you're coming?" she said with a lilt in her voice that implied she enjoyed this scene entirely too much.

He gave a low growl.

She laughed.

He was screwed.

Mach showed up at precisely that moment. He took a long look at Becca double fisting the beverage of the night. "No-oh-oh." He removed both cups from her grasp. "Avoid the punch, they were dumping a crap load of stuff in it. Stick with the medication punch."

"Medication punch?" Tanner asked.

Linx wasn't sure that he wanted to know. Actually, he was certain he didn't want to know.

"For those with pharmaceutical prescriptions," Babushka chimed in, scooting between him and Becca so they had to separate. "We don't add the good stuff." She made a gag sound, as though this were a repulsive idea not to have the good stuff.

Mach lifted his cup. "It's just like when I was a kid. Like the orange drink my mom used to make out of powder and water."

"Good to know," Becca said, eyeing the beverage table. "I'm glad I brought my own drinks."

She set her cup down on one of the tables, sly like. No one else noticed, but Linx did. He slipped her his cup as well. She did the same with his.

"Shall we sit and drink my purse beverages?" She asked, arm still linked with his, her side pressed along his side in a way that made him not really care if he got any cake after all.

He pulled out a folding chair for her. Then, cautiously, sat next to her.

She handed him the ginger ale from her purse and grabbed a sparkling water for herself. He popped the top on his can, took a long drink, and eyed the cake table.

Babushka shuffled toward them. She patted her hands together, clapping quietly with glee. "You are at Etta's table."

"Oh, I'm sorry." Becca started to stand. "We didn't know."

Linx followed suit.

Babushka pointed her wrinkled finger at Becca and Linx and then waived it toward their chairs, "You vill sit. She vill be happy to have customers."

He glanced to the chair. Then to Becca. She did the same. They both came to the same conclusion because they both sat.

"What is Etta teaching at this table?" he asked, the metal folding chair suddenly uncomfortable against his ass. Truth was, he was sort of afraid of the answer, but held out hope it involved frosting and carbohydrates. Maybe Etta was a baker.

"Lap dances." Babushka lifted her hands. "Of course."

Becca barked a laugh. Loud.

Linx did not laugh.

"You two are together?" Babushka asked.

Becca seemed to freeze a bit at that question. "Um."

"Yeah, we're working that part out," Linx said, giving Becca's shoulders a squeeze. "Becca here is on vacation. She's here because I promised cake."

Becca cleared her throat. Then she grinned like she'd just found out she sat at the cake table. "I'd… be willing to learn to give a dance. That would be fun. Very vacation-y."

He wasn't convinced.

"I thought you liked me," he said low.

Becca's eyes sparkled like the elderly had spiked the punch with champagne instead of vodka. "I have a hunch here that it's going to be more fun for me than for you."

"And you?" Babushka directed this question to him. "Vill you dance for her?"

He cleared his throat. Twice. "No. But… I'd be willing to learn."

Becca clapped him on the shoulder. "And, just like that, this night just got fun."

She looked to him with expectant glee.

"You *vill* learn." Babyshka winked heavily. Her eyelid stuck briefly at the bottom long enough that he grew concerned for her wellbeing. It took a solid moment, but she recovered and hustled away, leaving them both sitting in their folding chairs with no clue what came next.

"I'm uh…" Tanner cleared his throat and pointed toward the cake table.

"Me too," Mach added, motoring straight to the table and not looking back.

Those traitors were going to eat all the freaking cake.

Babushka quickly returned with an elderly woman who, thankfully, didn't resemble his grandmother.

"This is Etta." Babushka gestured to Etta. "She gives good dance."

Uh. No. Uh uh. He started to stand, but Becca's hand moved to his shoulder, holding him in place. "Hold on there, Speed Racer."

"Etta is going to dance for Linx?" Becca asked, entirely too sweetly. She let her hand drop from his shoulder.

Babushka shook her head. "No, she vill teach him to dance for *you*."

Becca expression went slack. She held her hand to her chest. "Me?"

Becca stared at him for a long beat, a dare practically broadcasting between them. The parameters of the agreement hashed out with only that glance. Fine. Fuck it. He'd do it, and he'd enjoy it.

"I'm in," he said as he ran his teeth along the edge of his lip.

Becca was still doing the talking-with-only-a-glance thing to him. She wanted this. He wanted this. This was going to be fun. He was going to enjoy the hell out of dancing for Becca.

Etta rubbed her gnarled hands together. "The first rule of lap dancing is that you don't use your cootie cat when you grind. Rug burn after a night of dancing is uncomfortable for everyone."

Yeah, he'd just bet it was.

"I have a question." He raised his right hand like he was back in high school in Mr. Carpenter's chemistry class. "Where exactly would I find my cootie cat?"

Etta scowled, looked at his crotch, then back to his face. "Your love dart."

He choked a little on his own spit.

"Right." He nodded, recovering quickly. "Don't use my love dart when I grind."

Becca bit her lips together, but her shoulders shook.

"If he doesn't use his love dart, what should he use?" Becca asked, all total bullshit innocence.

"You've got good meat on your thighs. Put it to use." Etta

nodded at his aforementioned thighs, which made Linx glance down.

"Don't use my love dart, got it. Use my thighs, instead," Linx said, all confidence, as though he was an A-plus student.

He'd never been an A-plus student in anything but music.

"Smile at the lady." Etta held her hand toward Becca, flashing a dentured smile in illustration.

Linx followed her lead and did the same.

Becca did, too. She was a beautiful woman, but the smile she flashed looked like something from a thriller flick. Like she was going to sink those teeth in places he wouldn't enjoy.

She was totally screwing with him. And he liked it.

Her normal, not-going-to-munch-your-nuts smile remained in place as she waggled her eyebrows at him.

He responded in kind.

That got him a chuckle. There. Much better.

"Now, you must explain the rules to the lady." Etta said.

Linx paused in their flirtation. "What rules?"

"I always make the man sit on his hands." Etta held her palms to her ass in illustration. "You should have her do the same.

"Sit on your hands." Linx instructed Becca.

She did as she was told. He preferred to be the boss in all things bedroom, so Becca following his direction made his love dart stir and his fly tighten.

"Tell her not to touch your love dart," Etta said.

Linx swallowed away the laugh threatening to spill. Serious. Be serious. "Don't touch my love dart." He paused. "Yet." He added a hand motion that looked like two arrows pointing to his groin for effect.

"Wouldn't dream of it," she said, clearly all in on this gig.

"Tell her you'll do the touching, not her." Etta glanced between the two of them again. "But run your hands over your rutabagas while you do it."

Linx blinked hard. He'd heard the parts of the body

called many, many things. He didn't understand where he kept his rutabagas.

"I don't know what that means," he said.

"Your chest." Etta gripped her breasts in illustration. An illustration he could have lived his entire life without seeing.

He glanced to where Mach and Tanner filled their plates with entirely too much cake. The bastards.

"The hearse is almost here," Babushka said into a karaoke machine he hadn't noticed before. "We'll meet out front in two minutes."

Hearse? What in the hell was going on at this place?

Becca started to stand, but Linx pinned her back in her chair with a glance. She sat on her hands again, like a good little Becca.

Etta glanced toward the door as the throng of elderly headed that way. "Wait here. I'll be back."

"What did she mean, the hearse is here?" Becca asked in a whisper. "Did someone…?"

The question hung there because it seemed entirely inappropriate for them all to be dancing, decorating penis cookies, and drinking CBD oil if someone had bit it.

"No." Etta waved her hand. "Everyone is alive. Wait here."

"Where are they going?" Linx murmured, mostly to himself.

"They're going to see who wins the pool," Tanner said around a mouth of cake.

Linx glared at him and his mouthful of carbohydrates.

"What pool?" he asked before Becca could. If Becca asked it then Tanner would freeze up and probably wouldn't be able to speak.

"They all place a bet," Tanner said. "On how long it'll take the funeral home to send out a hearse when they report a death."

"She said no one died." Becca's forehead wrinkled in obvious concern. "Do you know something else?"

Tanner shoveled another forkful of cake in his mouth when Becca spoke. Shit. He'd also gone red again.

Linx hoped like hell there wasn't a corpse on hand. That would really turn the night to crap.

"No one died." Mach had finished his cake, so he wasn't inhaling it in his gullet. "It's a game."

"A game?" Becca asked, which was good because Linx's tongue and mouth didn't seem to be useable at the moment. He froze in place.

This would end up on Inside Edition. He felt it in his bones.

"No, no one's dead. It's like an old person lottery," Mach explained.

"An old person lottery?" Becca asked.

"Why does she keep repeating everything I say in question form?" Mach turned to Linx as though he would have the answer.

He didn't because it made no fucking sense.

"There is no logic in any of this, that's why." Becca tossed her arms wide. Unfortunately, that movement stretched her t-shirt across her…rutabagas…which momentarily distracted him.

"It's just a game," Tanner said, getting control over himself. His cheeks were now only a light pink instead of bright red.

"I put my money on five minutes ago. I'm out. Tanner was out a half hour ago." Mach hooked a thumb toward Tanner.

Tanner swallowed and stopped shoveling cake. "I didn't know they weren't in a hurry. Don't worry, Becca, it's just a game. Harmless."

"I bet the funeral home doesn't think it's harmless." Mach

eyed the door. "Is it a crime to report a dead body? If it is, would that make us accomplices?"

"I should call my friend, she's a lawyer." Becca dug through her purse and pulled out her phone. She paused before she turned it on. Stopping and dropping it decidedly back in her bag. "You know what?" She slung her purse over her shoulder. "We should all just leave. In case."

She caught Linx's glance, and he knew exactly what she meant.

"Escape," he said, offering her his hand to help her stand.

"Quickly." She gripped his hand, bolting out the side door of the room.

Mach and Tanner were behind them, he was sure. Unless they paused for extra cake.

They probably paused for cake.

Becca didn't seem like she was in the mood to go back to grab a to-go slice, so he didn't ask. The two of them snuck across the snow-covered grass like they were covert agents until his Porsche was in sight.

"Linx?" Becca whispered from behind him.

He turned.

She pegged him with a snowball, right in the chest.

He stared at where the flecks of snow resided on his coat. Was she serious right now? Snowball fight during an escape?

Scratching at his jaw, he strode toward her.

She giggled. "I dare you to have a snowball fight with me."

Oh, is that how she was going to play their escape?

He continued sauntering toward her like they weren't escaping a retirement home lap dance session. She dodged him, but he was faster. He grabbed her waist before she slipped away and held her against him as they fell to the snow-covered lawn. Becca landed on top of him with a soft thud.

"You dare me, huh?" he asked, brushing a piece of hair from her forehead.

She bit at her lip. "Yes?"

He didn't hit her with a snowball. That wouldn't be fair because, even if she dared him, he was something of a savant when it came to kicking ass in a snowball war. Ask his sister, she'd tell anyone. Given that he actually wanted Becca to speak to him again, he went this route: the face to face, eye-fuck route that ended with him kissing the hell out of her there in the snowbank. One longing look between them and their mouths met in a tangle. Her warm breath was a reprieve from the cold all around them.

Much better than a snowball fight.

He broke the kiss, stood, and pulled her to her feet.

Then they sprinted to the car.

He still hadn't had any damn cake. But he had Becca, so it turned out he actually came out on top.

Chapter 13

Becca

Becca latched her seatbelt before Linx had even slid into his side of the Porsche. The kiss in the snow had been amazing, but Brek had been right—Babushka was a loony tune. A fun looney tune, but Becca had worked a six-hour shift, and she didn't want to end up in the starring role of one Babushka's jailhouse stories.

Unless talking about rutabagas and Linx's love dart counted as a story.

It probably counted. They still needed to skedaddle

"Well, wasn't that just a ball of fun?" Becca still grinned. What could she say? The whole shebang had totally been worth the price of admission. Especially, ahem, the ending in the snow.

Linx revved the engine as they pulled onto the street.

His attempt at asserting his masculinity in a show of male fortitude was adorable. She didn't say that because mentioning that he used his vehicle as a method of assuring her—a member of the opposite sex and someone in whom he clearly held copulation interest—would set him more on edge.

Since she wanted to spend more time with him, she didn't want to do anything to jeopardize her situation. She had extra ginger ale in her mini-fridge. She would invite him up. Her futon wasn't one of his mattresses, but it could still be fun.

Then their fling could finally get down to business. She wasn't about to let the chance to spend a real night with a rock star slip through her fingers or get nicked away.

As long as he didn't have another show of masculinity with his Porsche engine too close to her apartment. That would draw the attention of her parents, which would make it a whole thing. The absolute last thing she wanted was her dad coming outside to find out why there was a Porsche parked there.

"Do you mind not doing the engine masculinity thing when you get to the block where I live?" Becca said as they pulled to a stop at a light across from Whole Foods.

"Masculinity thing?" he asked.

"The revving of the engine." She patted Portia's dashboard.

He frowned. "I tapped on the gas."

Uh huh. Yeah, and she just wore lace underwear to work that day because it made her feel pretty.

"Okay." She wouldn't push it. She shouldn't have said anything to begin with. "Just, you know, don't do it quite that hard when we get closer to my place."

Unless you don't want to come up. But if that's the case, I'll be super disappointed…

"I wasn't planning on it." Linx clicked on his blinker and totally did the rev thing again as he turned onto Speer Boulevard. "But while we're discussing it, can I ask *why* you made this request?"

Ah, fine. *Because I want to grope you and not alert my parents, I have company.* "Dad's got his poker buddies over. Apparently, they play all night and don't care for interruptions."

Also, I don't want him to know you're visiting.

"Do you want to crash at my place?" Linx asked. Did he sound… hopeful? He almost sounded hopeful. Given their romp in the snow, he was probably hopeful.

Actually, she was hopeful, too. His place would be much more comfortable than hers, and then he wouldn't have to take off early to check in with Gibson.

Becca picked at a stray denim thread on her knee. "I don't want to put you out."

"It's just me and the cat." He glanced from the road to her for a brief second. "I like company."

He reached for her hand. This time she let him. Because this time the move had an undercurrent of promise for the night. For the record, that undercurrent was ahhhh-mazing. His thumb stroked the fleshy part between her thumb and forefinger. Who knew that was such an arousal point? All her textbooks about human sexuality did not mention this erogenous zone. They needed to do a reprint. Immediately.

Or, perhaps, this was just Linx. Maybe this was what it was like when they touched. Stroked. Spent the time together on the drive across town touching, not talking, until they pulled into his garage.

They sat in the silence of his garage for a weight-filled moment.

"Becca." He unbuckled and un-clicked her seatbelt so the whisp of the fabric zipping through the loop over her shoulder was the only sound in the car's cab.

She cleared her throat. "Yeah?"

He rested his hand against the column of her neck. "Come upstairs with me."

Whoo boy, this was getting intense.

Her heart thudded as she wrapped her arms around his neck. "Okay."

"If there's anything you need, all you have to do is ask." His voice turned husky. Husky in a way she'd never heard before. If he could layer that husky sound onto every track he ever recorded, his music would go platinum in less than a week. He slipped on the sly half smile she was fond of, the one she was beginning to adore. The one that stripped her bare.

"Oh?" she asked, doing her absolute best to keep her voice steady.

"The snow was fun." He inched closer to her, running his hand along her neck, his forefinger tracing to the front and drifting to the indentation at the base of her throat. "But I wonder what it would feel like to kiss you in a Porsche."

He moved his hand away, and she swore he might as well have tapped her directly on her sweet spot. His touch had powers over her that she needed to get a handle on.

"Funny," she said, clearing her throat.

"What's funny?" he asked, his finger back in action, tracing along the apple of her cheek, all the way to her earlobe.

The ache between her legs would need attention if he kept up this type of foreplay.

God, she hoped it was foreplay, and he'd see it through.

His thumb traced along the bottom edge of her lip, gently pressing the skin there.

She shifted in her seat. Her cootie cat was about to throw a hissy fit if it didn't get some attention soon.

"I was just wondering what it would feel like to have you inside me in a Porsche," she said, as his breath traced along the edge of her jaw.

Oh, *fuuuuck*. She went there. Bad Becca. Also, good job, Becca. She gave herself an inner high five.

He chuckled. "You say things to me that make me wonder where I've been all these years."

"On tour, waiting for the head Ten to show up." She said it as a joke. Except it didn't sound funny when they were alone in his car, and the air zapped between them, and her thighs ached from being pressed together. It sounded more like a promise.

The damn half smile reappeared on his face. She let out that little groan that she only made when she was about to come. The space between them diminished as he arched over the middle console.

Huh, maybe she was about to have an orgasm right there in his passenger seat. That was ridiculous though because he hadn't even touched her between her legs.

Oh, well, yep, he remedied that. His hand slid over the fabric of her pants and between her legs. The light touch made her moan and arch into him, greedy, wanting more.

Her breath caught painfully in her lungs, like she'd been running a full marathon and she'd done zero training. The feeling didn't last long because Linx finally—thank goodness, finally—full-court pressed his mouth to hers. Her entire body heated, and she moaned against his mouth.

He kept his hand between her legs, easing the pressure building there.

Logistics in the small space were iffy. Next time she made out with a guy in a vehicle, she'd have to ensure it was an SUV or something with more leg room so they could do this with a little more ease. That way she wouldn't have to press her neck against the doorjamb to arch fully against him.

"Maybe we should go inside? I can show you my love dart," he said, the words gruff.

She arched against his hand, nearly ready to be undone. "I sort of hate that description."

"Microphone?" he asked. "Maybe that's what I should call it."

She ran her hands between them, down to the waistband of his jeans, toying with the trail of hair there. "Your dedication to music is admirable."

"It is, isn't it?" He arched up into her hand.

His package pressed into her palm and Holy Hannah.

This *was not* a microphone. He was packing a full sound system down there.

She stroked his sound system as it hardened against her hand.

They needed to get out of this car because he had amazing beds inside.

Ah-mazing beds that would be more comfortable than this position. Except, oh God. Actually, he turned his hand against the bundle of nerves at the opening of her entrance and, you know, this spot was just fine. Perfection, actually.

Yes, she wasn't sure if she said the word or if she only thought it.

It didn't matter because she was about to have an orgasm in Cedric Lincoln's Porsche. She gripped his erection through his jeans, and he rubbed against her hand as she arched against his. Stars sparkled behind her eyelids as he grunted and thrust against her hand. She fell over the edge into the orgasm he'd been building for her since that first night at Brek's Bar.

He groaned a long sound as a wet warmth spread across her hand.

Huh. Okay, well, obviously he'd just gotten his cookies, too.

Linx relaxed against her, not pressing her into the seat any more uncomfortable than she'd been before, but definitely taking a moment to regroup.

"Holy shit," he said against her shoulder. "That was…"

"Yeah." She blew out a breath. "That was…"

He moved off of her with a lot of awkward. He took care with her though, drifting slow. Careful not to pull at her hair —which had to have been a total wreck—and helping to adjust her so she sat forward in the seat instead of skewed to the side.

He reached for her other hand, pulled it to his mouth to press a kiss against her knuckles.

She adjusted, moving until she was face to face with him, brushing her palm over his jaw, the light stubble biting into her skin.

She held his face with her hand, running it over his neck to his back. This was nice. The chemistry between them was phenomenal.

"You're a bit of a mess." She glanced to the wet spot just below his waistband.

"Shit." He sat back, a fresh look of horror etched into his expression.

She opened the glove box. "Do you have some napkins or something in here?"

"No, uh…" He held his hands wide. "Shit."

He was right. There was nothing in the glove box except his registration and an insurance card from State Farm.

"We can go inside and you can wash up?" she suggested. Maybe they could even take a wash-up shower together. That could be fun. More cookies could be had by both of them.

"I can't walk in my house like this. What if my cat sees me?" He sounded frantic.

She placed a hand on his forearm. "I don't think Gibson will care."

A fierce look of determination crossed his face as he ripped off the right sleeve of his t-shirt and wiped himself up.

That was sure one way to handle it. She probably would've suggested he use one of his socks before resorting to trashing his tee. But, whatever, he was a gazillionaire. He could buy a new t-shirt. He should also invest in some napkins for his glove box. Just sayin'.

They both let themselves out of the Porsche, her legs a little too much like gelatin as she recovered from her fall down orgasm mountain.

Linx got rid of the shirt sleeve in the garage trash. And then he stepped to her, wrapping her in his arms to hold her with a strength she hadn't realized she needed.

This was nice. This thing between them.

Nice being the least appropriate word ever. Phenomenal was more like it, but the intensity of that word made her chest feel tight and adrenaline flood her system with the beginning dredges of panic. This. Was. Temporary.

A pina colada on the ice cream sundae of her escape.

Nice it would have been. Safe and *nice.*

Exchanging gazes, she kissed him. Light, gentle, and with a touch of determination because she was going to enjoy the hell out of this night.

Chapter 14

Linx

"Your clothes from last night are still on the end of the bed in the guest room." Linx opened the door from the garage to the butler's pantry. Yes, he had one of those. No, he did not have a butler. Yes, he thought, the name was more than a little pretentious.

The room was still sorta neat. Mostly a bunch of extra granite counters and glass-paned cupboards that remained empty even after he'd moved in. He'd had nothing to put in them, even if he had wanted to use the space.

Becca finger combed her wrecked hair, which was unnecessary because he had every intention of messing it up again as soon as they hit his bedroom at the top of the stairs. Perhaps even before. They could take a detour on the sofa.

Come to think of it, if he did things right, she wouldn't need the clothes either.

Linx's now one-sleeved Metallica tee was long enough it covered the wet spot left on waistband of his jeans. He hadn't come like that in his pants since he was a teenager. Might as well crown him Mr. Momentum. With Becca, he had no restraint at all.

"Is there someone here?" Becca asked as they entered the kitchen.

The lights were on the low dimmer setting, and the television broadcast from the living room sounded like CNN.

He rapped a beat on the edge of the counter. "Nope. Lights and TV are for Gibson."

The lights stayed on a timer for the cat. The television was on one of those timer things, too, to keep Gibson company when Linx wasn't around. Mostly, he left it on the news to enrich Gib's mind. He, however, had a handy app on his phone he used to turn it off and on. Gibs hadn't chewed through those wires. Yet.

He sometimes fucked with his cat and changed the channel randomly while he was out. Figured if Gibs had opposable thumbs, he'd do the same, so it was fair game.

He used the app to turn up the rest of the lights in the house. Then he changed the television channel, just because he could.

"Are you hungry?" He started toward the fridge. His body needed at least a few minutes before it would be ready to go again. He wasn't exactly twenty-four anymore. Hell, he still had stamina, he just needed five minutes and a sandwich before he would be ready for round two.

"The goddamn thing keeps switching to C-SPAN. I swear the thing is possessed," a deep male voice said from his living room.

Linx stalled mid-step. Every molecule of his body paused like he'd clicked that button on the app.

That voice sounded like his dad.

No. No. No. Not a family visit. Not tonight.

Eyes closed, he sent up a mental request to any higher power currently available that his family not cock block him.

Higher powers probably didn't handle things like that, though.

"You're hitting the channel changer. Stop sitting on it, and it won't do that." *Fuuuck*, that was his mom. Definitely his mom.

He scrubbed his hand over his face, scratching at the way-past five o'clock shadow that grew from his jaw.

"Someone's here," Becca whispered, gripping the now-bare biceps of his sleeveless arm.

"It's my folks." He glared at the arched doorway that led from the kitchen to the living room, calculating whether he could get Becca back to the car with no one noticing.

"Your parents?" Becca's eyes bugged. Massive. As big as the bucket of water that was being tossed on their night. She went back to finger combing her hair. Faster this time.

Good call, since she looked like she'd just had almost-car-sex with him. He glanced to his jeans. Then to his sleeveless arm.

Shit.

He pulled at the hem of his tee.

"To the car," he said, shooing her back to the butler pantry for their second escape of the night. They could make out in his car some more and go back to her apartment. Better yet, they could check into a hotel or something. Some place no one but room service would interrupt, and no one knew where they were.

Room service had sandwiches.

An exceptional plan, except that was the moment his sister Courtney waltzed through to the kitchen holding a plastic bowl with popcorn remnants in the bottom.

She must've caught Linx and Becca in her periphery because she jolted and dropped the bowl. Unpopped kernels in the bottom bounced across the tile with a *tick, tick, tick.*

"Announce yourself." She held a hand to her chest. "Seriously, Cedric."

While he was not thrilled that his family interrupted his plans with Becca, he couldn't help the smile stretching across his lips. He loved his sister like a… well… a sister. His parents were awesome, too, in small amounts, every few months.

Reluctant, he released Becca's hand to kneel and snag the plastic bowl. He handed it back to Courtney.

"What are you doing here?" he asked. "And why are you up? Isn't it past your bedtime?"

It wasn't. His sister was a total night owl. His parents, on the other hand, were usually in bed by nine. It was most definitely past their bedtime.

She glanced to Becca and perked up like the German Shepherd puppy they'd adopted when they were kids. He'd named the mutt Stixx and they remained best friends all through Linx's teenage years.

Beside him, Becca still frantically tried to tame her hair.

"Are you the woman Linx told me about?" Court was all syrupy sweet, ready to turn on the Lincoln dazzle. She glanced to Linx. Then to his missing sleeve. "Did I interrupt…?"

"Court." He said her name low, a warning. Not that he expected she'd heed the warning, but a guy could hope. "This is Becca. Becca, this is Courtney. My sister."

Becca stopped messing with her hair and raised her brows in his direction. "*Am* I the woman you told her about?"

"The therapist waitress with the pretty smile." Courtney set the bowl on the counter and bounced on her bare feet. "Is that you?"

"Of course, she is." Linx glared at his sister. "And now we"—he gestured between Becca and himself—"are leaving before Mom and Dad"—he gestured to the living room—"know I'm here."

"What am I supposed to tell them?" Courtney smirked. "They're going to want to know where you are."

"Tell them about your intense desire to check into the

Four Seasons with my credit card tonight. Then wait for an invitation to breakfast tomorrow."

"When have we ever waited for an invitation?" Courtney asked, like he was the one who had gone bananas when it was the world around him.

She was right. His family didn't do invitations.

All he wanted for his evening was to eat cake and hang out with Becca. Also, change his jeans. Was that too much to ask?

"We never wait for an invitation," Courtney explained to Becca, the sweet seeping back in. "Because if we did, we'd never get to see him."

"That's not true." Except, he couldn't quite remember the last time he'd extended an invitation. He should make it a point to do that. Then again, perhaps, they should give him the opportunity. That was the problem. They never gave him the chance to invite them, what with the random showing up.

Granted, he liked it when they showed up. Except now. Right now, he wished they'd take him up on the Four Seasons offer.

"We'll meet up for breakfast," he conceded, since breakfast was his favorite meal of the day. "Tomorrow morning. I'll text you."

They could stay here the night with Gibson. He'd take Becca to the hotel. A magical place where they could finish what they started.

"Cedric!" his mom called from the living room. "Is that you?"

"I didn't hear anything." His dad's reply muffled through the walls.

Courtney blinked her innocent Bambi eyes at him. "What's your plan now that they know you're here?"

"You could tell them I wasn't here," he suggested. "That I wasn't coming home tonight."

Courtney shook her head.

"What about Gibson?" Courtney asked. "You were just going to leave him here alone all by himself?"

"No, I was not. Because *I* was planning to be here." He felt the old game between him and his sister starting up. This was how it had always been, the back and forth he always looked forward to with her.

"But that's not what you wanted me to tell Mom and Dad." Courtney's brain games, along with what he'd just done with Becca, were both jacking with his ability to think straight.

He leaned against the island countertop. "Tell them I have a cat sitter."

Courtney crossed her arms loosely. "If you're going to lie to Mom, you better get your story straight."

He growled, but they both knew he didn't mean it.

That's probably why Courtney clearly didn't care.

Becca smiled and watched like this was a nineties sitcom and she had a front-row seat. All they needed was canned laughter and they'd be golden.

"If anyone knows how to pull one over on Mom, it'd be you," he said because Courtney was, in truth, the best at that.

"Because I think things through before I add them to my story." She slipped a wink to Becca. "He hasn't learned that his lie is getting deep." She squinted at him. "You really think Mom won't sniff it out?"

The heavy feeling he always got in his chest whenever he even thought about lying to his mother started to press. His mother's special skill was uncovering his fibs. She probably even listed it on her resume. The woman was practically a walking, talking, human lie detector when it came to Linx.

That ability had really wrecked his chances of pulling anything over on her during his teen years. Courtney didn't have that problem—she could throw up smoke and mirrors better than anyone. Lucky for them all, she didn't do it often.

He was pretty sure. Who could really know when she was such a pro?

Becca watched him with what seemed to be increased interest.

"You're thinking hard over there," she said, bumping her arm against his.

"He does that." Courtney waved a hand and went about making another batch of microwave popcorn. "But soon he'll realize that there's only one choice. That choice is to say hello to our parents and welcome us with open arms."

"Open arms?" he asked.

"Yeah, open arms." She smirked, pulling the crinkling plastic wrapper off the bag of popcorn.

He held his arms wide. "Then come here and give your big brother a hug with his open arms."

She looked to Becca. "He wants to give me a noogie or a wet willy. I know his game. When he starts speaking about himself in the third person, it's time for me to walk away."

Noogie was the direction he leaned. And, yes, he was hoping her walking away with his parents was a solid option. But since Courtney had his number, he slung his arm around Becca instead. She seemed to melt into his side.

"Courtney?" Mom called. "Is Cedric here?"

"Hi, Mom," he called back, as cheery as his sister. "Just got home."

"Did you bring your lady friend with you?" Mom shouted across the house.

Linx elected not to respond to that by shouting across his house. Better that he keep his trap closed.

"You told Mom about Becca?" he whisper-asked.

Courtney popped the popcorn sleeve into the microwave and pressed start.

"I told *Dad*," she said.

"I told your mom. It was all me." Dad sauntered into the room and raised his guilty-as-all-fuck hand.

Becca ticked her head to the left a touch, taking an observing role that was much less fun that what he'd planned to do with her before his family showed up.

Mom wandered into the kitchen, heading straight for his dad. "Dad tried to keep the fact that you have a lady friend a secret, but you should all know by now your father with a secret is visible from the International Space Station."

Dad couldn't lie to Mom, either. Linx theorized it had something to do with the fact that they were both Lincoln men, and she had a sixth sense with them.

"Lady friend?" The edges of Becca's mouth twitched before she stopped them by biting her bottom lip.

He grunted in a not-really reply.

Linx made the introductions between Becca and his parents. To her credit, she rolled with this development as well as she'd done with the senior citizen lap dancing session earlier.

He appreciated that in a woman—the ability to go with the flow.

"It's not called a lady friend, Mom," Courtney said, her popcorn *pop, pop, popping* in the background. "It's called a girlfriend."

Becca paled. All the blood in her body drained to her toes. Just like that, she wasn't melting against his side. She was stiff as a stick of butter from the freezer.

There was that weight again. He and Becca hadn't had the girlfriend discussion. He cleared his throat, giving Becca extra space between them since that's what she seemed to need.

"Why would you do this to me, Courtney?" Linx pressed his palms into his eye sockets. "What did I ever do to you?"

"Do you want the list?" Courtney asked.

Becca laughed, gentle like. He felt that laugh in his soul, even if her complexion was still sans color. "Your family clearly loves you. They're just checking to be sure I'm not a serial killer or something."

Courtney gave Becca a knowing smile. The kind of smile that implied they were going to be good friends. The kind of smile that meant he was fucked.

"This is the first time you've ever seemed like you're making good choices," Courtney said. "Nice job, big brother."

Okay, that wasn't fair at all. He was the king of making good choices.

"I make good choices," he said, defending himself because it would be poor form if he brought Becca to his house to have almost-sex with her in his Porsche.

"Eh." Of course, it would be his father with the shoulder lift and the ambivalent lack of acknowledgement of Linx's life choices. "That's debatable."

Becca adjusted her purse on her shoulder and glanced to the butler's pantry like she debated how quickly she could get out of there. "I should probably head out."

"No," Linx said at the same time Courtney also said, "No."

Becca stalled, clearly unsure of the proper etiquette in such a situation. Hell, who fucking knew?

What he did know? He didn't want her to leave. He wanted to finish what they'd started.

"Cedric makes excellent choices," Mom said to Becca. "I mean, he's practically a household name." Mom gave Dad a knowing look. "You don't get to that level unless you make good choices."

"Thanks, Mom," Linx said. Mom could officially stay. Not that it mattered if he wanted to make it official. She'd do what she wanted to do, anyway.

Becca still looked unsure about sticking around.

Dammit.

"*He* could be a serial killer," Courtney added. "They become household names, too."

"I'm not thanking you." He stuck his tongue out at his sister because… yeah… old habits die hard.

"Did he tell you all about himself?" Courtney turned her focus back to Becca.

"He told me a little," Becca said. "But we're not—"

"Did he tell you he sucked his thumb until he was five?" Courtney asked.

This is how it ended. His career. His plans. Because he would murder his sister and go to jail, for forever and ever.

"It was a whole thing in kindergarten," his dad added.

"You're one to talk, Courtney." Linx shoved his hands on his hips. "You peed your pants on the school playground when you were six."

Becca's gaze ping ponged between his family and the butler's pantry like they were in the world championship ping-pong tournament.

Courtney's eyes went huge. "You went there. In front of your new girlfriend? Who just met me?"

Becca interrupted the family bickering, saying, "I think—"

"She was busy playing." Mom stepped in to quell the hurricane force brewing between her kids. "And Cedric had an intense oral fixation. He grew out of it."

Becca's mouth parted, but one short, "ha," emerged from her lips.

She totally knew he'd never grown out of it. He just got better at hiding it and not shoving his thumb in his gullet.

"Mom." Linx gave a headshake. "Stop."

"I'm just saying." Mom waved a hand.

Dad brushed his hands together. "Your mom is right." His gaze trailed to the missing shirt sleeve on Linx's right arm. "Where's your sleeve?"

"It's the new style," Mom said. "Everyone knows."

Courtney widened her eyes in Linx's direction and drew air circles near her ear with her finger. Becca clearly tried to pinch back her smirk. She failed, but at least her color had returned to normal.

"Since Linx has company, we should grab some dinner and give them time alone." Dad rubbed his hands together and headed for the door. "They wouldn't let me eat real food until you got here."

"We also wouldn't let him grab something quick at the airport," Courtney said to Becca.

"Because it's never quick with him," Mom continued.

Could somebody just make it stop already?

"You think you know everything," Dad hollered behind him.

Mom started back toward the living room. "Because most of the time I do."

"Do we get to meet your family while we're here?" Courtney asked, now that all attention was back on Becca. "We could have them over for dinner while we're in town?"

Becca slid her gaze to Linx, eyes wide. "I guess."

"One step at a time, yeah?" Linx asked, herding his family toward the front door, and, hopefully, their exit.

"This is fun." Dad practically danced a jig out the door.

Thank God, Mom followed him. "I think you're embarrassing them, Hank."

"I know we are." Courtney turned to look over her shoulder and blew a kiss to him and Becca. "We'll let ourselves in after we eat."

"You could get a hotel," Linx muttered, but they all knew he didn't mean it.

"What would be the fun in that?" Courtney asked, pulling the door behind her. "See you lovebirds in the morning."

"Oh, I won't—" Becca said, but the door clicked closed before she could finish whatever she was going to say.

With the family gone, Gibson stuck his head out from his

hideout under the sofa, seeming to check that the coast really was clear.

"Linx?" Becca asked.

He exhaled, loud. "Yeah?"

"Your family is insane." She sighed. "But I kinda like them."

He crossed his arms and glared at the now-closed door. "Let's see if that opinion sticks through breakfast tomorrow."

"I'm not having breakfast with you all tomorrow," she said, nibbling away at her lip again.

"Given that I'm planning on keeping you busy tonight in my bedroom, I'd say breakfast is a good idea."

Now that? That got him a full Becca grin. "I need to be up front here. I'm not looking for anything beyond what we were doing in the car. Well…maybe a little more. But—"

"It's just breakfast," he assured, hoping that it'd turn into more than breakfast but not wanting to scare her off.

"I was told there would be chocolate cake at some point?" she said.

Uh. Shit. He didn't have any on hand. He could have some delivered, but maybe… "What if I go down on you instead?"

Her eyebrows rose, but otherwise she kept her composure. Until she shifted, pressing her thighs together. "Until I get my cookies?"

"If by cookies, you mean until I make you come multiple times, then yes." He splayed his hands on either side of her waist, holding her there.

"I think that's a fair compromise," she said, her breath against his mouth.

Yes, yes, he agreed that it was.

Her stomach growled. That was his fault. He hadn't gotten her anything to eat when they got home. He needed to remedy that.

"I'm going to make you something to eat. Then I'm going to eat *you*," he said.

Becca hands gripped his arms tighter. "That sounds like a plan."

"And Becca? I've got a solid lock on the door. And the walls in this house are not thin. Make as much noise as you want." On that thought, he needed to get moving so he could enjoy something better than cake.

Her name was Becca.

Chapter 15

Becca

Linx headed back toward the kitchen.

Which was good because Becca was famished. Turned out a night of waitressing, learning to give lap dances, making out in the snow, meeting the family of a guy she was totally into, and an orgasm in an automobile really left a girl famished.

Her stress levels rose substantially during the whole family-girlfriend shebang. Now that they were gone, they'd reset to a more reasonable level.

"For the record, you only like my family because you've been around them for ten minutes. Give them time. They'll lose their appeal," Linx grumped.

She doubted that. Her radar for dysfunction was spot on—unless it came to her own family. Previously, that radar had also malfunctioned frequently with romantic prospects. Which made it a good thing that this was not that. This was just this. And this was very nice.

If she were being really honest, this whole thing was a total Nutter Butter. Her fantasy come to life. Life-holiday perfection.

She'd put boundaries in place with the men she dated. No sex until they'd gone on at least three dates. Usually, she held out to four or five.

Definitely no sleepovers—even in the guest bedroom.

The rules were exhausting and raised her stress levels way past five. Which was why, as long as they refrained from any additional girlfriend conversations, this thing she had going with Linx was refreshing. She was at a solid zero. No stress. No responsibility.

Bliss.

She slid onto a barstool while Linx unloaded his refrigerator onto the center island of the kitchen. He tossed a head of lettuce in his hands like it was a volleyball. Gibson hopped up on the barstool next to her, eyeballing the counter.

"Don't do it, Gibs." Linx pointed to him with the head of lettuce. "Gotta wipe your paws before you go wandering on the counters."

Gibson hopped over to Becca's lap instead, settling in and turning on his purr motor.

Linx went to assembling a couple of sandwiches with the cutlets, cheese, lettuce, tomato. The guy obviously took sandwich art as seriously as he took his music. And his cat.

"How do you feel about Europe?" he asked.

Becca didn't look up from where she gave Gibson her attention. "I like Europe."

Gibson was apparently tired of this conversation because he hopped off of her lap and disappeared around the corner to the living where C-SPAN still blared.

"Great. When should we leave?" he asked. The question should have been funny, but there was no humor in the word. "Is your passport up to date? We could go tomorrow. Ditch my family," he continued.

Um. No. A trip to Europe was not light. Not light at all.

"What about Gibson?" she asked, apparently channeling Courtney.

"We can take him with us." Linx added a top layer of bread to the sandwich and cut it in half with a butter knife.

She couldn't be entirely sure because she'd never traveled with a feline, but, "I don't think you can just take pets with you overseas. Don't they have to go through a process with quarantining and vet checks?"

Hadn't celebrities gotten into trouble with that before?

"Damn, there's so much I don't know about pet ownership." He slid the finished sandwich across the island to her. "They need to write a book about it."

"Would you read that book?" Becca asked, before digging into the art that was her dinner.

Linx tugged his lips to the side. "Probably not."

Holy crapola, like everything else he did, Linx's sandwich was phenomenal. "This is fantastic."

He grinned. Clearly, he already knew that. "Thanks."

"Gibson can stay here. Courtney owes me. I'll ask her nicely to watch him. If she says no, I'll ask Tanner or Mach to do it."

Becca shook her head. "Leaving town when your family just arrived wouldn't be very nice."

"But it would be fun." He finished slicing his dinner in half and bit into it.

They ate in silence. With anyone else, the silence would've been awkward. With Linx, the normalcy of it was refreshing. She dug this. Linx's mattresses. Linx's sandwiches.

Linx.

All of him.

He could sell this service to cruise ship passengers and make a fortune.

"Besides—" The word rumbled across his vocal cords like a great lyric to a song. "—I'm not feeling like I should be very nice tonight. A nice man would not have the intentions I have for you."

She gulped. "What, exactly, are your intentions?"

Yay, he had intentions for her. She had a hunch they'd be her brand of dirty.

He paused, set down his unfinished sandwich, and locked his gaze on hers. "You're going to yell my name. In my bed."

The moment stood still, neither of them moving. The only sound came from the living room where *Politics and Public Policy Today* played on the television.

She'd never had sex with C-SPAN on in the background. There was a first time for everything, though, because her thighs were heavy, and a buzz formed along the nerve endings between her legs.

"I'm not loud in bed." She shrugged, trying for *laissez-faire* and failing miserably.

Unfortunately, what she said sounded a little like a dare. It did nothing to break the moment or the dissolve the chemistry lesson going on in the air between them.

Linx moved around the counter with intention. He stalked her like she was prey and he was an alpha predator ready to lay claim.

This was ridiculous. This was not who she was. She was a therapist-slash-waitress who liked rock music. The one time she'd tried to hook up with a rock legend, she'd ended up giving him a night of free therapy.

She'd never been the woman who got stalked by a rock star in his kitchen after he made her a sandwich. After he'd given her an orgasm in his freaking garage. After he'd introduced her to his mom and dad and sister.

As he got closer, his brown eyes took her hostage. She had no desire to leave. To run. To be anyone other than Becca of this moment. Becca, who was happy to let this man ravage her.

She separated her thighs as he settled himself between them, standing between her legs. What the hell. She lifted her ankles and wrapped them around him so his fly pressed against her center. Turned out, being prey didn't really suck like she'd expected. Actually, she was kind of hoping he'd do that eating thing he'd been talking about.

Who needed cake anyway?

"Yet." He gently pulled back on her hair until her face lifted to his.

"What?" she asked because she didn't understand what the hell-o he was talking about.

"You're not loud in bed…yet." Holding the back of her head, he pressed a dizzying kiss against her mouth. The kiss heated beyond normal kitchen-kiss levels, to where neither of them really cared about anything other than the feel of them together.

Linx broke the kiss long enough to run his lips over and along her cheekbone.

She shivered. "Okay."

Yup, that's what she said. Becca, who was usually verbose and had no problem finding words. Something about him made words disappear from her head. He took up all the room and left no space for anything else.

Neither of them were really that hungry anymore—at least she wasn't and Linx didn't appear to be, what with the way his tongue was in her mouth and his thick erection pushed against her belly.

"Wait," she said, pressing her hand against his chest. "What if your family comes back?"

He nuzzled her neck. The echoing zing sizzling through her.

He pulled back again, leaving her dazed and more than a little confused.

"They're not coming back for a while. Courtney and I talk a big game, but she wouldn't bring them back so soon. Dad wouldn't let her, anyway. Not when he was promised food." He lifted Becca from the stool before she could say anything else.

She didn't know a ton about Linx, but she hadn't really

pegged him as a multitasker. He seemed more like the type of guy who worked on one thing at a time and gave it all of his attention.

Nope, she was wrong. He could kiss her, carry her, and manage his way up the flight of steps without dropping her. All at the same time.

"I am not," he said, between kisses. "Coming." He went back to kissing her more. "In my pants." Still more kissing. "Again."

"Good call," she said as his mouth roamed. "You'll run out of t-shirt sleeves if you keep that up."

Come on, that was funny. He barely cracked a smile, though. His pupils were large. His pulse was visible in his throat. Hers beat as a perfect mirror in her veins.

He kicked the door to his bedroom closed behind them, depositing her carefully onto the bed. He was always cautious with her. It made little sense. Didn't reconcile to the man she'd believed him to be. The man she'd been told he was.

She didn't need him to be careful, and since words weren't really her friend right then, she showed him with her mouth. Lips and teeth and fingernails along his back had his erection straining further against the fabric of his jeans.

Then it was a frenzy of clothes coming off between fiery mouths pressed to one another, hands everywhere, and a deep throbbing inside her that craved release.

"I need," she said as he helped pull her jeans from her feet.

"What do you need?" he asked, undoing his own jeans and stepping out of them.

"I need..." When he pulled down her panties to her knees and pressed his face to the core of her, using his tongue and fingers, she lost her sentence.

God, God, God. She thrust against his mouth, as he used his tongue in inventive ways that she wouldn't have expected. How did he…okay, nope, didn't matter. That was…

Holy shit.

She arched against his bed as the orgasm built.

"I'm going to…" she said on a gasp, closing her eyes and pressing her head into the bedspread.

Then he removed his face. His hands weren't doing their thing anymore, and he wasn't there...

A crackle of foil drew her attention to the side of the bed where he stood, naked, sheathing himself.

What the hell-o-kay…The bulk of his sound system was quite the sight.

Her throat went thick. She pressed her legs together against the ache he'd created before pulling away, but she couldn't seem to find any words to ask him why he'd done that.

His gaze locked on hers, the space between them disintegrating. He moved to her, knee to the deliciously cloud-like mattress, and he was over her. He pressed a kiss to the small heart tattoo at the top of her hip as she spread her legs. Wrapped her calves around his thighs. Held his gaze in hers as he lowered himself onto her, into her.

"God, Linx," she said on a moan. The heft of him met the tightness of her.

He entered her slowly with delicious care, eyes locked to hers.

"More." The pressure inside built again as she urged him with her calves. Seriously, sex with Linx was way better than therapy.

Then he gave her more. Gave her everything.

He thrusted into her as she arched back against him. The air in the room seemed to be thicker than it had been moments earlier.

And then she was falling.

"Linx," she said on a breath.

"When I'm inside you, my name is Cedric," he said. This seemed important to him.

She tried to focus on his expression, but she was quickly losing any control she had over her own body as the orgasm to end all orgasms rolled over her, through her, taking her past the edge.

"Cedric," she said his name, more desperate than before.

"Becca." He buried his face in her hair. "So tight."

Actually, he was just that big. The kind of big that dwarfed everything around it, but in a good way. Like a super comfortable leather chair that seemed too big for the room, but actually fit perfectly.

His movements became more frantic. Hers did, too.

The rough hair of his legs across her smooth skin was the only thing keeping her grounded at the moment. And then, nothing mattered except the feelings he elicited throughout her body.

She convulsed around him, gripping his back as he continued the in and out movements that drove her further.

Like she was flying. Sure, she was present in the room, but she couldn't be certain she didn't call out his name as her body reveled in his.

Then he followed, flying and falling with her until they landed together, utterly spent, panting, and cocooned in his amazing mattress.

Yes, it was that good.

Just like he was.

He trailed his fingertips over her navel, down to her pubic bone and back up again. "That was…"

"Yeah." She blew out a breath. "That was…"

"You're thinking hard over there," he said, quoting her words from earlier.

She turned her head on the pillow to face him. "I am."

"Whatcha thinking about?" The familiarity with which he touched her made her feel like a total tosser for being ready to run earlier.

"Can we be serious for a second?" she asked, interrupting the exploration of his fingertips along her ribs.

He glanced down the naked length of her laying in his bed. "Sure."

"I don't know. I don't know what you're thinking." She rolled, aligning their bodies. "But I need to be clear about where I'm at with this."

"Becca…" He kissed her on the forehead. Unfortunately, he removed his fingertips from their exploration. "Tell me what you want."

"Sorry." She covered her face with her hands. "I'm making this weird."

He pulled her hands away, again with a gentleness that seemed so unlike him. "Given the night we've had, I'm sure there's nothing you could say right now that would make this weird."

"Oh, I might surprise you." She laughed, but it was stilted.

"Do you want to do the label thing?" He rolled on top of her, not giving her his weight, but letting their bodies touch. "Boyfriend. Girlfriend. That thing?"

The problem was, she didn't. That's not what she wanted. She shook her head. "I just. I don't want anything serious. I just—" She pressed her fingertips against her temples. "I want to have fun in my life for a while."

"If that's what you want, I can make that happen." He rolled her to her back, lengthening over the top of her, but not giving her his full weight.

She nodded. "I mean, would that bother you?"

He closed his eyes, let out a long breath. "Not as long as you don't go having fun with other guys while we're having fun."

"I'd feel better if we are exclusive while we do this." Look at her communicating like she would have encouraged her clients to do. Ask for what you want. Be assertive.

"Given that I've got no intention of being with anyone else, I'd say exclusive is a good deal." His hands were back to roaming again.

Well. Great. Good talk. "Okay. Good. We're exclusive. And we're having fun."

"See, that wasn't weird." His smile stretched clear across his cheeks.

"It wasn't." Not much, anyway.

In truth, the whole thing felt odd. Unlike Cedric's finger, which seemed to know exactly where it was going as it played her, *she* couldn't put her finger on why everything felt slightly off center…

Chapter 16

Linx

"Whatcha doin'?" Linx emerged from the shower with a thick, white towel wrapped around his waist. He'd hoped Becca might join him, but she'd been fast asleep when he woke earlier.

The fatigue would be his fault. The thought made his mouth water for her. They'd had an active night, that was for sure.

She sat cross-legged on the bed, tying some kind of knots with thin strips of leather trailing from her purse.

"Macramé." She kept her focus on the loops of leather, frowning at the rope she worked on, then nodded and fed the end of the rope through a long loop. Then she smiled like the sun had just come out on a cloudy day.

"I have no idea what that is." He strode toward her and her project.

She held up the braided rope made of tiny strips of leather she'd knotted together to form an impressive chain.

He fingered the inches of rope she'd created. "This is amazing."

"It's just knots." She said the words as though this wasn't an impressive feat. For the record, it was artistry, and as one artist to another, he appreciated the skill involved.

"And I just make guitar riffs." He turned to find a pair of boxers in his dresser. "That is art."

She said nothing, her eyes returning to the lengths of leather and knots she created.

"What will you make with it?" he asked, pulling on his favorite pair.

"A bracelet, I think." She tilted her head as she examined the knotted leather, running it through her fingers.

"It'll be spectacular."

Their eyes met then, and she smiled. Blushed.

He complimented her jewelry, and she blushed? After the things they did last night—and she had most definitely not blushed during any of the more adventurous encounters—she blushed at his compliment.

What. Was. Up. With. That?

Though, none of their bedroom adventures had involved leather rope. If it made her blush, perhaps they should give it a try. He'd like to investigate further. Unfortunately, for both of them, his family returned late last night, and he needed to put on pants before breakfast.

With a sigh, he dressed in a pair of faded jeans.

As much as he'd like to lose himself in Becca again, his family expected him at breakfast soon. The last thing he wanted was for them to come looking for him.

Not that they didn't suspect he'd had a sleepover, but he didn't want them to make Becca feel like she didn't belong in his house.

Because Becca definitely belonged in his space.

Even if she wasn't ready to admit it yet. Her words said one thing, but the language she spoke with her body said something entirely different.

"I enjoy doing it," she said as her hands continued tying

more knots. Over, under, through, and around. Her fingertips practically hypnotized him. "Calms my mind," she continued. "Like meditating."

"I tried that once." It'd been an epic fail because he couldn't stop his mind from drifting. Drifting to the riffs he would play that night. Drifting to what he'd have for dinner later. Drifting to whether or not the next tour would hit Houston. Totally defeated the purpose of the practice.

"Meditating?" she asked, as though it surprised her that he'd attempted it.

"Yeah." He pulled on a t-shirt. This one still had two sleeves. For now. "Didn't work out."

Her hands continued working with the leather, seemingly on autopilot. "Only once?"

"Didn't really get the point of it, you know?" He moved back to the bed. The mattress shifted under his weight.

She stopped working, which was a shame because watching her hands was mesmerizing.

"I started when things got harder at work." She stared at the leather, though it didn't appear she really saw it. "A few extra hard cases made it hard for me to sleep at night. I needed to get out of my head."

He laid a hand on her calf. "Do you want to talk about it?"

"Isn't that my line?" She laughed low, but it didn't sound like she meant it. "People carry around some serious shit with them." She started knotting again, on auto pilot. "It's overwhelming sometimes to help them unpack it all."

He traced circles along the muscles of her calf, letting her continue on if she wanted. Or not. Her call.

"You don't have to solve the problems of the world." He gave her calf a squeeze.

She nodded. Then did another row of knots.

"I have a hunch," she said.

"What's that?"

"Your meditation is making music," she said this then kissed him.

Man, that kiss… He kissed her back. Becca's mouth on his was definitely a morning treat.

"You think music is my meditation?" he asked against her mouth.

She nodded. "I do."

Girl might have a point.

"And this is yours?" he asked, a glance to the inches of rope.

She nodded. "A hobby to help me get out of my head."

No, this was more than a hobby, just like his music was more than meditation. "You should sell these."

They weren't like the friendship bracelets Courtney made as a kid. Those were chintzy little things. This was definitely artwork.

She laughed. "Ha. No."

"Why not?" He'd bet she could make her fortune hocking bracelets and necklaces like this to the celebrity crowd. He made a mental note to ask Courtney. She always had an eye for start-ups and excellent business prospects.

People in his world didn't care about how much something cost to make. They cared about the experience of owning it.

"It's recycled leather." Becca slid it through her fingers once again. "I'd get a few dollars for it, tops."

He moved into her, "I'd pay more than that."

"You don't have to." She nodded to his wrist. "Give me your hand."

"Becca?" he asked.

"It's a gift." She tied the leather around his wrist.

"I can't take this from you." His throat clogged at the thought. He was the one who gave gifts. He was good at that. Getting them? He got them from his parents and his sister. Sometimes the label sent shit to him. But this…this was…

She pressed a kiss to his lips. "I think the words you're thinking of are, thank you."

"Thank you," he said, though it took all his vocal training to keep the words from cracking.

He fucking loved it. Not only that it was from her, but it was perfection.

"We should head down to breakfast." She moved from the bed to the bathroom. "Then I've got to go."

He'd asked the housekeeper to drop off new clothes for Becca and another welcome-to-Linx's-basket full of all the shit Courtney loved. His sister had good taste, so he figured Becca would probably like it, too.

All of it was now in his bathroom, waiting for Becca. He liked that. The feeling of taking care of another person. Hell, aside from music, it was his own form of macramé bracelet-making.

By the time she emerged showered, dressed, and ready for breakfast, he'd already fielded two calls from his management team, checking in about the Bax and Knox issues, and replied to what felt like three dozen e-mails.

The kitchen was quiet when they got there. This wasn't a total shock, given that his parents were not night owls and they'd been out late the night before. Staying up late meant sleeping in. Courtney was usually up early though, even when she stayed up late. His sister never seemed to need the sleep of a normal human.

Normal being a relative term he used to describe himself and his own needs.

"Can I start the coffee?" Becca asked, already heading to the coffeepot and grabbing the carafe from the hot plate.

He nodded. "Beans are in the cupboard above. Grinder is right next to them."

"You grind your own beans?" she asked. The concept seemed to perplex her. "That seems like an awful lot of extra work."

"The best things are always worth a little extra." He moved behind her, opening the cupboard above, and letting his body brush against hers as he grabbed the tin of coffee beans. He bought the kind from Italy that cost a little extra but were worth every penny once the brew cycle completed.

He let his chin drift to the top of her head, pressing a kiss there because he could.

"Linx," she whispered. "Your parents and your sister could walk in."

The front of his t-shirt brushed against the back of hers, the cotton abrading his nipples as he allowed his hand to drop to her waist. "I'm only getting the coffee."

Becca turned. Her nipples were the ones brushing the front of his tee this time.

Not to say that turned him on, but it turned him on.

"You're being naughty." She rolled up on her tippy toes to press a kiss to his lips.

Oh, yes. Looked like he wasn't the only one interested in misbehaving.

"What's for breakfast?" She asked, turning her attention back to the grinder and the coffee beans.

He'd never had green-eyed envy for coffee beans before, but it seemed he was a guy who was a touch jealous of anything that Becca gave her attention to that wasn't him.

That thought needed a stop-check. Bacon would do the trick.

"Oatmeal, bacon, maybe some toast." He grabbed the box of steel-cut oats from the pull-out pantry beside the fridge. "Since we did pancakes yesterday."

"Do you always go all out for breakfast?" she asked before pressing the button on the grinder.

He couldn't exactly answer her question while the grinder did its thing, so he waited. Totally eye-fucking her. That was acceptable because she did it right back to him.

When the grinder finished, he spoke, "Sometimes I fix a

shake. Sometimes I cook eggs. Depends." He ran his teeth over the edge of his lips.

"Depends on what?" she asked.

"If there's someone here worth cooking for."

The little dimples in her cheeks popped slightly. "That's sweet."

"You're sweet." He knew this from firsthand experience and a whole lotta experimenting with his tongue and mouth the night before.

"Good morning, son," Dad hollered from the top of the stairs. "We are coming downstairs now." There was some rustling and hushed whispers. "If your friend is still with you, know that we are about to enter the kitchen."

Linx glanced to Becca and held his fingertip up to his mouth, in the don't respond gesture. Because his dad would continue on and it'd probably be a riot.

She said she wanted fun. Welcome to his world. She was obviously holding back a chuckle, which made him stifle a laugh.

There was a long pause before Dad continued, enunciating every word. "You should give us a hint if it is safe to enter the room."

Linx smirked.

His family totally barged into his life. They could suffer a little for the intrusion. He also had every intention of changing the television back to C-SPAN remotely whenever his dad watched his detective shows.

"He's not subtle at all, is he?" Becca asked as she finished pouring the filtered water into the coffee pot and clicked it on.

"Nope." Linx loaded his oats into his Instant Pot. Yes, he had one. Yes, he used it all the time. No, it didn't mean he had to take punches off his man card. "We're in here, Dad." Linx said louder than necessary, but he raised his voice to match the obnoxious that was his father.

Mom and Dad bustled through the hallway, headed

toward them. He heard something about not making Becca uncomfortable from his mom. Then something about how he wasn't making anyone uncomfortable—that was from his dad.

"Good morning." Dad said before coming around the corner.

His father was missing a sleeve to his t-shirt. Linx gave a pointed look to his dad's missing right sleeve.

"I hear it's all the rage with the kids these days," Dad said.

"Morning, Dad." Linx shook his head and waited for the coffeepot to drip.

Becca pulled more mugs down from the cupboard. "Good morning."

"I trust you all got some good sleep?" Mom asked.

Dad nudged her with his elbow. "Don't mention sleep."

Mom gave him a look like he'd gone bonkers. Linx gave him the same look. Becca glanced up from arranging the mugs and gave him a small smile. "I slept great, thanks."

She hadn't, not really. Linx knew because they'd spent most of the night talking and… other things.

"Where's Courtney?" Linx poured himself a cup, even though it only filled half his mug.

"Courtney's right here." Courtney looked like a train had hit her, and then she got run over by a truck. Deep purple rings under her eyes showing she hadn't caught much shut eye at all. Her combed air was pulled tight against the nape of her neck. Usually, she was ready to roll in the morning.

"Courtney is speaking in the third person." Linx handed her his coffee as a peace offering, given that she looked like she'd been on the losing end of an all-night bender.

She shook her head, moving toward the refrigerator instead to grab a bottle of cherry-flavored seltzer water.

This was new. Courtney loved her morning coffee better than most anyone else he knew. Except, himself.

"Are you okay, sis?" Maybe they should take her temperature or something? He was sure he had a thermometer in his first aid kit.

He looked to his mom. She'd know what to do.

Mom watched Courtney like she was a hawk but said nothing.

This was also not normal. Usually, as soon as one of her chickies showed the slightest hint of being ill, Mom was all about the Tylenol and the thermometers and the questions about bowel habits.

"Hey," Courtney sipped at the glass of seltzer she'd poured for herself. "I have something I need to say."

"What's up, sweets?" Dad paused, putting the pan on the stove for the bacon Linx had laid out.

"Here's the thing." Courtney cleared her throat and fidgeted with the napkin holder in the center of the island. She glanced to Linx, then Becca, then Mom and Dad. "I need you not to freak out. Because I'm not freaking out."

"Now we're all freaking out, Courtney." Come on, it wasn't like Linx tried to growl. Not really. But the whole don't-freak-out command totally had him freaking out.

His heart stuck in his throat, so he couldn't actually ask her if she wasn't okay. And, clearly, she was not okay.

"Honey." Mom reached for Courtney's hand. "What's going on?"

"I'm pregnant." Courtney cleared her throat after dropping the bomb. "Before anyone says anything, I already decided to keep the baby."

No one moved. No one except Becca, who blinked. Hard. The only sounds came from the drip of the coffeemaker and the hiss of the Instant Pot letting off steam.

Courtney didn't have a steady guy in her life, as far as he knew. She'd been the band's tour publicist for years. While he figured she'd hooked up with men, there'd never been one that had stuck. None that she brought home. Except that one guy, years ago. But he was a regular jack-wagon dickhead.

Linx hadn't minded at all when she'd scraped him off her shoe.

For the first time since he saw her last night, Linx really looked at his sister. Courtney's shirt stretched a little extra around her belly.

"Who is the father?" Mom asked, her tone gentle, yet concerned.

Courtney's cheeks pinked. She quickly shook her head. "He won't be involved."

Linx hoped like hell it wasn't that guy. What was his name? Gary. Jerry. Maybe he should've paid more attention. He hadn't liked the dude, though, so he hadn't taken notes.

But a guy who knocked up his sister and then didn't want to step up stuck sideways in his craw. It took everything Linx had not to say something that he'd regret. His baby sister was going to be a mother, and that gobsmacked him. Sure, she was a woman, and he didn't have any doubt she had, well, as their mom would say, gentleman friends. But she was Courtney. She was his sister.

"Doesn't seem like he has much of a choice," Linx said, finally. Of all the things he could've said, it seemed like the most fitting and the least likely to piss everyone off.

"It'd be *better* if he's not involved." Courtney glanced longingly at his mug but sipped from her seltzer. "He's not the fatherly type."

"Does he know?" Dad asked in a tone that said, *do I need to go Law & Order on him?* The ripped shirt sleeve wrecked the badass vibe he was going for.

"I'll tell him once I'm further along. When I know it's going to stick. They say the first trimester is the riskiest. I figure I'll tell him after I'm through it. I'd like to keep it just with family for now. And Becca. Obviously." Courtney traced a thin stream of condensation down the edge of her glass with a thumbnail.

"This is going to be wonderful." Dad clapped his hands as

though to make it so. "I'm going to be a grandpa. This calls for celebration."

"Dad…" Courtney said. Apparently, the carbonation in her beverage held a load of appeal by the way she stared at it. "Let's not do that."

"How can we support you?" Mom asked, likely earning A-plus points from Becca.

"Just… you know, don't make a big thing about it." Courtney nodded. "And don't fry bacon around me in the morning."

No bacon. He could handle that. She didn't need to be around bacon if it bothered her. Linx strode to the pan of bacon, grabbed it with a potholder, strode to the back door, and tossed the whole shebang outside. There. "Done."

Courtney's eyes were enormous. Becca's, too. Mom just put her face in her hands.

"I was going to eat that." Dad crossed his arms.

"Not if it's making Courtney sick." Linx checked the timer on the oats. "Oatmeal okay, sis?"

"Oatmeal is great." Courtney glanced up at him, her eyes watery. "Can we change the subject?"

"Becca," Dad moved right into the next subject with no segue at all. "What do you do for work?"

Becca nibbled at her bottom lip. "I'm a therapist."

"I think that skill set might just come in handy today," Mom muttered, filling herself a cup of coffee.

Becca took in a deep breath. Then she let it out. "Yeah."

Chapter 17

Becca

Well, they could chalk that breakfast up to one of the most awkward experiences of her existence.

Courtney dropped her bombshell, and then everyone went about breakfast as though nothing happened. Aside from the half-cooked bacon strewn across the back patio, Courtney only picking at her oatmeal, and the unnatural silence that had them all contemplating how to split atoms—given the intensity of her thought processes—the breakfast could be called a success. Ha. Not really. Becca had sat through couple's counseling that ended in divorce with less tension in the air.

Linx turned to music, which, she guessed, was expected. He'd pulled out his guitar and tumbled into his own thoughts. Which was her cue to head out.

He'd set up shop on the floor with sheet music spread out around him. Some pages were blank, some had penciled in notes.

"I'm going to head home." She sat near his feet, away from the amassed pages of music.

He set the guitar aside. "I'll drive you."

She held up her phone. "Already called for a car. The shop has mine ready to go. They'll drop me there."

"Are you at Brek's today?" he asked.

She shook her head. "I have plans to take my mom to lunch and then have a very long nap."

"You can nap here." He tilted his chin toward the bed.

Cautious not to disturb his notes, she crawled up over his legs to kiss him. "You need to spend some Becca-free time with your family."

And she needed some Linx-free time because she worried that she could very well get attached to the man in a way that was not fling-y.

"You sure it's not that you need some family-free time without them?" He did set his guitar aside this time, kissing the stuffing out of her.

"I need a nap." She smiled against his mouth.

"Is it bad that I don't really want to stay here alone with them?" he asked.

Her happy-go-lucky Linx suddenly became Mr. Frowny Pants. Becca didn't know how Linx preferred his soothing. Finding out tipped them into relationship territory. So she did what she would never tell one of her clients to do—she went for the quick, precise escape.

"Not bad." She gave a final peck on his lips before crawling back down his body. "You can always come nap with me later, if you want."

He let her go. "Then we won't nap."

She grinned because he was correct. Then she yawned because she hadn't gotten hardly any sleep. She was knackered.

"When can I see you again?" he asked.

After last night? Her skin warmed. Anytime he wanted to, if the truth were told. "Text me later?"

He nodded, pulling his guitar back to his lap and strumming out a few chords while she slipped out of the room.

Moving past Gibson, who insisted she stop to rub his head, Becca kept her steps light as she turned the corner of the hallway, hoping to slip past the living room to the front door but… gah… Linx's dad holed up there watching television.

She back peddled. Literally, walking backward as silent as she could in Converse sneakers. The kitchen door worked as well as the front door. Slipping out that one made much more sense and required substantially fewer opportunities for uncomfortable exchanges with the parentals.

She slinked into the kitchen, checking the car icon on the app, and ran smack dab into Courtney.

Not literally. Courtney was sipping at a cup of hot tea, staring at her laptop.

Okay, well, this was fine. Courtney didn't want to talk about anything, anyway. They were, according to her specific requests, not to mention the unmentionable.

"Hey." Becca shrugged off her purse and set it on the dining room table next to where Courtney had set up a laptop and workstation. She rummaged through the bag, fishing out her fake, supposed-to-look-like Kate Spade sunglasses.

Courtney glanced up from her screen. "Hey."

She said nothing, seeming to dare Becca to speak first. Okay, Becca could speak first. That wasn't a problem. Turned out she didn't have to because Courtney asked, "You're really a counselor?"

Becca nodded. "Officially. Though, I'm taking a break."

"Seems like everyone is taking a break." Courtney continued working on her laptop. Becca checked the car icon again—it was a touch closer, but not much. "Linx is getting restless. I can feel it."

"On behalf of Dimefront fans everywhere, I hope they

get this figured out soon," Becca said. "Do you know the other guys?"

"I do the publicity for the band." Courtney smiled, but it didn't meet her eyes. "For now, at least. We'll see what happens with my life in the next few months." She went back to staring vacantly at the screen.

"I'm sure they'll make accommodations." Becca went for chipper, but to be honest, her stomach got a little sore because she didn't want Linx to be without his band much longer.

"I know we don't know each other well, but your brother is awesome." Becca blew out a breath from her cheeks. She wanted to sit, start an intake, offer to help Courtney process the intense emotions she had to be feeling. Except this was not a therapy session. Becca's job was not to fix anything or help anyone else fix anything, either. An intake would be stressful. So, in this moment, she was not a counselor. She could be a friend, though. "And your family is, too."

"Linx is an easy guy to care about," Courtney said, sounding like she totally believed her words. "My parents are okay." The way she said it indicated she thought they were much more than just, okay.

"They're worried about you," Becca said.

"Nothing to worry about." Courtney's smile didn't meet her eyes. "I've got it figured out."

That was probably not true, but Becca wouldn't push.

"I haven't really known your brother long, but I get the feeling he enjoys taking care of people," Becca said. Gibson took that moment to weave through her ankles. "And pets."

"No kidding." Courtney glanced to the cat walking a figure-eight around Becca's feet. "Cedric has always taken care of me." Courtney closed her laptop. She pulled the charging cord loose and wound it up. "I appreciate that he'll want to keep doing that. I think, though, that it's time that I started taking care of myself."

Becca could admire that.

"Can I help?" Becca asked. "If there's anything I can do to make all of this easier—"

"I don't need a therapist." Courtney gave a firm head shake.

"That's good because I can't be your therapist." Not after what she'd done with Courtney's brother.

Courtney raised her eyebrows in question.

Becca's phone pinged, announcing the car was only a few minutes away. "I can be your friend, though, if you want one."

Courtney's jaw slackened. She nodded. "I think I'd like that."

Good. This was good. Look at Becca, making friends, just like if she was at a bar on the beach. Okay, this was very different from that. Same concept, though.

"You seem nice, Becca." Courtney stared at Becca with the kind of assessing look that usually made a person's palm sweat. But it didn't when it came from Courtney.

"Thanks." Becca scratched at her eyebrow. "I think."

Courtney laughed. "Cedric doesn't have a great history with women. But you're different."

The itch to ask what Courtney meant about Linx's history intensified. *Not your business. Not your business.* Fine. Whatever. She was going to ask. "How am I different?"

"I mean, at least you get to use your name, right?" Courtney held her knuckles up for a fist bump.

Becca stilled, trying to figure out what the heck Courtney meant. "Sorry, what?"

"Your name." The brief smile forming on Courtney's mouth faltered.

"Why wouldn't I use my name?" Becca asked.

"He didn't tell you?" Courtney's face went pale. It wasn't because someone was cooking bacon.

Becca's phone pinged again. The car was at the end of the block now. "Tell me what?"

Now, it felt like she needed to know.

Courtney shook her head. The color still hadn't returned to her cheeks. "On that note, I've said entirely too much. You should ask him."

Becca did the thing she had perfected, where she could, with a look, get someone to continue speaking about a subject even though they'd planned to stop. She didn't use the technique often in her practice, but occasionally it came in handy. She couldn't say if it was the way she tilted her head, the way she softened her gaze, or the way she simply said nothing as she did those two things, but six times out of ten, it worked.

What the hell? She tried it now.

Courtney paused, let out a breath, and started talking.

"Linx used to have—" Courtney held up two hands in apparent surrender. "—women that he saw in the various tour cities."

Well, yeah, Becca had figured that much.

"We all called them by their city name, not their name."

Serious? That was... "That's a little degrading," Becca said, noting a bit of a sour taste along her taste buds.

"I don't know where it started, but it became a thing. They all wore their nicknames like a badge of honor—Houston, Paris..."

"Denver?" Becca asked.

"He hasn't mentioned Denver at all since he bought the house." Courtney let out a breath. "Or anyone else. You're special. You're different to him."

Becca had known Linx was a bit of a player. Heck, Bax had confirmed that for her. That's why he was a safe bet for her pina colada fling. Still, this didn't sit right, and there was a lot here to psychoanalyze. Later. For now, Becca had to get to her car.

"And now I have officially said too much." Courtney shivered a little. "You should ask him about it."

"Said too much about what?" Linx asked, slipping beside

Becca to plant a kiss at her temple. "What should she ask me?"

"I just said…" Courtney closed her laptop and stood from the stool. "You know what? I think I'm going to go throw up now."

Becca looked from Courtney's retreating form back to Linx.

"You don't get to use your pregnant status to run away, if we don't get to ask questions about it," Linx yelled behind her.

"Can and will," Courtney hollered back.

Becca's phone buzzed, announcing her car's arrival at the front gate.

Good. Perfect.

Because she didn't want to think about this, anyway.

Chapter 18

Becca

Becca hadn't asked Linx about Denver or any of the others. Partially because asking him would be awkward as hell. Mostly, though, because asking raised responsibility levels which would cause a dump of cortisol which would raise her stress levels. Thus, it was none of her business.

"You're just not going to ask him? You're not the least bit curious about these women?" Kellie had taken a stool at Brek's Bar. It was early—like late afternoon—and the place was empty except for the two of them and one cook in the kitchen. Brek moved in and out of the bar area, finishing up a handful of projects before the crowd started and he'd need to dive into bartending.

"You should ask him about it," Kellie said when Brek was out of earshot.

This had been Kellie's vote from the get-go. Their other friends were evenly divided amongst the ask and don't ask camps.

Becca was team don't-ask. Generally, she was team talk-it-out and communicate-the-hell-out-of-all-situations. This time… "It doesn't really matter, though, right? It's not like we have a future. Besides, the past should stay in the past."

That sounded remarkably like something a grown-ass adult would say.

"Isn't the past what has made us who we are? If we pick someone to spend time with, we should know where they've been, so we can understand where they are and where they're going?" Kellie apparently felt philosophical today. Which begged the question—what was she avoiding that she was up in Becca's business?

"You sound like me." Becca wiped the bar counter. They only had thirty minutes before the regulars started pouring in.

"I sound like super-smart you." Kellie sipped on her vodka martini with three olives.

It wasn't exactly quitting time, but Kellie worked remotely for her accounting firm and made her own hours.

"Linx and I have both made regrettable decisions. We don't need to dwell in the lost land of fuck-ups." What mattered was the decisions they made from now on. Decisions that would lead to a helluva lot more fun.

It'd been days since Courtney had announced her pregnancy. Days in which Becca and Linx had not had another sleepover. Oh, they'd had sex. Mostly at her apartment after she got off work. She'd installed a lock.

He wasn't driving her anymore—she had her car—but he followed her home to ensure she made it okay. She assured him she was perfectly safe, but he insisted. It was sweet, so she didn't balk.

He'd invited her to his house for another sleepover, but with her work schedule and odd hours, it hadn't worked out. That was the cover story. The reality was that she realized things between them were feeling not-so-surface anymore.

She had a lot of baggage to empty before she was ready

for anything serious. Turned out, she carried a lot of luggage, herself. While she'd spent years helping others unpack theirs, hers had languished in the hallway of her life.

Not that this was a total surprise, but this was why she'd left Portland—so she could figure out where the threads of her past led to her particular future.

Linx was proving to be a lovely distraction from doing any of the work for herself.

And that had to stop.

After a handful more orgasms.

Hey, self-care mattered, too. She preached that to her clients often, and Linx was nothing if not making her feel lovely.

Speaking of Linx, he sauntered through the door. Her stomach tightened as he eye canoodled only her and headed straight to where she stood.

"Whoa." Kellie watched the whole thing with rapt attention before going back to sipping her martini. "He looks at you like he wants to have you for dinner *and* breakfast."

Becca sighed. Yeah. He did. It was nice to be on the receiving end of one of those looks. It was the thing she hadn't realized that she wanted until Linx handed it to her. Which totally messed with her ability to keep that line in the sand drawn.

"The usual?" she asked, already grabbing the ginger ale in the Coors bottle she'd prepared when she got to work, in expectation that he'd stop by.

"Uh huh." He grinned, clearly pleased that she'd had his beverage of choice prepared.

"Becca." He leaned across the bar and waited.

She moved so he could kiss her firm on the mouth, not because they were serious, only because she liked to kiss him. Yes, she moaned. No, she wasn't sorry that she made the noise. Also, she was super happy that no one else was in the room except Kellie and a bouncer.

"Hey," she said.

"Hey," he replied.

He'd been spending time with his family. And time with Mach and Tanner helping them draft a few songs he could pitch to the label.

He kissed her again. This time it was a quick peck on the lips. The kind of familiar kiss that dipped a toe well past hook-up levels. He grabbed the stool next to Kellie and sat. "I'm also your bartender tonight. Brek asked if I'd help out." He turned to her friend, sitting there with googly eyes. "How are you, Kellie?"

"Me?" She pointed to herself. "Oh, I'm great. Just soaking all this in." She waved her finger in a circle between Becca and Linx.

Becca growled at her.

He chuckled. "Me, too, darlin'. Me, too."

Becca's heart seemed to grow butterfly wings so it could flutter around her chest, right down to her tummy. She told them to knock it off.

"If you're my bartender, you should get ready for work." She glanced with a pointed look to the apron hung on the hook beside the cash register.

In turn, he gave a pointed glance around the room. "Seems like I've got a little time to fraternize with Kellie."

Then he refocused on Becca and practically undressed her with only that look. Heck, she almost came on the spot. Which was totally inappropriate, given that she was on the clock.

Kellie cleared her throat.

"Do you have a brother or something?" Kellie asked. "Because if you do, I call dibs."

Becca folded bar towels instead of engaging further with Linx. She shook her head.

"No brother that I know of. I can ask Mom and Dad." Linx laughed and tipped the incognito ginger ale to his lips.

Kellie sighed. "Maybe keep your eye out for another rock star looking for a woman who can balance his checkbook and do his taxes."

He tapped the neck of his bottle to her glass in a mock toast. "Now *that*, I can do."

"Hey, uh…" Kellie raised her brows in Becca's direction. "Becca had something she wanted to ask you about something your sister mentioned."

Crapola. Kellie went there. Becca shook her head. "No, I didn't have anything to ask you."

Breathe in the hook-up. Breathe out responsibility. This would be her mantra.

"Oh, that's not true. Is it, Bec?" Kellie swirled the remaining olive in her martini like she wasn't being a total rat. "There are things she should ask you about."

"Nope." Becca folded another towel with a bit too much vigor. "I shouldn't."

Brek, bless him, took that moment to come do the handshake thing with Linx. They did the niceties and all the shit they always did when they first saw each other. Shooting the shit a little and basically just being friends.

Becca hoped that the distraction would prove to be what she needed to… well… distract him.

Unfortunately, nope. Once he and Brek had done their chatter, he settled his gaze on Becca.

"What was the thing you should you ask me?" He cut right to the point in that way of his that managed to be easygoing and attentive all at the same time.

Grr… Becca would have words with Kellie later.

Actually, gah. No. She wouldn't. Her friend meant well, even if her methods were questionable.

"Becca, serious. What's up?" The softness in Linx's eyes broke down any barrier she'd tried to erect.

Unfortunately, the concern flowing from Linx got Brek's

attention. He didn't go back to whatever he'd been doing before. He hooked a hip at the corner of the bar top and settled in to hear what was going on.

Fine. Blurgh.

"You call me Becca," she said.

Linx frowned. "Of course, I call you Becca."

"What's with the naming of your previous… uh…" She slid a sidelong glance to Kellie. "Female conquests…"

"Oh, fuck." Brek ran his palm over his face, all the way down to his chin. "She knows."

"I'm not following." Linx scrunched up his forehead, clearly thinking too hard and not getting what she was saying at all. "What does she know?"

Becca gulped. It wasn't a big deal. She wasn't even going to bring it up. But… "Courtney said that your previous…lady friends…had nicknames."

His expression darkened as though a thundercloud of memory rolled in.

"The city thing?" he asked.

Becca nodded, hoping weirdly that it was just the city thing. Why was her stomach souring so badly with this conversation?

"Here's the thing," he said, staring up at the ceiling of the bar. The Budweiser sign behind him flickered a little, seemingly as uncomfortable with the conversation as the two of them were.

He looked to Brek with a glance that seemed to plead for help.

Brek just gave a slight head shake. "Just own it, man."

"Who's Denver?" Becca asked.

There. She'd owned it. Direct and to the point.

Linx

Oh no, he wasn't going there. Not when things were good between him and Becca. Instead, he played possum—roll over and pretend he was dead and didn't understand what was going on in the world.

"Denver is a place," he said.

Becca rolled her eyes to the ceiling. She'd become adept at that maneuver. "The person, you Nutter Butter."

Linx tapped out a rhythm on the bar with his knuckles. One of the songs he'd been working on with Mach and Tanner. He didn't chance a glance to Becca or Kellie.

"Own it," Brek said again.

"Your friend is giving expert advice." Kellie said. "Get it out there."

"Promise you won't be mad?" he asked Becca.

"No." She did, however, stop folding the towels and gave him all of her attention.

He couldn't be sure if this was a good thing or a not good thing.

He sighed. "Okay, I'll tell you, anyway."

"This is gonna be good," Brek said, his words monotone.

"Denver was a woman," Linx said. Got it all out there. No secrets between them was a great way to lay the foundation of a future. Not that this was a secret. He just hadn't told her. "She is a woman."

Becca didn't move. She did the thing she did that made a guy want to keep talking when he really didn't want to keep talking.

"I don't see her anymore." He glanced to Brek for help.

Brek was, as expected, no help. Not with that shit-eating grin on his face. Oh, yes, he was enjoying this entirely too much.

He looked to Kellie. At least she had a semblance of sympathy in her expression.

"I haven't seen her since before I met you." Linx fiddled with his beer bottle.

Not only did Becca remain perfectly still, she also continued staring at him like Courtney did that time Gibson had hacked up a hairball into her favorite pair of shoes.

"This woman's name isn't really Denver, though, right?" Becca asked, her forehead all scrunched up.

Fuck a toaster, he was going to have to give details.

"No." He stretched out the word. "Her name is Brittney. The guys called her Denver because she was from Denver." Easy peasy. Nothing serious. Nothing to worry about.

Yet, his pulse hit above-average beats per minute. He knew this because he could hear each beat in his eardrums.

"Tell her about Paris and New Jersey," Brek chimed in.

Brek needed to skedaddle home to his wife and baby and everything that wasn't busting Linx's balls.

Brek, however, didn't appear to have any intention of evacuation. He raised his eyebrows in Linx's direction, and it was official.

Linx was going to murder his *former* band manager.

Becca squinted. "How many did you have?"

"Okay." Linx held up his hands. "I can see how this looks bad."

"You can?" Becca asked all therapist-y. It wouldn't surprise him if she asked a follow-up question about how he felt.

Kellie was the only one who had his back when she said, "I think we should let Linx finish."

Was Linx going to do the honest thing? The right thing? Tell Becca?

Yes, yes, he was going to do that. He glanced to Becca. She waited patiently, no expression on her beautiful face.

"I had... uh... hookups when we were on tour," Linx said, finally.

He didn't say more.

For once, Brek didn't say more.

Becca also didn't say more.

Kellie said nothing.

They all sat there. Not talking. Marinating in awkward that bordered what he went through with his family when Courtney announced she was knocked up.

"I feel like there's more to this story," Becca said, finally. She didn't sound pissed, though. It's not like she could've thought she was his first. They'd, uh, established that already.

"C'mon, Linx. It's not that bad. Not like Bax and his jewelry." Brek nodded along with this assertion.

Linx loved the guy like a brother, but he was ready to deck him right about then.

"Bax and his jewelry?" Becca asked. "I feel the plot thickening."

Bax had his own system of giving his hookups special thank-you-for-banging-me jewelry. They were absolutely not going to discuss Bax and his jewelry. Which meant…

"I didn't enjoy hooking up with randoms. So,"—Linx coughed—"if I met a woman I liked, I visited her when I came to town."

"Visited her?" Brek asked, chuckling. Good to see Brek seemed to find this turn of conversation funny.

"And I bought them dinner." Linx went back to fiddling with his beer bottle. "And we all knew the score. Knew what we were doing." He continued fussing with the paper. "It wasn't like I misled any of them. We all got our—how did you say? Cookies from the jar."

Brek shook his head. "Not helping your case, man."

Kellie had her face held in her palms. "This is my fault. The reason I should not be allowed to speak."

Becca, meanwhile, held still, her face neutral.

"Huh," she said, after a beat. She ran her tongue along the inside of her upper lip.

Normally, that movement would do special things to his insides that would then make him want to do special things to her. Instead, he replied, "Huh?"

"What did the other guys do?" Becca asked.

"They picked random women for their one-night stands," Brek said, cheerful as all get out.

"Huh," Becca said, again.

"You keep saying that," Linx said with a low growl. He didn't see why any of this mattered.

"I'm processing this new data." She shrugged.

Linx set his beer bottle aside and reached for Becca's hands. She didn't seem pissed, just reflective.

"I know all of their names," he said. "The city thing was a thing the guys started because they didn't want to remember their names. The women I was with weren't looking for serious, either."

Brek let out a low groan. "You are not making this better. You should stop explaining and go back to bein' an idiot."

"Huh," Becca said, yet again, glancing between the two of them and tilting her head to the side.

Becca was all about communication, so the lack of communication freaked him right the hell out.

"See, you're doing the huh thing still." He tugged at her chin so she looked at him again. Her eyes were soft, and a tick of a grin edged at the side of her mouth.

He wanted to press kisses all over her mouth, but Brek was still right there and Becca didn't seem to be into the PDA thing.

"I am trying to decide if you were being rock star-responsible or a douche-canoe," she said, breaking his trance from staring at her lipstick.

"Definitely rock star-responsible," Kellie said, raising her right hand. "I'm voting rock star-responsible."

"He means rock star-lazy." Brek said, reminding them all that he was still there, hadn't left, and was itching to get his nose broken.

"I like to think of it as rocker particular," Linx said, only to Becca.

Maybe if he just ignored Brek, like Gibson ignored Linx when he was pissed, then Brek would take the hint and leave.

Either that, or he'd have Linx neutered.

On second thought, this plan might not be the best option.

With Linx's skeletons rattling in the wind, Brek finished his shit and took off to the kitchen. Kellie went to flirting with some guy near the jukebox. Linx grabbed an apron and went to work. Since it was a weeknight, the bar wasn't busy. Becca helped him out when the orders got a little nuts, but otherwise he had it handled.

"Tanner and Mach are gonna play a set," he said between the rush of orders, now that they were in a lull. "I shot them a text since we're slow and they need the experience."

"You're going to play with them?" she asked. The question was most definitely a question, but it also seemed to be a request.

"You want me to sing to you?" he asked, letting his body brush hers as he moved to grab a fresh bottle of Jameson.

She turned. The front of her Brek's Bar shirt brushed against his pecs. "You can always sing to me."

"Then consider it done."

The boys got settled on stage. Once things chilled, he grabbed a guitar and went to work with them—though, it was the furthest thing from work. Not when he was playing, and Becca was appreciating it.

And just when the world felt oh so very, very content—Becca filled a couple of beers on tap, Linx jammed with Tanner and Mach, and Kellie flirted with some other guy at the bar—the world tilted funny.

Bax and Knox—the other members of Dimefront—strode through the front door with manager Hans.

One glance to Linx making music with guys a decade their junior, and their expressions turned dark.

They did not look happy. Not at all.

Chapter 19

Linx

The part that pissed Linx off was not that his bandmates shot eye daggers at him every fifteen fucking seconds. No, that was fine. He could glare as well as the rest of them.

The part that pissed him off was they sat at the bar with Becca. His Becca.

Before he grabbed a barstool with the guys, Bax had wrapped her in a bear hug that lifted her right off her feet. Obviously, he remembered her, and that pissed Linx off even more. Bax had no business hugging *his* Becca.

Brek played interference but didn't seem pleased with the impromptu visit from Bax and Knox. Probably because he asked that when A-list planned on showing up, they give him a shout so he could increase security. Linx always played by those rules.

Bax and Knox obviously didn't. Because if they'd given a shout, Brek would've fucking mentioned it.

Becca must've felt the tension flowing through the bar, but she didn't let it slow her down. Knox flirted with her like she was a prospect for one of his one-night-only after shows.

Though Linx couldn't hear her, she had her passively-attentive-but-not-giving-him-anything-more-than-surface-attention expression on.

Linx was on the fourth—and final—refrain when Kellie approached the group. Knox turned his attention to her. Unfortunately, for everyone involved, Kellie ate up his advances.

Shit.

Kellie was pretty. Blond hair, blue eyed, heavy-makeup pretty. The kind of pretty that most guys would fall face-over-feet for.

Her rapt attention on Knox wasn't a total shock, given that he had a reputation for only being a dick when he wanted to or when he was hangry. He could be decent, too. With a little effort, he could pull himself out of asshole territory permanently. He just had no desire to do that.

The song ended and, thank fuck, the set was complete.

Linx gave a nod to Mach. "You and Tanner want to meet the rest of Dimefront?"

Maybe it made Linx a bit of a chicken's ass because he had ulterior motives. Those being that he'd very much like to have extra back up when he engaged with his bandmates.

"Yeah, sure," Mach said. Obviously, he was trying to play it cool. Linx appreciated that.

"You in?" he asked Tanner.

Tanner's grin stretched wide. "Oh yeah."

He balanced his sticks on the snare. Then he ran his palms along the sides of his way-too-popstar-for-a-rocker haircut and stood.

"Give me five with the guys, then I'll do an intro?" Linx asked.

He glanced to Bax and Knox. They were practically drilling holes in him with the intensity of their stares.

Linx wanted to take his time rolling cords that didn't need put away, chatting with a few patrons who didn't really seem to care who he was, but he wanted to get this over with. And check in with Becca.

Becca mattered most, so he beat it to where she stood next to Brek.

He didn't say hello to the guys at first, even as they tracked his progress across the room. The weight of their gaze on him was heavy. They couldn't find a moment to respond to him over the past months, they could fucking deal.

Also, he was making a point.

He moved around the lip of the bar to where Becca and Brek watched him coming. He wanted to kiss Becca, claim her as his. Let the boys know that she belonged to him. Let them see that he had a woman with a heart of fucking gold and a band who got his love of music. He had it all. They could take their extended hiatuses and suck it.

But claiming Becca in the middle of her shift would only be a show of who had the bigger dick. He respected her opinion of him a helluva lot more than that of his bandmates. So he refrained.

"Becca," he said her name instead of kissing the hell out of her. "Thanks for covering for me."

Becca tilted her head to the side. She had his number. Of course, she did. She was Becca.

Therefore, she took matters into her own hands, rolling up on her toes to press a kiss to his mouth. "Anytime, Cedric."

Becca gave him a side squeeze before turning back to work. If he hadn't known better, he'd say that she just claimed *him*. And it felt fucking amazing.

"Guys." He tied a Brek's Bar apron around his waist. "Have you been helped?"

Knox slid his gaze to Bax. Bax seemed as shocked as Knox.

"You're *working* here?" Bax asked.

"Part-time bartender," Brek said, pulling a Coors from the tap. "Helps me out when I'm short staffed."

Brek gave Linx a look that said everything. He had his back. Whatever happened, he had his back. Linx swallowed hard against a surge of emotion. Yeah, he had it all.

"If you're hiring, maybe I need a part-time gig. I could deal here." Knox held his fist out to bump Linx's.

An olive branch in knuckle form. Huh. Alright then. He met Knox's knuckles with his own.

"I thought I'd moved on from you people," Brek grumbled. "But you're still here."

Linx was pretty sure he didn't mean it. Because with all of Dimefront there, Brek and Hans could likely talk them into an impromptu set.

"What's with the shit going on onstage?" Bax asked, like Linx had been the one who called for the hiatus in the first place.

It shouldn't have made Linx happy that he had stirred a batch of jealousy in Bax. Hell, maybe if Bax and Knox saw what he had with this gig, they'd take music serious again.

Linx feigned innocence. "Shit? Onstage?"

"Who's the band?" Knox asked, sincere and not being a dick. "They've got good sound."

"They're friends." Linx crossed his arms. While he appreciated that Knox played good cop, he wasn't ready to offer his forgiveness yet. "Don't want to get rusty."

The thing was, usually Linx was the peacemaker for Dimefront. He smoothed things over. Made everyone else comfortable. Did his thing, bored as all shit while Bax and Knox made the calls of when and where the band played.

But he was done with that. He was having fun for a fucking change. Mach and Tanner didn't bitch and moan and take off every two minutes. Becca was everything he'd ever wanted. And Brek had his back.

He wanted the band to work shit out, but they had to try, too. He was done shouldering that weight.

"The contract says we don't play with any bands not on

the label without permission." Bax stared at the foam of his untouched beer. "Seems like your stunt on the stage is a breach of that."

The hell was he going on about? He was playing with two guys, helping them out in the industry. He wasn't violating his fucking contract with Dimefront. Linx opened his mouth to say just that—

"This is not the place to have this meeting." Brek pointed to the kitchen. "What do you say we go somewhere there aren't ears who can hear everything you say?"

They had shit to sort, but they always seemed to have shit to sort. This was the first time any of them had brought up legal shit. This was exhausting, and frankly, it was getting old. That realization hit Linx right in the solar plexus. Until now, he'd cared more about keeping the band together more than nearly anything else in the world. Maybe he needed new priorities…

"Becca can hear this. I don't care if Kellie hears," Linx said. The more witnesses the better, as far as he was concerned. With Bax's attitude and Linx's unwillingness to budge this time, Knox would have to be the peacemaker. Knox was not a peacemaker. Which meant there was a shit storm brewing.

Brek stepped closer to Linx, leaning in to whisper, "Not talking about the girls. I don't have enough bouncers tonight to keep you safe and handle a public brawl."

Shouting was a high probability, given that Knox was a hot head. They hadn't had a fist fight in years. Then again, that meant they were probably overdue.

"We're not going to get physical." Bax held his hands up in a show of surrender that they all knew was total shit. They may not be a band that threw punches, but Bax would be the first to throw a fist if he got his panties in too tight of a wad.

Linx wasn't convinced. Not at all.

Knox glared at Bax as though he wasn't convinced.

Fuck it, Brek didn't seem convinced, either. "Linx knows where to find the break room."

Becca gripped Linx's arm, gave it a squeeze, and then a not-so-subtle push toward the back.

"You should listen to Brek," she said. "I'll handle things here." Becca looped her arm around Linx's waist. "Let me know if you guys need a top off."

"Son of a bitch." Brek stared across the room.

Linx turned to see what he'd found. One of his bouncers was in a heated debate with Babushka. When had she arrived?

"I've gotta deal with this." Brek tossed down a bar towel and stalked around the edge of the counter. "Don't talk about important shit without me."

Linx nodded.

"Fine," he grumbled and ambled toward the kitchen, through to the staff break space. He strode the entire way, not looking behind to see if Bax, Hans, and Knox followed. He heard the clomp of boots and knew those sounds well enough from a decade of hitting the stage together to know they were there.

"The guys I'm playing with want to meet you." Linx shoved his hands on his waist. "When we're done here."

Bax didn't sit, but he leaned against the wall. Like he was totally relaxed. The tick at his jaw was the tell that he was not at ease. "You seemed cozy up there on stage with them."

"Take it down, Bax," Hans warned.

"I was." Linx crossed his arms. "They're good guys. Excellent musicians. They'll sign with a label soon." He'd bet his favorite guitar on that.

Knox grabbed a chair, flipped it around, and straddled it. "I'd like to meet 'em."

"Don't like the look of what was happening up there." Bax stared into space . "Felt like it was more than just a set with noobs."

"They get the music," Linx said. "They perform for the sound, not because of what it can do for them."

Not for the payout it could bring.

"You're saying that's what I do?" Bax asked.

Hans and Knox had the decency to look troubled at Linx's words.

Neither said anything for a long beat.

Finally, Hans piped up. "Talked with the guys. We're ready to get back to work."

"Oh, well, then by all means, let's get back to work." Linx stretched his arms wide with what he hoped was clearly mock enthusiasm.

Bax frowned. "Figured we'd come tell you in person. Didn't expect to find you having extracurricular fun with another group."

Mach and Tanner were more than another group. They were what making music was supposed to be.

Linx took in Bax and Knox for the first time in a long time. And he got it. Saw it.

Dimefront became something other than music a long time ago, and the path they'd been on led them to a place he was not digging.

He swallowed. Hard.

He wanted Dimefront more than anything. At least, that's what he'd been telling himself. But he would not keep dancing this dance with these guys.

"If we're going to keep taking a hiatus from Dimefront, I'm going to have to find a new gig." He pushed past the ache in his chest and said the words. They needed to be said. The group needed to decide where they were going from here.

"You should know, Em left him." Hans folded his hands together on the table, keeping his focus on Linx. "You all have been doing your shit, and Bax's world collapsed."

How the hell had Linx not heard about this? How was it not all over the tabloids?

He looked to Bax. All the fire had drained from Bax's attempt at a confrontation. He nodded.

Linx ran his hand over his hair. "Fuck, man. I'm sorry…"

"Just cut him some slack, yeah?" Hans asked.

Knox kicked back in his chair until it was on two legs instead of four. "There's shit he needs to catch you up on."

Clearly. Man, that sucked. Bax was into Em, and she was all in with him.

"I'm sorry she took off." Linx moved forward and clapped Bax on the shoulder, holding his hand there in solidarity with his bandmate. "That fuckin' sucks."

"We've all got crap to deal with." Bax looked up then. The vacant look in his eyes was haunting. "A lot can change in a couple of months."

"You think we can call a truce on whatever this is with you guys?" Hans asked. "Because I don't like it."

Bax nodded. "I'm game for a truce."

"When we go back to work, we need a new agreement." Linx dropped to a chair across from Knox. "Something that spells out vacations, time off, all that. So I'm not stuck twirling my thumbs while you assholes do your own thing."

"Fair." Knox nodded.

Bax finally relaxed a little. "Fair."

Okay, look at this, they'd sorted shit without Brek even being in the room. They were practically adulting the hell out of this situation. Someone should give them a gold fucking star on the door.

"I see you met a girl." Knox gave Linx a knowing, not-an-asshole grin that Linx didn't realize he'd missed. "I wanna hear about her."

"Becca." Linx nodded. This was good. Truce was good. Getting back to making music was good. "You'll dig her. She's the best."

"Glad you found that." Bax sat on the chair between both of them. "Serious. You deserve a dose of happy."

Looked like the band was on the road to back together. It should've felt great, but all Linx could think about was when they went back in the studio and back on tour. How long until the sour seeped in again? How much he'd miss Becca. How much he'd hate missing sets with Tanner and Mach. The relief just wasn't there.

And what in the hell was he supposed to do with that?

He rubbed at his temples. He'd try. That's what he'd do. Hopefully, the guys would be on board with trying.

"Mom and Dad are in town." Linx picked at the edge of the vinyl table with his thumbnail. "You should stop by the house. There's food."

"Food's good." Knox lifted his fist for a bump.

Linx obliged.

"Heads up, Courtney's here, too." Linx slid a glance to Bax. Was it his imagination, or did Bax blanch a little at that? Then again, he and Courtney were oil and water. If oil and water caused a combustion that could take out an entire city block. Those two had been in some serious shouting matches over the years.

"Go easy on her, she's having a rough time," Linx added.

"What's up with Courtney?" Hans asked.

Bax sat straighter, all ears about Linx's sister.

Did he tell them she was pregnant? He shouldn't. She said to keep it to the family. Then again, they were family. And if they were going to be around, he needed Bax to not be a total dick to her.

"Keep it on the down low. She's not telling the dad yet." He leaned in, talking low even though no one else could hear. "She's pregnant. Keeping the baby. Living with me in Denver, for now."

The air in the room chilled like one of the cooks had left open the walk-in freezer.

"Fuck," Hans said, kicking off from the wall.

The color drained from Bax's face, and his eyes got so big the whites were visible.

"She's *what*?" Bax sputtered. The strong words were quiet, filled with shock, and doused in emotion.

What in the hell was going on with Bax? Linx had known the guy for dozens of years and had never seen his veneer crack the way it just did.

His movements suddenly jerky, Bax stood. His chair clattered to the ground. He moved mechanically to set it up. "Where is she?"

"You wanna tell me what's going on?" Linx asked, his chest tight and his fingertips numb. He stretched them open and closed in an attempt to restore feeling. It didn't work.

Linx looked between Bax and Knox. Back to Bax, who looked like he'd just got caught with his dick in his hand.

"Is this the part where you tell Linx you banged his sister?" Knox's glare at Bax was like a switchblade. "Or should I?"

It didn't seem possible, but Bax lost more color. He pressed the heels of his hands against his lower jaw. "This cannot be happening."

Linx's lungs seemed to stop processing air. *The fuck? Bax and Courtney?*

No. That wasn't possible. The guys had an unwritten code. All of them honored family. Hell, even Lennox, their first drummer, abided by that rule. He didn't follow any of the other rules, but he damn well followed that one.

"Tell me you didn't sleep with Courtney." For all that was holy, he couldn't wrap his brain around the idea that Bax had been the one to screw his sister. Literally, and now figuratively, with the baby coming.

He'd rather it was that Alan What's-his-name. And he despised that guy.

Bax held up his hands. "It's not what you think."

Linx didn't yell, even though he wanted to. He was

remarkably calm, given the maelstrom beginning to pound in his blood vessels. He stood, too slowly. Too slowly. Too calm, given what was happening inside. Blood rushing through his ears swished so loud, he was sure he'd heard Knox wrong. Misunderstood the whole shebang.

"Linx, take a breather." Hans used his let's-all-be-reasonable manager tone.

Linx wasn't having it.

"Is that why Em left?" Linx asked, ready to punch a hole in the pretty boy face of his lead singer.

At the mention of Em, Bax jerked like Linx had struck him. "Courtney and I hooked up after Em left." He moved his hands to his hair, as though he was trying to hold his brain together. "I didn't fuck around on her."

"Em did." Knox stood, moving between Bax and Linx like he was acting as a bouncer.

"It's true," Hans moved next to Knox. "She was the one with a side gig while she planned her wedding to Bax."

"That's not what this is about now." Bax seemed to come to some kind of conclusion. "This is about Courtney. She's pregnant? I need to see her."

"No." Linx shoved his hands on his hips, spread his stance, and met Bax's eyes. "She comes to you. When and if she's ready, she makes the move. You leave her the hell alone."

Bax shook his head. "Can't do that."

"Can we *please* take a breather?" Hans asked, his hand pressing against Linx's chest.

Knox hadn't moved. Apparently, it'd been Linx who stepped forward. His body was ready to go big brother on Bax, even if his mind hadn't yet come to that conclusion.

"You knocked up my sister." Blood rushed in his ears. "You jacked with the band."

"Linx. Breathe." Knox had a look of terror across his

mug, like he knew this was the end and suddenly he didn't want that freedom he was always bitching about.

Too. Bad.

Looking at Bax...Linx just...couldn't bring himself to care if they all ever made music again together. This was what it felt like to be numb. He just didn't fucking care.

"Dimefront is done." Linx slashed his hand through the air.

Bax flinched.

Hans looked like someone had punched him in the love dart.

Knox shook his head. "Not accepting that."

"Serious. Over. *Done.*" It was his call this time. "Bax wanted to talk about contracts. I read the goddamned contract. Any of us want to call it? It's done. I'm calling."

There was no way in hell he'd take the stage again with Bax.

No. Way. In. Hell.

"Whoa." Brek strode through the door and held up his hands.

The numb wore off, and Linx needed to get to Becca. Pain radiated from the area of his heart. She'd know what to say to make it better.

"I thought we agreed no decisions until I came to referee?" Brek asked, eyes on Knox. Likely because Knox was the only one in the room who was thinking clearly at the time.

"That was before Bax knocked up my sister." Linx closed his eyes. Done. He needed to be done.

He opened them, but the haze of pain was there. Stronger than before.

Brek cringed and took in Bax. He had the look of a father who was disappointed in his kid. "Tell me this isn't real."

"We don't know for sure." Knox stood. "We'll have to talk to Courtney."

"No one talks to Courtney until Courtney makes that

move." Linx would call her, fess up to his fuck up, and then hire security and a whole football team of attorneys for her so she never had to see Bax again. Unless she wanted to. In which case, he hoped he never had to see the guy again.

"The kid is mine." Bax stared at his shoes. He swallowed hard, his Adam's apple bobbing. "I need to talk to her."

"That's not happening until she says it happens." Linx shoved his finger toward Bax. "Stay the fuck away from my family."

He said it. He meant it. He wasn't going to budge.

Chapter 20

Becca

Oh. Damn.

Linx stalked from the break room. He looked like he was ready to throw a punch.

Becca grabbed the attention of the nearest bouncer and gestured toward Linx. The bouncer slipped into the shadows, following the resident rock star.

At least there was that.

For the first time since her life-vacation started, she gave no thought to stress levels or the responsibility index based on her actions. Linx looked wrecked. She wanted to be there for him. Period. She moved a little slower because…she gulped… dammit. She cared about him a helluva lot more than she should.

She shook off the realization. She'd evaluate the consequences of that later.

"Cover for me?" Becca asked the other waitress on that night.

She nodded. Becca pulled off her apron as Linx approached.

He walked straight to her and lifted his hand to her neck. "Have a sec?"

"For you, I do." She snatched his hand in hers. "Where should we go?"

"Walk." He gestured to the door. "Some place that's not here."

Becca nodded. "Yeah. Sure."

"What the hell happened back there?" Mach asked, approaching with an abundance of caution. "You look like somebody pissed in your beer."

"Bad night." Linx's Adam's apple bobbed. "Can't do the intro like I promised."

"It's cool." Tanner glanced to Becca as she grabbed coats and gloves. Tanner's eyes were a little wider than usual. "Another time."

"Yeah." Linx nodded, taking his coat from Becca. "Another time. Excellent set tonight. Let's connect tomorrow."

Becca's stomach hurt for him. Wrecked. He looked wrecked.

What on earth had gone on back there?

He headed for the exit, her gloved hand in his bare palm. She glanced back to Tanner and Mach, who were twin mirrors of concern.

He needed to process whatever was going on in his head. She got that. She also wanted to know how she could help him. They walked for a sold three minutes, dodging ice patches and snow banks before she couldn't take the silence anymore.

"What happened?"

He shook his head. "Band's done. Dimefront's over."

Say what?

"Linx." She pulled his hand.

He stopped. She held his gaze to hers and refused to break that thread between them.

If she was in session, she would've let him lead. Let him set the pace. They weren't in session, though.

"Tell me," she said, squeezing his hand at the same time she spoke.

"Courtney's baby is Bax's." He glanced to the sidewalk, scraping the tip of his boot in the tiny pebbles of gravel. "That's what he said."

"But you haven't talked to Courtney." Becca stepped in front of him.

He shook his head. "I will. Need to give her a heads up that I accidentally told the father of her baby."

Sometimes, when people got mired down in their problems, they needed to name the emotion before they could move through it.

"You're pissed," she said.

He nodded. "He messed with my sister." He pointed to his chest. "My sister."

"Linx." Becca reached for his other hand so she held them both. "Courtney was in the room, too."

He turned and took three steps. Then he turned and took two steps back. "We had a deal. Family is everything. We don't fuck with that."

He told her about Em and Bax. The ending of their engagement. The unsteady truce between the Dimefront guys that lasted only moments before it shattered.

"Oh, Linx." She lifted her hand to the leather on his chest. "This is not yours to carry alone. There are three of you on that team. Three of you who make it work."

He stared at the sidewalk again. His expression vacant.

Her heart ached for him. "Want me to buy you some chocolate?" She pointed to the convenience store up the block. "My treat?"

They settled on their selections, and she paid for them. He didn't balk or try to take out his wallet, which was a good indication of just how wrecked he was.

Linx grabbed the plastic sack and handed her a Snickers bar. She ran her thumb along the seam of the wrapper. He didn't wait. He yanked the wrapper off his Twix then bit into the two chocolate, caramel, cookie bars with one bite.

She tilted her head to the side.

"What?" he asked, looking back at the bars.

"What is it with you massacring candy bars?" Becca asked.

Seriously, she understood he was going through something of a crisis, but did no one teach him how to eat chocolate bars properly?

"Huh?" He studied the rest.

She pointed to it. "That's not how you eat that."

He scowled at the candy like it had offended him. "How would you eat it?"

Uh. "One bar at a time, like a normal person."

"When has anyone ever accused me of being normal?" The edges of his mouth twitched at that.

She relaxed the slightest touch. He was going to be okay. It'd take time, but he was going to be okay.

"Are you okay?" she asked. The bar's jukebox played the low notes of Nirvana singing "Come As You Are." The sound drifted onto the sidewalk.

"Fine." He went about eating the next bites of candy bar much less like a Neanderthal and more like she would've done it.

For some reason, that bothered her.

"Never mind." She nodded to what was left of the candy. "Eat it the way you were."

"I'm getting mixed signals here." He nudged her with his shoulder.

She didn't want to, but, "I need to get back to work."

"Tell Brek I'll come back later?" He glanced to the lot where his Porsche sat. "Need to go have a sit-down with Courtney."

Becca nodded. She rolled up on her toes and pressed a kiss to his mouth. "I know everyone always says it's going to be fine. But I believe it will be."

He hugged her tight. There on the sidewalk in front of Brek's, he wrapped his arms around her and didn't let go for a long, long time.

Becca

Linx was drinking, and it wasn't ginger ale. Last call had been two hours ago. That's when he showed up. He hadn't brought his Porsche, and she wasn't sure who dropped him off. He immediately went behind the bar and grabbed the bottle of Jameson. He hadn't exactly been slamming the hooch, but he wasn't going light, either.

Everyone else had gone home. She'd promised Brek she would stay with Linx so Brek could get home to Velma and their toddler. Then she locked up.

Then she waited while Linx made music. Becca sighed and folded more bar towels.

Linx set up shop on the stage, sitting on the floor like he had in his bedroom, and working on a song she'd never heard.

She kept her focus on him: alone on the stage, long hair hanging over his shoulders, scruff that headed into beard territory peppering his cheekbones. He played a few notes on the guitar. He crooned to himself. Then played a few more. Then he made notes on a pad of paper.

She worried at her lip as he sipped on another shot. Not tossing it back. He sipped and savored like they were in Colorado's wine country, enjoying a sampling at St. Kathryn Cellars.

At various intervals, she'd brought him pretzels, a burger,

another candy bar. He touched none of it. Like the rocker he was, he was only interested in the whiskey. Ginger ale wasn't cutting it.

Brek had watched all of this with little stress lines she'd never seen before etching the space between his eyebrows. He assured her Linx would sort himself out. She wasn't sure if he said it for her benefit or his own. Nothing else was said about whatever the hell-o had happened with the band in the breakroom.

She pressed her tongue against her top two teeth. *Say nothing. Don't ask. Not your business.*

She wanted to know what happened with Courtney. She wouldn't ask.

She wanted to know what happened with Dimefront. She wouldn't ask.

She wanted to know how to help Linx. She wouldn't ask.

The fact of the matter was… she didn't know how to ask. This wasn't what they had. The asking thing. But she couldn't leave him alone. Refused to leave him with anyone else. Brek. Mach. Tanner. Knox. Even Hans, the band manager who seemed to take everything extra serious. They'd all offered to stick around with him.

She sent them away.

For better or for worse, her heart was becoming entangled with this man; and though she hadn't processed it and wasn't sure exactly what it was that they had together, she wouldn't leave him alone in his own head.

After Linx left earlier, Bax stomped out of the bar. Knox and Hans, however, stuck around and had a beer (or three) with Mach and Tanner. They all seemed to hit it off. The only indicator that Knox carried any stress was his constant glances toward the door. Who he expected, wanted, or hoped would walk in, was anyone's guess.

Hans, on the other hand seemed to be a whole bundle of wound-up, stressed-out energy. She was pretty sure that's why he stuck around the bar for Brek's extended happy hour.

Linx finished a few bars of music. He sipped his Jameson.

She set down the last of the towels and headed for him. He tracked her the entire way until she moved behind him and he couldn't see her anymore. Then he let his head rest against her breasts.

"Play me a song?" she asked, trailing her hands along the cotton of his t-shirt with enough pressure to feel the corded muscles underneath.

He seemed to relax into her palm, so she continued touching him. Kneading the muscles of his shoulders. "You're in knots."

"You are the queen of knots," he murmured, holding up the wrist housing the leather bracelet she'd made for him.

She scoffed. "I tie them. I'm not good at the untying."

"I think you'd be surprised at how good you are at that." He grasped her wrist, turning to hold her against him. Inhaling deeply.

God, he felt good. Like a permanent life vacation.

On that note, she stilled.

He wasn't permanent. He was Linx. She'd best remember that, or this brief fling would break her heart. An ache in the vicinity of her chest warned that it may be too late.

"What do you want to hear?" His words rumbled against her neck as he spoke against her skin.

"Whatever you want to play."

Extracting herself from his arms, she toed off her sneakers and removed her socks. Her feet were killing her, and she was only yay far from going the orthotic route of her mother. Then she sat on the stage in front of him, cross-legged. He played Fleetwood Mac's "Dreams," and she clapped, giving a loud whoop with her hands held around her mouth to amplify the sound.

That got her a Linx grin.

Then he sang.

Oh, man, did he sing.

The song was mostly slow, but with an upbeat riff spaced throughout that he played with the precision of the professional he was. The soul he poured into the lyrics? She blinked back a whole heap of emotion threatening to spill right out of her eyelids.

Tears continued to sting as he sang about loneliness and stillness. She felt those words down in her marrow. And when he finished, he played two extra notes she was certain didn't belong in the song, but somehow fit. Neither of them said anything as the last note dissolved into the air. He let the guitar hang from the strap and pressed his palms to his cheeks in a way that made her heart hurt. For him. For the band. For Courtney. For…herself.

"How can I help you?" she whispered.

He drank her in like she was the Jameson, but he wanted to slam it instead of sip.

She could live with that.

"Take off your shirt," he said, the words gruff. Low. Nearly a growl.

At any other time in her life she would've thought he was daring her, but somehow she knew that's not what this was. She'd asked a question. He gave an answer.

She drew a deep breath. First, she was technically at her place of work. Therefore, by the laws of keeping her employment, she should probably keep her top on.

However.

The bar was empty and locked up tight. Since she was on vacation, she was allowed to do things that pushed the envelope. And, most important, she had a rock star requesting comfort.

Second—there was no second. She could do this. Would give this to him. She removed her shirt, pulling the Brek's Bar tee over her head and tossing it to the side.

Linx stared at her shirtless torso, running his tongue over his lips.

"What else?" she asked, the words so husky they didn't even sound like her.

"Hair down."

She pulled the ponytail from her hair, flicking the holder to the rest of the pile.

Keeping her gaze on Linx, she didn't ask what was next. She waited for him to make the call.

"Bra," he said, the heat in his gaze illustrating exactly what he wanted to do to her.

She'd never—not ever—thought she'd be this intimate with a rock god onstage with his guitar. Yet, here she was. Oh, yes. Maybe she did have a way to comfort him. A way that would reduce both their stress levels. Those lap dance lessons might come in handy.

She popped the clasp at the back of her bra and tossed it to the pile, too. He stopped playing, stared at her breasts, eyes flaring.

"Tell me what you want, Cedric." She shook her head, hair falling loose and covering the tops of her breasts.

He set aside his guitar. The wood kissed the stage with a small tap that echoed through the vacant space. "I want to be in you."

"I want that, too." She stood, going for the full lap-dance-spectacular. Running her hands up and over her breasts, toying briefly with her nipples until they pebbled, she held Linx's eyes with her own.

"Sit on your hands," she instructed, still toying with her nipples as she spoke.

Warmth pooled between her legs, her panties damp with her wanting.

He did not sit on his hands. Oh no. Instead, he pulled his shirt off over his head, tossing it with her clothes. Her pulse sped up at the sight of his bare chest. Why did a man who could make music the way he could need abs like those?

Don't ask, Becca. Go with the flow.

Once his shirt joined the pile, *then* he sat on his hands.

Gah, this was likely the most erotic thing she'd ever experienced. And she still had her damn pants on.

That just wouldn't work for what she had planned for him. Spoiler: she was going to give him the best damn lap dance he'd ever had in his life. She'd see to it.

Slowly, she pushed her hands along the skin of her body, down over the curve of her breasts, past her torso, to her navel. Then further.

Linx followed the movement of her hands with a gaze that practically burned her skin with the heat it produced.

She unclasped her jeans, pulled them over her hips and kicked them aside. She was sure there was no way to take off jeans in a way that looked like a decent striptease. Lucky for her, she'd worn a lace thong that would more than make up for the awkwardness of stripping off her pants.

Attempting striptease brilliance, she inched the lace down her thighs, over her knees, past her calves, and kicked them aside.

Meanwhile, Linx sat on his hands while the complete sound system in his pants stood at attention. He needed relief. Relief she had every intention of giving. Eventually.

Dropping her hands from her breasts, she strutted to him. He looked up at her, but otherwise remained neutral. She resolved that he would *not* remain neutral for long.

So she danced on him, humming as she moved. She may not have been able to sing for the life of her, but she could hum right along with the best of them. Grinding and pressing, letting her body show him what she wouldn't allow her mind to think. He hummed along with her, the two of them creating a melody that worked. Oh God. It worked. He panted, his hands no longer under his ass. Oh no, they were all over Becca. His mouth found her breast and, oh, God. *Yes, yes, yes.* She held his head to her breast, letting him tongue and suck, feeling an echo of each tug between her thighs until she breathed faster, too.

"I'm going to come," she said on a gasp as his tongue did an impressive maneuver against the sensitive nub of her nipple that had her internal muscles primed and ready for release.

"Hold on," he commanded.

Oh God. She held on. Gripping the inside of her thighs against the outside of his. Allowing the girth of him to push against the core of her through the layer of boxers and jeans he still wore.

"You're going to lie on this stage." He moved her, laying her so her back was to the hard-scuffed wood.

She allowed it.

His legs on either side of hers, he leaned until his mouth was against hers. "You're going to put your hand between your legs while I get rid of my pants."

Oh, okay. If she was going to totally go for wanton, might as well dive in. She'd done lots of things with men before, but she'd never touched herself in front of her partners.

Linx guided her hand to the spot he intended, rubbing her with her own fingers, pushing them inside her. The internal muscles clenched and seized.

She. Was. Going. To. Come.

"Cedric," she said on a breath, her hand moving inside her with the help of his.

"Keep going," he said the words, gruff and harsh, as the warmth of his hand over hers disappeared.

The sound of a zipper, followed by the unmistakable rip of foil, were the soundtrack as she brought herself to the edge.

Then he was there, kneeling over her, spreading her thighs, removing her hand. He licked at the fingers he'd had her use—drawing them in his mouth deep before releasing them. She would've liked to have a coherent thought at that moment. Some way to vocalize how turned on she was by all of this. Unfortunately, her mind seemed to have reverted to some primitive state that allowed only feeling. The buzz throughout her body was enough. She was certain Linx felt it, too.

They needed no words. No explanation of what came next. No worry for the future.

The hard length of his erection slid inside her, and they moved together in a rhythm that had them both climbing. Until he pushed them both over the edge.

And. It. Was. Glorious.

Chapter 21

Becca

Linx broke off a piece of the Kit Kat bar she'd brought over earlier. Of course, he broke it against the grain. *Neanderthal.* This time she didn't mind because it was just…Linx.

He'd grabbed his boxers. She'd grabbed her panties. And then they did the second thing she'd never done on a stage: they cuddled. He slid behind her, her back to his chest. She leaned against him as he felt up every inch of her belly. This time the touch wasn't leading anywhere—not yet. It just. It just *was.*

And she wasn't sure what to do with that.

He nudged her lips with a bit of chocolate. She opened, nipping a little at the tips of his fingers when he slid the candy against her tongue. She turned to look up at him as the chocolate melted against her tongue.

The haunted look behind his eyes still shone through, but not like before. Stage sex had helped. Because stage sex was exceptional. Her new favorite kind of sex. And, as always, Linx's aftercare program was on point.

"How are the knots doing?" she asked, turning to face

him and running her hands to his back, feeling for more knots to untie. She could pull off a few more lap dances if he needed them.

He shoved his face into her neck, inhaling deep. "Better."

Rolling to the side, his back to the stage, Becca splayed on top of him.

He didn't speak, just stared at the darkened lights over the stage. She pressed her ear to his chest, listening as his heart thudded.

What she needed to do was get a handle on herself because she'd fallen in deep with this guy. Somehow, in the middle of stage sex, they'd blasted right through her promises to herself that she'd ditched responsibility.

"What are you thinking?" she asked.

He sighed. "That I can't believe you spent an entire night with that asshole."

Wait. What? She pulled back. "You said you weren't pissed about Bax."

He growled against her skin. "Fuck no. I'm pissed about us."

Hold up. What was he going on about?

"Us?" She studied his expression.

He pulled her down and pressed her head back against his chest. "All that wasted time."

"Linx?" Becca asked, firming herself to ask the question she'd been dying for an answer to all day. "Can I ask you something?"

"Anything."

She pressed two palms against his chest to lift herself over him. "The other day. The first time you kissed me and we didn't…you know. In your kitchen. Are you sure that wasn't really about Bax?"

He scratched at his temple, which stunk because that meant he pulled his hand away from her body. "I assumed you had cuddle time with Bax."

She said nothing, didn't move, so he would continue.

He went back to starting at the ceiling. "And I figured that meant you kind of liked him."

She waited for him to continue. He didn't right away. But she had tons of practice waiting for others to talk first. Here, it seemed more than a little important.

Finally, he pulled her tight against him and spoke into the hair at her temple. "I worried that you would rather have him than me. That I'm just the guy in front of you, not the one you want."

At that, she softened. The hard edges of her dedication to stress-free vacation living melted a little more.

"Not that I really mind being a consolation prize. Usually," he continued. "But with you...it wasn't something I'd be able to move on from. Being with you when you'd rather be with…him."

Becca straddled his stomach and sat up, cowgirl-style. "I don't want to be with him."

His lazy gaze trailed over her. "Well, I know that now."

"Can we dig deeper into this?" she asked, nearly at a whisper.

"Can we not?" He pressed the bulge of his erection against her center. His desire for another go was as obvious as the night was dark and morning was just around the corner. Her pulse beat hard in her ears as desire shoved her rational brain to the side.

"You want to know why I really didn't go further?" Linx repeated her question, but he didn't glance to her. Not at first. Finally, he moved his gaze to her. "More than the shit with that guy." He wouldn't say Bax's name. Hadn't said it since he came back from his chat with Courtney. "I held back because *you* matter."

The pulse pounding in her ears stuttered.

"I matter?" she asked. Actually, it sounded more like a squeak. Who was really paying that much attention?

Linx, apparently. His expression warmed—a softness in contrast to the hard planes of his jawline.

"I haven't had a lot of women in my bed who mattered beyond what we shared with our bodies," he said, gripping her waist, pressing her against him.

Do not evaluate his statements. Do not do it. Don't psychoanalyze. This is not an intake session. He's not a patient.

"You're different. I don't want to screw that up," he continued.

She shouldn't have, but she tried to dissect his words. She came up empty. The buzzing in her ears did not allow her to think clearly.

"I don't understand," she said.

"I like you. A whole lot." That got her the wide Linx grin she should just go on ahead and patent. "You matter." He reached his hand to her chin and traced his fingertip along her neck. "I don't want to screw up what I hope could come of you and me."

Right. He was saying that if she were to unpack his emotional baggage, he might not take the suitcases and leave? Was that what he was saying?

Because if that's what he was saying, that was dangerous for her heart.

He didn't talk for a long moment. Neither did she.

"I'm feeling my way through this," he said, finally. "I don't want to go too fast. Too slow. I want to be what you need me to be."

Oh. That was… that was… huh.

"Without Dimefront, I can focus on us." He tucked a lock of hair behind her ear.

She swallowed and refused to succumb to the intense desire to grab her clothes, grab her keys, and run away. "This isn't reality."

His eyebrows furrowed together. "Why?"

Why? "Because it's fun."

"Can't life be fun?" He asked as he ran his hands up and down her bare sides as though she were a skittish animal he was doing his best not to spook.

Too bad, though. She was already spooked.

"Life is hard, Linx."

He moved his hands when she attempted to stand. Letting her go. Which was good because she had a lot to think about.

"Vacations are fun. Life. It just isn't." She crossed her arms near her belly as he rose from the stage floor.

"Someday, I hope you realize how wrong you are." He moved to her, tilting her chin up to him.

"Linx." She reached for his hand where it rested against her cheek, tracing the mountains and valleys of his knuckles. "I'm going to be honest here." God, he'd been through hell, she didn't want to add to that. But he had to know. "I don't know what I want."

Because, God love her, she didn't.

Other than to run far away.

But what exactly was she running from? She pressed her hands against her temples.

"Do you want to go?" he asked, seeming to read her thoughts.

She nodded.

"Then let's get you home." He tugged his shirt over his head. "But, Becca?"

It took every ounce of intention, but she looked at him. Really looked at him. The devastation of losing his band. The hope of a future with her.

"Yes?"

"When you figure it out, I'll be waiting."

He meant that. No doubt he meant that.

And she didn't know what to do with it. So she took him home.

The sun was still not thinking about touching the sky when Becca pulled into Linx's drive. She didn't take the driveway around to the garage. She pulled up to the front door instead.

"Do you want to come in?" he asked. "Sleep here for a while?"

She did. But she couldn't. She needed time to reflect. Time to figure out what was going on with her. She shook her head. "You need to sleep without distraction."

He looked at her like he knew her number. He so knew her number.

He leaned across the gearshift in the middle of her cheap sedan and kissed her full on the mouth. "When you're ready, give me a sign."

She gripped the steering wheel tighter. "What we have… it's…"

Temporary. A flash of desire. A blip on the radar. A feeling that will fade.

"It's perfection," he said, finishing her unfinished sentence. And with that, he opened the car door and meandered to the front door of his house.

And Becca? Becca watched until he went inside.

He didn't look back.

Neither did she, as she drove away.

Chapter 22

Linx

Forty-nine hours, twenty-five minutes—the time since Becca dropped him at his front door. He'd been serious. The next move was hers. That didn't stop his fingertips from itching to text her. His craving for a ginger ale in a Coors bottle at Brek's was, frankly, becoming a ridiculous.

He was holding out, but he didn't know how much longer it'd last.

If there was a silver lining in having a band implode while his girl wasn't reaching out to him, it was that he'd made a helluva lot of good music in all the time he wasn't sleeping. The broody kind of tunes with extra helpings of angst.

Unfortunately, he didn't have a band he wanted to test them with.

He'd heard from his agent. Then he'd heard from the attorney his agent had hired for him. Then he'd heard from the label. Linx had been told in no uncertain terms, making music publicly with Tanner and Mach could, technically, be considered a breach of his Dimefront contract. They couldn't prevent him from playing with them in private, but the consensus had been that he needed to not do anything to tick off the label. It'd look bad for him, and it could affect their shot at a deal later on.

That fucking sucked.

On top of that, Knox fought the dissolution of Dimefront. Which made no fucking sense at all, given that *he* was the one who always talked about leaving so he could do other shit. After a long chat with Hans, it became abundantly clear—Linx's escape clause wasn't a *Get Out of Jail Free* card. He couldn't just call it quits without owing many people a shit ton of money.

He didn't like owing others a shit ton of money, so he was going to have to go back to the studio with Knox and Bax. But he would hold out on a tour. Too close. Too much time with these assholes.

Linx did his best to block Knox out of his mind. He bit on the blue guitar pick between his teeth to free his hands up so he could write a few notes on the pad he'd been filling.

A tap on the door drew his attention away from the music.

"What?" he asked.

Uh huh, he was being unreasonably grouchy. Fuck it. He'd earned this mood.

The door pushed open, and Knox strode through like he wasn't in the midst of threatening to sue the hell out of Linx.

"The fuck do you want?" Linx asked, moving his gaze to the yellow pad of legal paper where he'd been making notes about the song.

Knox crossed his arms. "I know you're pissed."

Oh, yeah? He knew that. Good. Linx said nothing in return. Knox hadn't fucking earned a response.

"I'm sorry." Knox uncrossed his arms and shifted on his socked feet.

Mom must've caught him at the door and made him take off his shoes. She had a whole thing about that. Linx didn't get it, but he rolled with whatever made her happy while she visited.

Linx still said nothing.

Knox held out a finger and began counting, "One, I'm sorry for sayin' I wanted out of Dimefront. Two, I'm sorry for not tellin' you we were coming to Denver before we showed up. Three, I'm sorry for that time I hooked up with London. Four, I'm sorry I threw out all of your guitar picks in Belgium and replaced them with peanut butter M&Ms. Five, I'm sorry I didn't give you a heads up about what went down with Bax and Courtney when I found out." He knelt in a squat, ass to heels so he was at eye level with Linx. "I miss anything?"

Linx set aside his guitar. He ran his palms over his face. "No."

"You have something you want to say to me?" Knox asked.

Given that Linx hadn't fucked with Knox on any of the tours, and he didn't keep secrets, he had nothing to say. Still, it took a pair of brass balls to walk in here and apologize. "Apology accepted. Now fuck off."

Accepting the apology didn't mean that he was ever going to go on tour again with—

"Good enough." Knox tossed a business card on the ground in front of Linx.

Then he stood. "See you there."

He left, saying nothing else.

Linx went back to playing and writing his song, not looking at the card. But the pull of whatever the hell it was finally overtook his desire not to know. He looked.

The business card of a music studio near LoDo. On the back, someone—not Knox, the handwriting was way too easy to read to be his—noted a time.

4:30.

That's all it said.

They had summoned him. He hated that.

Fine, he'd show. He'd show, and he'd make music.

But he didn't have to like it.

AT FOUR-THIRTY-FIVE, Linx slunk through the front doors of the recording studio, hands stuffed in his hoodie. He pulled the thing off once he was inside. Sure, he'd shown up with plenty of time to be early, but he jacked around on his phone, hoping Becca would text. The guys would have to wait. Petty, yes, but they'd made him wait long enough.

Becca still hadn't reached out, so his mood soured worse than it'd been that morning. And that was saying something.

He pulled open the door to the sound booth. Bax and Knox were already in the studio. They weren't shooting the shit and playing warm-ups like he'd expected. They were sitting in a circle with Hans and their emotional-support, Brek.

Linx pulled open the door to the recording booth, and all the chatter stopped.

"Linx." Bax stood. He had a look of relief that he could just wipe right the hell off his face. "Thank fuck you came." He held out his hand for Linx.

A peace offering. An olive branch Linx wasn't ready to consider.

Therefore, Linx didn't shake it. He stared at it then glanced up to the face of the man who had once been his friend.

Saying nothing, he walked to the side of the room where his bass was still in the case. He'd had it couriered over earlier and gave explicit instructions that no one touch it without him present. He may not have had a reputation of being serious about much, but he was serious about this, and he'd made that clear enough times that no one screwed with it.

"I'm sorry," Bax said to Linx's back. "I fucked up. I'm trying to make it right."

"You assholes want to make music? By all means, let's make music." Linx jerked the bass out of the case with more force than necessary. He squeezed the neck. Hard.

Fuck, he needed to break something. He didn't want it to be his instrument. He was seriously considering Bax's nose.

"I said." Bax stepped forward, palms up. "I'm sorry."

"Sorry for what?" Linx asked, going through the motions of set-up—the cords, the tuning, setting the mic stand—but not feeling anything but numb inside.

"I'm sorry for jacking you around about the band," Bax said, sincere, ignoring Knox. "Taking off with Em. Leaving you hanging."

Linx glared at him. It wasn't *him* he was pissed about. Courtney hadn't been able to eat anything until well into the afternoon. She was miserable because his former buddy couldn't keep his dick in his pants.

"Yeah, well..not accepted." Linx played a couple of cords. Totally out of fucking tune.

"Apologize for dicking around with his sister." Knox ground his back teeth together, visibly. "Start with that one instead."

"We move the band to Denver." Bax said, widening his stance. "Knox is in. Hans is in. Brek's already here to help us sort our shit when it gets too serious. You're here. Courtney's here."

Linx glanced to him at the mention of his sister.

Bax had the decency to look wrecked. "You may not believe this, but I care about her. I care what happens to her. I care about the baby. I care about what you think, too."

"You touched her." Linx swallowed against the betrayal. "Family is off limits. We all know that. But you fucking touched her."

"Hey." Knox kicked off from his stool and moved next to

Bax. "Seems to me there were two people there. You're not pissed at Courtney for—" Whatever he was going to say, apparently he thought better of it. "—doing the dirty with this fuck face."

Bax sighed. "I'll eat your shit because I deserve it. But I want to do what's right for her. Not because she's your sister, or she works with the band…because she's Courtney and she deserves better."

"That's the fucking truth," Linx said, under his breath.

"Whatever she needs, even if that means I stay away until she's ready to let me in." Bax's throat worked.

Did his eyes mist? His eyes totally misted.

Fuck.

He was sorry.

And Knox wasn't wrong. Linx had laid all the blame at Bax's feet because it was easier.

"I screwed up, and I want to fix it," Bax said. The sincerity in his tone seemed pure enough.

Knox nodded. "If coming here's what it's gonna take to save this thing we've got between us? I'm in."

Linx was already convinced the thing they had between them was dead and atrophied. "I'm playing out my contract. It'll be through next year."

"It doesn't have to be like this." Knox stepped forward. Then thought better of it, stepping back.

"I don't play at the whim of the band," Linx said through gritted teeth. "I don't anymore. Not after this is done. I'm tired of the bullshit." He pointed to Knox. "You're in and out more than a gigolo." He turned his finger to Bax. "And you're not much better." He shook his head. Held up his hands. "I'm done with this."

Bax shoved his hands at his hips. "We come to Denver. Work from here. We all agree to a new contract—three months. We have three months to make it work. It doesn't work? Any of us can walk at any time."

That would've been fan-fucking-tastic about three months ago.

"No." Linx pulled the strap of his bass over his shoulder. "Can we make music now?"

"Linx's guys become new members of Dimefront." Brek stood, calm as all shit. Like the band he'd helped shape wasn't about to dive into its own grave.

"Everyone gets a full vote, right from the beginning. You three. Mach, Tanner. If they decide they want to join up," Hans said, standing alongside Brek as a united team.

"Oh, they'll join up," Knox said. He seemed sure. How the hell was he so certain? "We all know Linx is the heart of the band. Bax is the brain. I'm the asshole. We've got an opening for a soul. I think they'll fill it just fine. That'll make them…what?"

"The soul," Hans said, certain as all hell.

"And if it doesn't work out?" Linx asked. "Three months in, it doesn't work out? Then what?"

"Then I'll manage you, Mach, and Tanner. New band. New gig. They're serious, and they've shown it." Hans crossed his arms at his chest. "That's the offer."

Brek started toward the door to the recording booth. "I guess what you boys need to do to save your band—if it's that important to you—is make some fucking magic."

Chapter 23

Becca

"Dammit." The knot on the bracelet slipped, wrecking the last three rows. Becca tossed it to the side of her futon with the other piece she'd been working on.

Before she met Linx, she wouldn't have used the word indecisive to describe herself, but for some reason she wasn't able to make a coherent decision about how to approach him. Them.

Gah.

She'd had this client once, a younger girl who was really into one boy at her high school. She'd told Becca, "He makes my breath stop whenever he looks at me. Is that normal?"

Becca had asked her to define what normal was in her world. That had never happened to Becca personally, so she hadn't felt like it would be normal for her.

That was before Linx.

Unless this is just what he does. Pulls women into his trap and tosses them aside when he's done.

No, her internal monologue could go ahead and hush. That's not who he was. With him, she had the breath-stopping thing. Being with him was the end of a long, long aimless walk she didn't really believe had an ending point. Being without him was like jumping back on that aimless trail.

This epiphany scared the snot out of her and made her anxiety bubble grow.

She glanced to her phone for what felt like the billionth time that day. She needed to text him. Needed to hear his voice. Wanted to feel his touch.

Or maybe this was the lack of sleep talking. She should call a colleague. Ask for a consult so she could get something to help her rest.

Except, she didn't want to sleep. Sleep was worse than being awake. When she slept, a little niggle in the back of her mind had Bax's voice telling her what a player Linx was. How he went through women like they were Cherry Coke, and how he tended to string them along before dumping them on their face in the middle of the highway while his tour bus chugged merrily along.

That last part was totally her interpretation of what Bax had said. It didn't matter because Linx was just a rock star she crushed on. Now, though, it mattered. He was a rock star she was falling arse over tit for.

Yes, it mattered a lot.

"Becca?" Mom called, her steps already headed up the stairs to Becca's loft. "You up, sweets?" Mom kept her voice upbeat, but she'd been worried, and it showed in the cautious way she'd called.

"I'm here." Becca's right foot had fallen asleep from the way she sat on the futon. She shook it to wake it up. Her latest project had been a necklace gift for one of Velma's co-workers. Velma had found some unique, hand-carved beads for Becca to work into the piece. Honestly? It looked fantastic. She nearly wished she didn't have to sell it.

But she needed to sell it. Her tips were jacked since she'd driven Linx home. Given that her brain was in a perpetual fog, she wasn't her normal, accurate, waitressy self. Twice last night she'd messed up drink orders. That was not her normal. Brek knew it, too. He said nothing, but Velma had been showing up more often, sitting at the bar to chat with Becca while she worked.

Velma didn't sit at the bar. She just didn't.

Becca hobbled toward the door, working her foot in circles to get the blood flowing again. She let her mom in, not that she needed to. Mom would let herself in since the fancy new lock wasn't engaged. But it gave Becca a sense of autonomy to have some control over her own door.

"Hey, Mom." She held her arms wide, giving her mom the hug she knew she'd want.

Mom gave a quick squeeze then hustled through with a tray of oatmeal chocolate chip cookies—her specialty. She used granola instead of normal oatmeal, and the results spoke for themselves. Becca wanted to eat the entire plate full. She wouldn't, but oh boy, did she want to.

"I brought these as a peace offering in case your dad gives you more junk about interrupting his poker game." Mom pinched her lips to the side. "I keep telling him to let it go. But you know how he is. All you have to do is ask him."

Right, also, Becca spaced that her dad was hosting poker the other night. She played Dimefront music way too loud, apparently wrecking her dad's concentration. Multiple times since, she'd heard all about the fifty dollars he lost thanks to her love of rock music.

"I'll give him fifty dollars to stop talking about it." Becca toyed with the edge of her fingernail polish that had chipped. Crud, when had that happened?

"Don't worry." Mom began folding the bin of Becca's clothes she hadn't gotten around to dealing with. "I gave Belinda's husband a hundred-dollar bill to lose to him this week. Once he wins again, you'll be off the hook and we'll all hear about how good he is at the game."

Uh. "Thanks? I guess."

"No problem." Mom held up a pair of lace panties to fold, looked at Becca with her eyes wide and a small smile showing her approval. Then she folded them and set them with the other laundry.

"How's the jewelry coming along?" Mom nodded to the futon where the remnants were strewn.

Becca sighed. Knots were not enough to keep her mind off of Linx. She didn't think they ever would be. And she couldn't reconcile that with what she knew of reality. Deep down, on some internal level, she understood she'd created a smokescreen protection system. Her subconscious had installed it because the truth of the matter was—she could easily fall in love with Cedric Lincoln.

Digging a little deeper? She was already halfway there.

And instead of announcing that to him, she'd spent the past week holed up in her apartment anytime she wasn't at work, thinking of him. Listening to his music, like she was a tween. Hell, she should probably buy one of his posters to hang above her bed and just get that part over with.

He hadn't texted because he'd given his ultimatum.

She hadn't texted because she was being difficult.

Too bad she'd gone into therapy work instead of music because she could've cornered the market on angsty, regrettable love songs.

"Can we talk about Linx now?" Mom asked off-hand, but it was more than abundant that's why she'd come up. "Or is he still off-limits?"

"Mom." Becca shook her head. Subtle, but hopefully, obvious.

"Off-limits, then," Mom said to the laundry. "Can we talk about your job search?"

Becca had scoured the internet job listings for a therapist with her credentials. Turned out, she was in high demand.

She could go back to her job in Portland, stick around in Denver, or go anywhere, it seemed.

She didn't want to go anywhere. She wanted to go see her rock star. Throw the ball he'd set firmly in her court and make the move she was certain she wanted more than those oatmeal cookies.

"Sure. We can discuss the search." Becca moved to help Mom with the basket of laundry. It was that or messing up another row of Velma's gift bracelet. Her hands were itching to do *something*. "Nothing to talk about, though. I haven't applied for anything."

She couldn't bring herself to want to apply.

"You want to run again, though. Don't you?" Mom looked up from the sweater she wrangled.

Becca gulped. "Maybe."

Yes.

"Baby girl." Mom dropped the sweater, reached for Becca's hand, and squeezed. "Wherever you go, you'll still be there."

She'd still be there missing Linx. She felt like she'd just sucked on a cotton ball at the realization.

"Are you therapizing me?" Becca asked because that sounded remarkably like something she would've said to one of her patients.

"Maybe." Mom shrugged. The sly-mom grin tickled the edges of her mouth. "Although, I didn't go to school like you did. What do I know?"

A lot, apparently.

"I think I'm falling in love with Linx," Becca whispered.

Mom was mid-reach for Becca's favorite pair of Lululemon yoga pants she'd grabbed for a steal on ThredUp. She stalled. Stopped. Then frowned. "Well, yes. That's a given."

"I didn't know," Becca continued whispering for reasons she didn't want to dive into because all answers led to Linx.

And her heart breaking because of him utterly terrified her.

Mom's jaw fell a few millimeters, her lips parted slightly in clear surprise.

"What do you mean, it's a given?" Becca asked.

"Are we just realizing this?" Mom slid her gaze around the empty room. "I thought you knew?"

A whole sock seemed to lodge in Becca's larynx. She blinked back tears. No. She didn't know. Not until now. Not really. "What do I do? I'm supposed to be on vacation from my life, not falling for unavailable men."

Mom returned her focus to the Lululemons. "Sorry, I missed the part where Linx is unavailable?"

"He's a musician."

"And you're a counselor."

"And he's had strings of women."

"Then he'll know what to do in the… ahem… bedroom." Mom rolled her eyes. The look didn't suit her. She sighed. "You're thinking way too hard about this."

"I'm on vacation." Holidays didn't require thought. That's the whole reason a girl went on a vacation.

"Says who? Seems like you're living a good life here. You were happier than I've ever seen you. Until a few days ago."

Becca *had* been happy. Shit. Ugh. Gah.

"This could be your life. What you have with Linx and wherever that takes you."

Becca shook her head, a little too forcefully. "It's not supposed to be."

"When do we do what we're supposed to do?" Mom made a yuck sound. "Build a life you don't need a vacation from. That's the whole point."

It was Becca's turn for her mouth to slip open. Had her mother just solved the riddle of life while folding laundry in a loft above her garage?

The ache in Becca's throat intensified. The wanting of

something and not knowing how to have it. She knew what she needed to do to get it, all she had to do was send a text. But how did she make it work long-term?

"What does that look like? The vacation-free life thing?"

Mom's eyes went soft. "Seems like for you, it looks like Linx."

Becca swallowed a whole lot of crow because it did look a lot like life with Linx. "I've got a lot to sort through."

"Then dump it out here and let's sort." Mom gestured to the pile of laundry.

Um. This was going to take reflection. Time. Processing. "That's not how it works."

"Why not?"

"It's just not."

"Maybe it is and *you* haven't realized it."

"I tell you what, I bet you that if you call that boy right now, he'll pick up on the first ring." Mom stared pointedly at Becca's phone.

"I'm not going to do that." Becca picked at the chip in her nail polish again.

Mom shrugged. "I could make it a dare. Then you have to do it."

Becca pressed her hands to her cheeks. "What if he's moved on from me?"

Mom looked like Becca had lost her marbles all over the apartment floor. "Then go *get* him."

"I can't exactly be a rock star groupie as a career." Becca drew a deep breath. Then she released it.

Mom did the pinching of the lips to the side thing again. "Why not?"

Because it pays nothing. I need to eat and have a place to sleep.

Because I'm scared.

There it was. Damn, but her mom was good.

"When you go get him, don't do it quiet-like." Mom set

the empty laundry basket aside. “Make your point. Make it loud.”

Becca squared her shoulders. She could do this.

She gave her mom the biggest hug she could, and she held on tight.

Then she called Linx’s sister because she had some work to do.

Chapter 24

Becca

"You're sure you want to do this?" Courtney asked. After Mom left, Courtney came over. They'd spent some time brainstorming how to best approach Linx. The concept for the night's engagement had been Courtney's idea, but Becca was on board because it was *perfect.*

Therefore, when Courtney asked if she was still in, she nodded.

"He's coming?" Becca looked to the door. Linx hadn't arrived. The rest of the band had—minus Bax—but Courtney had asked him to ensure Linx showed.

Bax seemed to be willing to do anything for Courtney. Courtney wasn't convinced that would last—to put it mildly. She'd used inventive language to describe her feelings about Bax. Their relationship—if one were to call it that—was complicated. Becca had hoped that they'd work through their challenges, but it'd take work. Lots and lots of work.

Tanner stalked to Becca. He was Frowny McFrowny. Nope, he didn't look happy. Crud. Her plan relied on the band's support.

"Britney Spears?" Tanner didn't turn red for once as he spoke to her. "Serious?"

Becca nodded and pressed her lips together.

"Anything else. Pick anything else." Tanner started listing famous rock ballads.

Becca glanced to the door as another patron entered. It wasn't Linx.

"Britney remains the plan. The song fits."

Tanner rubbed at his temples. "She's fuckin' serious."

Aww… apparently a few days into his tenure as the official Dimefront drummer had given Tanner a burst of confidence and a dose of attitude. Adorable, really.

"I am *fucking* serious." Becca made wide eyes at him.

He made wide eyes at her.

Then he mumbled something about the things he agreed to for the cause and stomped off. He may not have been happy about her song choice, but he went straight to the stage to do a mic check.

She wasn't working that night, so she'd foregone her Brek's Bar tee for a low-cut red blouse that fit tight at the waist and her bust, with flared sleeves.

Courtney wandered to Becca, staring at her phone. "Bax said they got hung up, but they're coming."

Good. That was good. *Deep breaths, Becca.*

"You and Bax are okay?" Becca asked, deflecting her attention from her own problems to those of her new friend.

Courtney glanced to her belly then back to Becca. A ghost of a storm passed across her eyes. "I wouldn't say we're good. Speaking, yes. Good." She lifted a shoulder. "Debatable." She shivered. "This isn't about me, though. Tonight is about you and my brother."

Her brother. Becca swallowed the lump lodged in her throat since she'd decided to do this. To take the risk. To live life as a permanent vacation.

That was the moment Linx strode through the door of

the bar, the neon Budweiser sign casting a blue halo around him.

Oh, man, the universe really had done a fantastic job with him. Becca's mouth went dry at the sight, just like it did the first time she saw him standing there.

Bax came in behind him and stood blocking the door, arms crossed. His gaze flitted to Courtney then to his boots.

Linx didn't pause when he walked in. One look at Becca, and his shoulders dropped. He turned to leave.

Bax, however, got lead singer points for refusing to budge. He shook his head and pointed to the stage. Linx turned to see what he was pointing at.

Becca hurried to the microphone onstage.

"Excuse me," she said. Her breath puffed over the sound system. She moved her mouth away a few centimeters. "I… uh…" *Do it. Come on.* "There's been a dare. Uh, Cedric, if you'd hold a second." Her throat worked against the fear he'd walk out the door anyway.

Linx had a look of utter shock on his face—eyes wide, mouth parted, jaw slack. He didn't continue his forward momentum to the exit. Instead, he paused, apparently waiting to see where she was going with this.

Knox immediately dove into the opening piano bars for "Baby One More Time." *Bah bum, bum, bum.* Tanner was right behind him with the beat. And Becca? Becca dove in, pulling the microphone from the stand and strutting to the edge of the stage, facing Linx. Then, as she sang about how she shouldn't have let him go à la Queen Britney circa 1999, Linx's hard edges softened. The edges of his lips twitched. He covered his mouth with his palm. Shook his head, but kept his gaze locked on her. She waggled her finger, indicating he should come up on stage with her.

The rest of what she had planned required his participation.

Perma-grin back in place, he strode to her, up the steps of

the stage. She pointed to the chair she'd placed for this very reason, directing him to it. He looked to her and looked to the guys on stage, but moved in the direction she showed.

She sashayed to him, pushed him to a chair, and began a PG-ish version of the lap dance she'd given him there on that very spot while she sang her exceptionally off-key version of Britney's song.

The elderly crew in the front row let out a whole slew of catcalls and whistles. And when the song ended, Linx pulled her to his lap and kissed the stuffing out of her.

That got more catcalls and whistles.

Then Bax took the stage with the rest of the band, jumping into one of the Dimefront favorites, effectively taking all attention away from Linx and Becca.

She made a mental note to thank him later.

"Is that the sign I've been waiting for?" Linx asked, his voice gravelly.

She nodded.

"Thank fuck." He pressed his forehead to hers.

"Do you think I have any promise in the industry?" she asked.

He chuckled. "Not a chance. But you can sing to me whenever you want."

"Actually, according to your rules, you owe me a song," she said, her lips against his mouth. "The whole tit-for-tat. Someone does something for you, you do something for them."

He full-court grinned. "I've been reconsidering those rules."

"Nu uh." She tapped the side of his jaw with her forefinger. "That's not how it works."

"Becca?" His expression turned serious. The Adam's apple in his throat bobbed. "Are you in this with me?"

God, how had this even been a question? Why had she waited to make her move?

"I am." She nodded. Pressed her face into his neck. "But I'm a little afraid of you, to be honest," she added.

That got his attention.

"Why afraid?" he asked, pulling her back to study her face.

Because more often than not, emotions made little sense. Sometimes the way the body processed them made even less sense. And sometimes the only thing that made *any* sense was the thing that a person knew might end up in heartbreak. "Because I don't want to go slow, but I don't want to go fast, either. I don't really know what I want."

This was presently the story of her life.

"Then we'll feel this out together." Not a question. He stated this declaration as fact.

Her throat went thick. "One metaphorical foot in front of the other."

"I promise, no matter what happens next, I'll do my best not to fuck it up." He was gripping her waist like she was his lifeline. Like if he let go of her, his entire world could break apart into pieces.

She could, in fact, totally relate.

"Isn't that what we all do? Usually. We do our best?" she asked.

He shook his head. "Not me. I do the minimum required and sail through the rest."

She draped her arms around his shoulders. "I don't believe that for a second."

He turned his palm over and held it there until she slipped her fingers against his. Her hand fit perfectly there.

"I have a proposition for you." He ran his thumb over her knuckles.

Yes, they were on a stage. Yes, she was sitting in his lap. Yes, this time there were people in the room. No, she didn't care. She still nibbled at his ear. "Oh, yeah?"

He cleared his throat. "There's a job opportunity

available."

"What's that?" She pulled back to gauge if he was serious.

"Manager of keeping the band from losing their shit regularly." He grinned. "We're gonna give it one more go with Dimefront. See if we can make it work."

"This is a good thing, right?"

He nodded, but his teeth were gritted. "I want you with me. You'll get to use that master's degree of yours."

She bit at her bottom lip.

"We're a bit of a rowdy crew." He continued rubbing her knuckles. "But the job comes with a full package—health insurance, retirement, time off…"

"And you?"

"Yeah, the job comes with me." He grinned.

It felt…Dammit, it felt amazing. The sunshine of his attention was becoming her personal drug of choice.

She inhaled a deep breath and let it out. Then she said, "Sorry, I can't take the job."

He frowned. "Why?"

"Because I'm a therapist." Thanks to her mother and her auxiliary lunch, Becca had an idea. She called her old boss and pitched it. He loved the concept. Together they would develop a virtual life-coaching platform with certified therapists. Teaching everyday people to put a voice to their emotions with a heavy focus on figuring out what made a person thrive.

She'd be able to help patients again, and still live a life outside of work. She'd have…balance.

Linx frowned, his shoulders drooping. "You're going back to Portland?"

No. She wasn't. Not for anything other than work trips and visits with her friends.

"I'm going to work, virtually. Wherever there's WIFI." She traced the leather bracelet she'd given him, still on his wrist.

"We have WIFI on the tour bus." He gave her the lightest of nose rubs with his own.

Then he looped her arms around his neck and, one arm under her knees, the other around her back, he rose from the chair.

"That's probably a good thing, then, huh?"

"My girlfriend's gonna be a guru." He grinned at that. "I dig it."

"Maybe I'll even get my own table at the retirement home." She chuckled.

He shivered. "Hard no from me."

"We should get out of here," she said, low. "You can take me on an actual date this time."

"Do you want to go on an actual date?" He sounded surprised. Like it hadn't occurred to him.

They were moving toward the exit. And they were a them.

"Yeah. I do," she said.

"Where do you want to go?" he asked, as Courtney held open the door for them and ushered them outside.

She shrugged. Anywhere, as long as he was with her.

"Courtney's here, and Mom and Dad took a few days to go up to Estes Park. Mom's always wanted to stay at the Stanley Hotel." The wicked smile stretching across his mouth gave away his intentions for some time alone. They were excellent intentions. Who needed a proper date right off the bat, anyway?

Not when this was only the start. They had all the time in the world to go on that real date.

"My place?" he suggested, as he carried her toward his Porsche.

"Okay. That sounds fun." She pulled back slightly, her gaze meeting his. Then a little half smile quirked at the side of her mouth.

Oh. Yes. This was only the beginning.

Epilogue

Linx

Later that night…

He'd stopped on the way home for chocolate cake. Then he'd enjoyed it in his bed with his Becca. Then he'd enjoyed *her*.

She reached up to trace his cheek with her fingertip. "Now that you've got a girlfriend, do you have to break up with all your others? The cities?"

Hah. No.

"It's not like that. No expectations. If I was in town, I'd call. Sometimes they'd be in a relationship. I don't stick my dick in somebody else's garden, so we didn't catch up on those trips."

"That's a lovely mental picture." Becca's eyes sparkled. He did an internal fist pump because she was back, and life was pretty fucking sunny.

He cleared his throat. "Sometimes I'd be busy or seeing someone."

Becca smirked.

"Hey, it happened."

"Uh huh. I bet it did." She stroked the skin of his chest even as she ribbed him with the sarcasm in her words.

"Do you want me to contact them all and tell them I'm in a serious, committed relationship?" Linx asked.

"Would you just send a mass e-mail or something?" Becca asked. "Oh. Maybe there will be a club." At the idea, she propped herself up on her elbow. "I want to join the club. I bet you don't know that I love joining clubs."

She was a nut.

"You can't join." He squeezed her waist. "It'll be for my exes, and you're still with me."

"Maybe I want to compare notes." She tried to wink. The effort she made was adorable, but this was not a skill she possessed, apparently, because she did it about as well as she sang.

Which was to say, A for effort. A participation trophy for showing up.

"Can we be done with this conversation now?" Linx asked.

"That's probably for the best." Becca stretched out beside him.

The fact that this was his life, that she was his life, that Dimefront was moving forward with something that felt more like conviction than they'd had in years…it all felt foreign. Foreign, but right. Perfection.

Becca pressed a kiss into the curve of his neck.

"You're with me now," she whispered into his ear.

"I am," he murmured.

"I don't care who came before." She nibbled at his ear in that way she did that drove him absolutely crazy with lust.

He moved until their bodies pressed together, careful like he always was when it came to the things that mattered to him.

Then he turned and flipped his woman so she was on her back, underneath him.

She wrapped her legs around his waist.

His heart dipped in his rib cage at her willingness to embrace all the parts of him. The good. The bad. The old. The new.

He pressed a kiss to her forehead before he said, "You're my world now. I don't need cities."

They didn't speak for a long time.

"Is this real?" she asked.

He pressed his face into her hair. "I fucking hope it is."

She smiled against his mouth. "You're good at this. You know that?"

"Which part?" He nibbled at her jawline like she'd done at his ear.

"The making-me-believe-in-happy-endings part." Then she pressed her mouth to his.

Happy endings were the fucking best.

There's more Becca & Linx!

A special bonus scene Christina created especially for newsletter subscribers!

Claim the bonus scene at:
ChristinaHovland.com/played-bonus

Acknowledgments

Ever since *Going Down on One Knee*, I've wanted to write a Dimefront series. This is the start of that endeavor, and I'm loving these boys even more than when I had the kernel of an idea all those years ago. Courtney will get her HEA soon in *Knocked Up by the Rockstar*.

Thanks, as always, to my kids and to my husband, Steve, for understanding that when my resting author face is in place, I need to be writing. I couldn't do this job without your love, support, and constant proof that HEAs are real.

Mom and Seren, thank you for loving my books and encouraging me on this author journey. I love you both.

Mad props to Cedric who told me I should use his name. Thanks for being a friend and supporter.

Thank you to my critique team and beta readers: Eden French, Serena Bell, A.Y. Chao, Dylann Crush, Patricia Dane, C.R. Grissom, Jody Holford, Diane Holiday, Deb Smolha, Renee Ann Miller, and Becky Wesnidge.

Thanks to Takis for always being available to help me with my Russian and all of the ideas for Babushka.

Thanks always to the fantabulous Dr. Victoria for always seeing to the medical needs of my fictional characters.

My agent, Emily Sylvan Kim, continues to be the rock star advocate of my writing. I am so grateful to you, Emily, and to all of the Prospect Agency staff.

Holly Ingraham, what can I say? Editing this book during a pandemic while homeschooling small children and doing a full home remodel was nothing more than a feat of greatness. I am so grateful you are my editor.

L.A. Mitchell. Whew. We did it. AND WITH TIME TO SPARE! I may not always tell you how much I appreciate your honest feedback on my stories—usually because I'm cussing like Brek as I fix the issues—but, oh, how I do appreciate you. Thank you for helping me make this story shine.

Shasta Schafer, as always, is brilliant and has the most gorgeous soul you'll ever have the privilege of knowing. Thank you for being my final eyes before press.

Courtney, Dallas, Leeann, Lindsay, Sarah—thank you for always being online with a listening ear for me. *I lub you!*

Karie, I hope we're in the hot tub right now with a cocktail. Serious. Thank you for being my best friend.

Kiele, you know why you'll always be my person and the voice of reason I need in my life. *MUAH*

And, it means more than anything that I get to thank ***YOU***, my rock star reader. I get to live my dream because you buy my books.

Also by Christina Hovland

The Mile High Matched Series

Rock Hard Cowboy, Mile High Matched, Book .5

Going Down on One Knee, Mile High Matched, Book 1

Blow Me Away, Mile High Matched, Book 2

Take It Off the Menu, Mile High Matched, Book 3

Do Me a Favor, Mile High Matched, Book 4

Ball Sacked, Mile High Matched, Book 4.5

The Mile High Rocked Series

Played by the Rockstar, Mile High Rocked, Book 1

From Entangled Publishing

The Honeymoon Trap

Rachel Out of Office

About the Author

Christina Hovland lives her own version of a fairy tale—an artisan chocolatier by day and romance writer by night. Born in Colorado, Christina received a degree in journalism from Colorado State University. Before opening her chocolate company, Christina's career spanned from the television newsroom to managing an award-winning public relations firm. She's a recovering overachiever and perfectionist with a love of cupcakes and dinner she doesn't have to cook herself. A 2017 Golden Heart® finalist, she lives in Colorado with her first-boyfriend-turned-husband, four children, and the sweetest dogs around.

ChristinaHovland.com
Twitter.com/HovlandWrites
Facebook.com/HovlandWrites
Instagram.com/HovlandWrites
Goodreads.com/HovlandWrites
bookbub.com/profile/christina-hovland

Enjoyed the Story?

Turn the page for chapter one of Going Down on One Knee!

Going Down on One Knee

Number-crunching Velma Johnson's perfectly planned life is right on course.

That's a lie. Sure, she's got the lucrative job. She's got the posh apartment. But her sister nabbed Velma's Mr. Right. There has to be a man out there for Velma. Hopefully, one who's hunky, wears pressed suits, and has a diversified financial portfolio. He'll be exactly like, well... her sister's new fiancé.

Badass biker Brek Montgomery blazes a trail across the country, managing Dimefront, one of the biggest rock bands of his generation. With the band on hiatus, Brek rolls into Denver to pay a quick visit to his family and friends. But when Brek's sister suddenly gets put on bed rest, she convinces Brek to take over her wedding planning business for the duration of her pregnancy.

Staying in Denver and dealing with bridezillas was not what Brek had in mind when he passed through town, but there is one particular maid-of-honor who might make his stay worthwhile.

Velma finds herself strangely attracted to the man planning her sister's wedding. Problem is, he ticks none of the boxes on her well-crafted list. Brek is rough around the edges, he cusses, and doesn't even have a 401(k). But trying something crazy might get her out of the rut of her dating life--so long as she lays down boundaries up front and sticks to her plan...

Going Down on One Knee

CHAPTER ONE, THE COUNTDOWN BEGINS

Three words. Three. Little. Words. Nothing important.

Okay, so the three words were important. Massive, really.

"Congratulations, you two," Velma Johnson rehearsed aloud to the vase of a dozen yellow roses gripped in her arms. With a reaffirming gulp of Denver's crisp spring air, she hustled through the open-air parking garage to the security door of her apartment building.

Her sister, Claire, had big news. To be exact, Claire and her boyfriend, Dean, had big news. Velma had a feeling she knew exactly what their news would be—they were moving in together. The next step in their relationship. Tension in Velma's neck strung tight at the thought.

A successful career and a posh apartment she could eventually rent out as an investment were steps one and two of Velma's elaborate five-year plan. She had ticked both those boxes. Dean, three kids, and moving to a two-story house just outside of Denver had been steps three through seven.

Not anymore. Now, her sister was moving in with the man Velma had crushed on for years. The one Velma measured all others against. The one she sang Prince and Madonna songs with at the office.

Yes, they were moving in together. That's why Claire had called yesterday and asked to take her to dinner. Velma had insisted they meet at her place instead. Her invitation had nothing to do with the fact she liked having Dean visit her apartment—even if he was with her sister. She'd offered because it made sense they'd want a private location for their big reveal. And when the announcement came that they'd be embracing that next relationship milestone…well, being on her home turf sounded pretty darn appealing.

Just as she reached the security door, the sound of a motorcycle that clearly had no muffler cut through her thoughts. She turned. The bike pulled up next to her car—into the parking spot meant for her guests. A super-muscled, badass-mother-trucker of a biker swung his leg over the side of the motorcycle and stood.

Her heart stopped with a *thunk*.

Vin-Diesel-biker-dude pulled off his helmet and—sweet mother of Mary, had the temperature jumped by ten degrees? She got the picture: he rode a motorcycle, hit the gym twice a day. The type she avoided because she did not do badass. She preferred the suspenders-and-slacks kind of man. Except, at that moment, she debated how important that preference really was to her.

Focus, Velma. Head held high, she approached him. "Excuse me? Sir? You can't park there."

He frowned at the number marking the spot.

Normally she wouldn't mind sharing the space, but with Claire, Dean, and his friend Brek coming to dinner, she needed both of her parking spaces.

This man was obviously not Dean's friend. Dean's friends were all buttoned-up, suit-wearing, Wednesday-afternoon golfers. She was nearly certain.

The black leather jacket and jeans ripped at this guy's knees looked horribly out of place next to her Prius. His longish, rock-'n'-roll blond hair was nicer than hers (although his could use a trim). She didn't even mind the dragon tattoo creeping around the side of his neck or the layer of mud coating his motorcycle boots. Everything about the man screamed masculine.

Velma shifted the heavy vase in her grip. *Fudge.* Which of her neighbors was letting their guests use her spot this time?

"No, see, that's the spot for my apartment." Oh, how she wanted to rub at the headache pulsing at her forehead. She didn't have time for this. Not today. "I'm sorry, it's just that my sister and her boyfriend and his friend are coming for dinner because my sister has big news. And while I have no idea what that news is, it's important to her. So that makes it important to me. Which is why I put on a pork roast, bought roses, and got out my crystal wine goblets. That's what you do when your sister has big news, you know? Never mind she's practically living my five-year plan without even trying, and I'm over here without even a boyfriend. *That* was not part of my plan. At this point, I should be at least six months into dating my future husband."

Oh God. She was rambling. And he was staring at her with a half grin that made her skin flush. Seriously, the way the man smiled should be outlawed.

She ducked her head. "Anyway, I have company coming and I kind of need my spot."

"Five-year plan?" he asked. As though that was the important part of what she'd just spit out.

This is how one makes an absolute idiot of oneself. "You know what? It's fine. You can stay right there. Don't worry about it." She shifted the flowers again and turned on her heel.

See? People said she was inflexible, but here she was, absolutely rolling with it. She smiled at her flexibility.

"One sec," Motorcycle Dude called. "This is the number they gave me."

She paused midstride and turned around.

He ticked his head to the side. "Velvet?"

Oh dear. She could easily be swayed by the gravelly way he said her name. Well, the nickname her family called her—despite her repeated cease-and-desist requests.

"Um, yes?" She gripped the glass vase harder with her clammy hands.

"Brek." He looked at her like she should know him and pointed to his chest. "Dean's friend."

Velma stared.

Oh.

This was Brek? She'd expected him to wear khaki pants and drive a Camry. He reached into one of his saddlebags and held up a six-pack of Coors and a four-pack of Bartles & Jaymes fuzzy-navel-flavored wine coolers. "Claire asked me to bring the beer and wine, since I'm crashing your party."

Wine coolers? She stared some more. *Be flexible,* she reminded herself. *Flexible. Flexible. Flexible.*

"Great. Fuzzy navel pairs perfectly with pork roast." Cheeks burning and arms full, she managed to open the security door.

"So, you're Claire's sister?" His lazy gaze trailed over her.

"The one and only."

His deep-blue eyes rivaled the color of the razzleberry lollipops she loved. The kind that made her mouth water just thinking about them and… *Focus, Velma.*

"Can I come up, Velvet?" His deep voice held a subtle hint of roughness.

"Velma," she corrected. "You're a little early. I'm so behind. Normally, I'm much more together."

"I can come back later." Brek's eyes softened, totally contrary to his outer badassery.

"No. I am officially the queen of flexibility. It's not a problem."

He did the darn grin thing again. She silently instructed her body to ignore it.

"Queen of flexibility. That ought to be interesting," he

mumbled mostly to himself but loud enough for her to hear. He stepped next to her, balanced the beer and "wine" against the impressive muscles of one arm, and slid the vase she carried into the crook of his other arm.

"Thanks." This time it was her turn to mumble.

Without looking back, she led him up the stairs to her apartment. Another glance his way, and she'd probably trip face-first into the wall or something equally embarrassing. To prevent herself from taking another peek, she focused on sticking the key in the keyhole of her apartment door as though it took every ounce of her concentration.

There. The door swung open. He stepped through the doorframe, close enough for her to catch the scent of leather and Irish Spring soap. Close enough for her to reach out and touch the stubble running over his jawline. Close enough for her to—she shook her head to dislodge the abrupt light-headedness.

"This place is huge." With a long whistle, he set everything down on her dining room table.

Vaulted ceilings, open concept, white walls and sofa, with pops of jewel tones in her carefully selected décor; it must all appear so unnecessary to a guy like him. But these were her things, proof of everything she had worked so hard to achieve.

Brek walked into the kitchen and glanced to the slow cooker on the counter. "This smells amazing, Velvet. You a chef?"

"Velma," she corrected him again, slipping on an apron with the words *Domestic Diva* embroidered on the front. "And no, I just like to cook."

Velma took in the dinner she'd spent the afternoon planning and preparing. Vegetables had been roasted in the oven, and a chocolate cream pie was setting in the fridge. Not the pudding kind, either. A real, honest-to-goodness, made-from-whipping-cream-and-two-kinds-of-chocolate pie. She hoped she could eat those leftovers while she binge-watched Rodgers and Hammerstein musicals later.

"Then what do you do, Vel*ma*?" His emphasis on the last syllable made her wish her name wasn't so frumpy.

"For employment?" she asked.

"Yeah…or pleasure."

The expression on his face and the way he drew out the word "pleasure" made her toes curl in her sandals.

Right, employment. He'd asked about her work.

"I'm a financial planner," she replied.

Brek rubbed his hands together. "Like Dean?"

"Yup." She and Dean had worked together for years. "Our offices are across the hall from each other. That's how Dean met Claire." Claire had come to visit Velma at work and had wandered into Dean's office by accident.

That was the day Velma's dream of becoming Mrs. Dean Stuart died—all because she had waited too long to make her move and lost her chance.

Mr. Right had met her sister and they'd ended up together, making kissy faces during Thanksgiving dinner.

Actually, they never made kissy faces. The two of them were much too classy for that.

Brek leaned his hip against her granite countertop and crossed his leather-covered arms. "No idea what Dean does at his job, either, but I'm sure you're both fantastic at it."

"We help people with their financial portfolios. Annuities, estate plans, investment management, things like that. What about you?"

"I'm in the music industry." He snagged one of the crystal wine goblets she'd put out earlier and swaggered toward her.

Her stomach did a loop the loop. The swagger affected her more than expected. "You play in a band?"

"Nah. I play guitar, but not professionally. I manage a band." He popped the top off a wine cooler and poured it all the way to the tippy top of the glass. Then he edged inside her personal-space bubble and handed her the glass.

"Thanks." Normally, she didn't drink much—especially on Sundays. Monday marked the start of the week, with new chances and opportunities. She preferred to start it at her best, not hung over with a headache.

Then again, tonight was the night of change. Big-news change. My-sister's-moving-in-with-my-dream-man change. So Velma would have a wine cooler—no use in wasting it when Brek had already poured it—and ignore her attraction to Dean. Steps to a new life filled with…finding a new man who was as perfect for her as Dean was. Baby steps and all that.

Brek slipped off his jacket and tossed it over one of the island barstools. Tattoos ran from the short sleeves of his black T-shirt to his wrists. They looked tribal, mostly wild, and super-hot. If one liked tattoos. Which, she reminded herself, she did not.

"Claire says you two are twins?" Brek asked.

"Uh-huh," she muttered around a gulp of carbonated peach drink.

"You and Claire don't look like twins," Brek said.

Velma pulled a stack of small, hand-painted dessert plates from her for-company-only dish cupboard. "We're not identical."

"No kidding," he replied, serious. "It's the eyes."

Ha. Hardly just the eyes. Velma's eyes were muted gray, like a painter had finished painting for the day and just didn't feel like adding more cyan to the palette. Claire's were a rich brown. More than that, Claire was thin and Velma, well…she was Velma. All curves, like her mother. No matter how many calories she counted or steps the app on her phone registered, the curves stayed put. Velma's hair was dirty blonde. Not the attractive kind, either. In-desperate-need-of-highlights blonde was more like it. Claire's hair was a beautiful deep-chestnut color.

"Why does Claire call you Velvet?" Brek asked.

She sighed and paused, plate in hand. "Family nickname. No matter how many times I ask them to stop."

"Velma." He seemed to be testing the name, letting it melt on his tongue like warm chocolate on a vanilla sundae.

"Not a name I'd lie about." She set out the last of the plates on the table.

"I like it. It's original." The low, rumbly words made her lungs constrict in a warm way she refused to acknowledge.

"Unfortunately, it's not even original." She pulled a cutting board from the pantry. "Claire was born first, so she got the cool name. I was born three minutes later and got Velma."

"It's an interesting name."

"Velma was my grandmother's name. But there couldn't be two of us in the same family, so they all call me Velvet."

"I like Velvet," he said.

She scrunched up her nose. "I don't."

When she was a child, everyone bought her clothes with cheap velvet fabric. They itched. She hated them. As far as she was concerned, velvet was scratchy and uncomfortable.

"This news. Any idea what it is?" Velma asked.

"You don't know?" Brek replied.

"No idea." Except she was absolutely certain they were taking the next step in their relationship by moving in together, and maybe getting a puppy.

Brek popped the top on a Coors. "I figured you and Claire shared everything."

"Nope." Not this time. "Claire just said she has big news."

"Maybe she's knocked up," Brek suggested.

Velma's heart skipped five beats. She grabbed a knife and sliced into an onion with renewed energy. "No way."

"I don't know." He ran a palm over the back of his neck. "Seems reasonable to me."

"Then you don't know Claire. She's way too involved in her career to get pregnant right now." Velma set the onions aside and went to work on chopping carrots to top the salad.

Brek motioned to the cutting board. "Can I help you with anything?"

"Do you know how to julienne carrots?" Velma replied.

"Nope." He shrugged. "But I know how to cook a steak."

She laughed. "Well, tonight it's pork roast, so I'll have to take a rain check on your culinary skills."

"Absolutely. Next time I'm in town, I'll grill you up a steak." He raised his beer to her.

She stared at him. He couldn't actually be serious.

He was serious.

"Maybe they called us here because Dean needs a kidney?" he asked.

"He doesn't need a kidney." Although, Velma would probably give him one if needed. She had a remarkably hard time telling him no. "They're probably just…" *Say it out loud, Velma.* She sighed. "Just moving in together."

"Nah. They wouldn't have dragged me here for that. Maybe their big news is they're gonna try to hook us up."

"You and me?" Velma pointed the knife at Brek, then back to herself.

Of all the options, that one was the most reasonable. And, yet, totally unreasonable. No way would Claire pair the two of them together.

"You said you don't have a guy." Brek's tone turned serious.

Her body irrationally responded to his apparent interest with tingles.

"No." Of course, she didn't have a guy.

She'd had lots of first dates lately.

"I get the feeling you need some help loosening up. Enjoy

some time away from your five-year-husband-seeking plan. There's a club downtown with a great band playing later. We should go." Brek's gaze raked over her.

His pointed interest was actually…nice. Still, there was no way she would go clubbing later. Brek wasn't her type. Not only because of the tattoos or the extreme need for a licensed barber or his ripped jeans. No, it was more the general sense of unease he stirred within her. Also, it was Sunday. What kind of a club was open on a Sunday night? Definitely not one she should visit.

"You stressed about the dinner?" he asked.

"No," she lied through her teeth.

"You're stressed about the dinner," he declared. "I get that, but there's nothing to worry about."

For a half second, she believed there was nothing to worry about. Truth was, there was always something to worry about. Starting with her clothes. She needed to change into something that wasn't yoga pants before her sister arrived in what would undoubtedly be a perfect sundress.

"I'm only in town for a few days anyway," he continued. "We'll get through the part where Claire and Dean do the awkward you-two-should-get-to-know-each-other schtick. We'll eat and then we'll send them on their way. You don't want to go to a club? That's fine. I'll stick around. What do you say, Velma?"

The way he said her name felt like silk against her skin. Silk was so much nicer than velvet.

She tried to tug off her apron, but her hair was stuck in the tie at the back of her neck. Crud. Another tug. Her hair was really stuck. "You want to go clubbing on a Sunday night?"

"Absolutely." He nodded to where her hair was caught. "Need some help?"

"Yes, please." She pressed her eyes closed.

He looped a finger under the little bow tying the apron at

the back of her neck. His calloused fingertip traced the ribbon along her shoulder to the collar of her sweater, unraveling the knot of hair and sending little shivers along his path of exploration.

Maybe she could get away to the club for a little while. It wasn't like she had better things to do. "Where is this cl—"

"Hey, Velvet." Her sister, Claire, shoved open the front door. "Hi, Brek. You made it. Dean's so excited you're here."

"Did you lose him?" Brek squeezed Velma's shoulder.

A hit of sizzle deep in her belly echoed the motion of his touch.

"He's parking the car." Claire closed the door and sauntered to the kitchen with her svelte build and Audrey Hepburn grace. "Okay, I know I've made you wait. But…" Claire bit at the light-pink lipstick on her bottom lip. "Surprise!" She held out her fingers with a little jazz hand motion.

An *engagement* ring perched on the fourth finger of Claire's left hand.

Velma's heart skidded to her toes. She blinked hard. No, it couldn't be.

A ring.

A wedding.

Satin and lace, champagne toasts and flower girls.

This wasn't a puppy. And it was so much more than an apartment.

Velma reached for Claire's hand, her throat constricting. "Oh my gosh."

"I know, right?" Claire squeezed Velma's fingers. "I had to tell you in person."

"Oh. My. Gosh." Velma said again, this time more slowly. She looked straight into Claire's eyes and saw it—excitement and love for Dean. Happiness. Velma glued a grin onto her face. Her sister was happy. That was all that mattered. "Claire. It's perfect."

"I'm gonna go find Dean." Brek caught Velma's gaze and winked. "Now that the cat's out of the bag."

"Wait, you knew about this?" Velma asked.

"Hell yeah, I knew." Brek opened the door. "Didn't want to ruin Claire's surprise, though."

"So you asked me out instead?" Velma asked.

Claire scrunched up her forehead. "Brek asked you out? Like on a date?"

"Oh look, it's Dean." Brek feigned innocence as he held the door wide. "I'm officially saved by the groom."

"She finally told her?" Dean strode inside and glanced to where Velma stood in a swirling vortex of time.

"Uh-huh." Claire nodded, her eyes misted over.

A suit. Dean wore a tailored suit complete with shined cap-toed shoes and gold cuff links. Each black hair on his head lay precisely where it should. He was absolute perfection.

Velma swallowed the heaviness in her throat and tried to pretend it was from excitement for her sister.

"Well, then—hey, sis." Dean strutted toward Velma and wrapped her in a hug. "Claire made me keep my mouth shut for a whole week."

Velma's insides did a little flutter that was totally unacceptable. Time moved at the speed of a sloth. Like watching a car accident happen in real time, when everything went slow and then fast again all at once. "You've been engaged for a week and didn't say anything?"

They'd sat through a load of sales meetings. Two client lunches where he'd driven them both to the restaurant. He'd never given any indication he'd freaking proposed to her sister. They'd discussed retirement plans and supplemental income sources. He hadn't mentioned anything that would've even whispered of proposal news.

"Believe me, it was hard keeping my mouth shut. Can you

believe you're going to be my little sister?" His breath brushed against the top of her head.

"Uh…nope," Velma said through gritted teeth.

"It's great, isn't it?" Dean leaned back and scanned her face.

Her knees went weak, like a cheesy movie heroine.

"It is great. Totally. Great. I'm so excited." Velma stepped away from him, refusing to show anything but happiness for her sister's sake. Any feelings from now on would be purely of the appropriate sisterly kind.

Claire and Dean were engaged.

Yup, Velma's Mr. Right was going to marry her sister.

Enjoyed the sample?
Going Down on One Knee is Available Now!

Going Down on One Knee